# THE Vashallen Chronicles

## Retrieval

Published by Mission Point Press
2554 Chandler Rd.
Traverse City, MI 49696
(231) 421-9513
www.MissionPointPress.com

Design by Sarah Meiers

ISBN 978-1-958363-80-5
Library of Congress Control Number 2023904010

Printed in the United States of America

# THE Vashallen Chronicles

## Retrieval

## D.S. MOON

MISSION POINT PRESS

# A few words of thanks:

To Gary, who said I could.

To Andrew Bain, for sound advice
and encouragement.

To my parents, who taught me
to just be me.

# Prologue

Patrain was happy. The garden she had painstakingly designed and grown in preparation for her joining day was exactly as she'd envisioned it. In a few hours her guests would arrive; she imagined with great satisfaction how they would marvel at the beauty she had created to honor her Ventir on this important day.

Mother appeared in the greenhouse door. Patrain smiled and waved. Mother didn't return her greeting, only motioned Patrain forth as she turned, melting into the dark interior of the greenhouse. Curiosity pulled the young bride forward.

In the moist warmth of the greenhouse, Mother was tending pots of anglardin moss, burning away stray tendrils. Anglardin moss was a beautiful potted plant, hardy and lush, but allowed to grow wild it quickly choked out other vegetation. Patrain watched with confusion, wondering why her mother thought this lesson necessary on today of all days. She already knew anglardin moss needed careful tending. She tilted her head in question, and the vision of her mother wavered. Light drained from the room. Patrain's vision shrank until the dark burning orbs of Mother's eyes filled her view.

Before her stood a dark visage with an infinite stare.

It probed her soul. A silent scream from the vision's maw assaulted her senses, and Patrain threw her hands up to cover her ears, tears running down her cheeks. The scream ended. The dark visage raised one thin arm, pointing to the garden.

Patrain tore her gaze from the horrific sight. Through the glass she saw her beautiful garden, overgrown with anglardin moss. No, no, no! All her hard work! One thought broke through Patrain's anguish: Surely Mother couldn't believe she had been so careless? Patrain whirled around. Mother was gone. The greenhouse was empty except for the moss clippings littering the floor.

Patrain Adderigus awoke abruptly. She sat straight up in bed, her breathing ragged, and ran a shaky hand over her forehead, pushing damp hair from her face. It had been a dream, just a dream. She breathed a sigh of relief but couldn't quell the urge that compelled her to leap from the warmth of her bed. She hurried to the window to check on her garden, the garden in which she would say her vows in a matter of hours.

## Chapter One

# Starship Revival

A subtle vibration radiated across the deck, generated as the Revival's powerful engines briefly engaged. The maneuver adjusted the starship's orbit around Callisto, one of Jupiter's Galilean moons. The uncloaked starship nestled safely between Jupiter and Callisto, undetected by Earth. The planet and moon had provided the perfect cover during the Revival's mission, allowing her crew to preserve power, but now even Shay's mastery couldn't eke another year from their fuel reserves. It was time to prepare for their return to Devet IV.

Lanaq, the Revival's only organic crew member, paced slowly back and forth across the command deck, waiting patiently, while Shay, the ship's AI, completed the orbital procedure.

When the ship fell silent once more, the AI's liquid voice filled the command deck: "We have achieved optimal orbit, and all readings are within normal parameters." Shay spoke as the shadow of Callisto stretched across the ship's view screen.

"Define optimal, please."

"Our current position will keep us hidden from Earth for the next thirty days. Further adjustment will not be required before we are ready to break orbit for the return voyage."

"Thank you, Shay. That is indeed optimal." Lanaq was fairly certain his wry humor was lost on Shay. Designed to be his companion during the long mission, her sisterly chiding often kept him on his toes. Just as often, her company kept him sane. "With the ship secured, there is no reason to delay. Begin the awakening process for the occupied medical bays in infirmary one," he authorized solemnly.

Lanaq's mission to Earth, the third planet in a small solar system in the Milky Way galaxy, was one of watching and waiting. He had watched, observing human history from the age of the pharaohs to the days of the first female president of the Earth government, and he had waited, ever-so-patiently, anticipating the day Project Ferax would begin producing viable Vashallen candidates.

Project Ferax had taken much longer to bear fruit than the three thousand years he had acted as pilot. Begun over three hundred thousand years ago, the project had only started generating Vashallen candidates in the last few hundred years.

He had fifty-three of those candidates aboard ship. Lanaq was troubled by the small number of Vashallen he had been able to gather. A vocal faction at odds with the current regime would almost certainly argue fifty-three was a small number, especially considering the time and effort invested in the project. Lanaq was convinced the quality of the candidates should outweigh the quantity, but he was realistic. He knew his mission would be under scrutiny upon his return. The Quorum would have questions. He didn't think they would like his answers.

Having authorized the awakening of the Vashallen, Lanaq spent a moment in quiet reflection. He would soon have a solemn task to perform, and it weighed heavily on his conscience. Beyond selecting the candidates, beyond reviving them, it was his responsibility to explain Project Ferax to the Vashallen.

Lanaq had prepared himself to provide explanations and reassurances to the Vashallen. He'd organized the relevant information in his head, planning how he would answer questions. Truth be told, he had practiced the conversations, both in his head and aloud. Shay had caught and teased him just like a big sister, but she'd helped him refine his delivery. Now that the moment was fast approaching for him to explain his species' actions to the fifty-three females currently slumbering in stasis ten decks below his feet, Lanaq feared he would be unequal to the task.

His blood pressure spiked. Fear made his heart pound, an unfamiliar state for Lanaq. He recalled his mother's parting advice: "Calm is he who is ready." Perhaps she anticipated the disquiet he would feel at this moment. He took a deep breath to steady himself, then recited the mantra she'd taught him.

Lanaq released his breath. His pulse slowed, and his mind became tranquil. "Shay, I'm going down to the infirmary to oversee the revival process. Please relay a progress report every five minutes and begin bringing the androids online."

"Acknowledged. However, I am required to remind you of the Quorum mandate. Only the synths are allowed to be present during the Vashallen's first contact."

Frustration tinged Lanaq's response, though he knew Shay was only following the Quorum's guidelines. "I don't intend to break protocol. I'll leave before the final awakening. After three thousand years, I want to be present for at least part of the process."

"So, you aren't headed down to the infirmary to see one particular sleeping beauty?" The teasing sarcasm dripped into Lanaq's ear.

"I never should have let you pick that movie. Thousands upon thousands of choices, and you pick one you can tease me with for decades."

"It seemed apropos."

The doors whooshed open at his approach but leaving the bridge didn't mean he could escape Shay's all-too-human derisive snort, which followed him down the corridor. Lanaq quickened his pace toward the lift, eager to make the most of the moments remaining to him. His time with the Vashallen, once they were awake, was strictly prescribed by the Quorum. His orders allowed him contact only as necessary to make the Devetian case to the women, and to answer their questions. He would follow that order to the best of his ability, but he couldn't deny the pull he felt toward Beatrix, the first Vashallen candidate he'd chosen, and he couldn't help the feeling of hope that flared in his chest. The lift doors opened as he approached, Lanaq entering and indicating the infirmary as his destination.

Located ten decks down, the infirmary was a cavernous, heavily fortified room running down the port side of the starship. It was currently divided into one hundred medical bays, each bay containing a single stasis bed and its accompanying apparatus. An identical room was located on the starboard side of the ship. It lay completely silent and empty.

Lanaq stepped out of his thoughts and into the hallway as the lift reached its destination. He approached the doors to the infirmary, which parted silently, allowing him entrance. The room was shadowed, except for the soft glow of equipment. Ambient light bathed the faces visible through the transparent portion of the stasis units, the silence in the infirmary broken only by the hiss and whir of machinery. As Lanaq traversed the room, soft blue light tubes, located around the perimeter, began to glow, brightening in intensity until the space was adequately lit.

The medical units maintaining the health of the Vashallen were active, beginning the revival process. He traversed the room, doing a physical check of each Vashallen, assessing their individual progress. He left bed one for last, so that he might linger, gaze at the supine form housed within. Shay was right, Beatrix *was* his sleeping beauty.

At the time of her retrieval, Beatrix had been forty-seven and dying of breast cancer. Now, watching her through the glass, Lanaq could see the revival process having its effect on her outward appearance. Her skin appeared plumper, her hair more vibrantly strawberry. Most important were the changes that weren't outwardly apparent. When Beatrix awoke, she would no longer be plagued by disease. For all intents and purposes, she would instead be a healthy, reproductively viable young woman.

The monitor above Beatrix's stasis unit gave an extended low chirp. Dragging his gaze away from her face, Lanaq noted the information on the display. Stage one of Beatrix's revival was complete.

The amount of time needed to finish revival was contingent upon a wide variety of factors; consequently, each Vashallen would complete the process at a different rate, though they would all be awakened as one.

On this matter the Quorum had fiercely debated, as they did about most things, finally deciding that the Vashallen were best served by being awakened all together rather than individually. They thought it would be less alarming for the women.

"Lanaq, this is your first five-minute update." Shay's tone was sweet honey. Lanaq had spent three thousand years listening to the nuances of inflection in the AI's voice; he heard the underlying sarcasm.

"I swear Mother had you programmed to be annoying."

"Of course she did. She was wise enough to know every young man should have an older sister to keep him straight."

"I always imagined an older sister would be kinder, less annoying."

"I will ignore that last comment, as I know you are pining over meeting a certain Vashallen." Lanaq barely heard Shay's retort as he gazed down at Beatrix. "Two Vashallen have successfully completed the revival process. Another three have entered the final phase. I estimate twenty-six minutes before they can be collectively awakened."

The slight reprimand in Shay's tone made Lanaq realize he was so focused on Beatrix that he hadn't even registered the other monitors. He straightened, acknowledging that he had no real need to be in the infirmary. Shay was in control of this phase of the process, and his presence was superfluous. He had just wanted to be close to Beatrix.

The doors to the infirmary slid open again. The attendants, ten androids with female features, entered the room. Once again, it was the Quorum who determined that attendants with a female appearance might be less stressful for the Vashallen. Lanaq was still unnerved by the physical genderization of the androids; it felt unnatural.

He watched the efficient attendants go about their assigned duties, preparing the room by laying out fresh clothing and filling drinking glasses, though their true task was to be a safe, reassuring presence once the women wakened.

More monitors signaled revival completion as Shay began her next update. "Twenty-eight Vashallen have successfully completed the revival process, and are ready for awakening. I have a revised estimation of completion in thirteen minutes. Everything is going well, Lanaq. I see no indication of failure in any of the revivals."

Lanaq knew Shay was trying to reassure him. "Thank you. I will return to the command deck immediately." He turned toward the doors, but paused to address the attendants, who moved fluidly around the room: "Take good care of them," he instructed needlessly. Of course the attendants would take perfect care of their charges, because that was exactly what they had been programmed to do. Lanaq sighed. He was reluctant to miss the momentous awakening that was about to take place. Duty required he must. Taking a last look to fix the memory in his mind, he stepped through the infirmary doors, which slid closed with a definitive snick.

Inside the infirmary, thirteen minutes and fourteen seconds later, the upper portion of each medical bed slid open and slowly retracted into the wall. The unused stasis pods disappeared into the floor, replaced by comfortable sofas, armchairs, and dining tables. Attendants stood ready, positioned at even intervals along a center aisle. A barely audible hiss from each bed indicated the reversal agent was being administered to the women. The awakening of the Vashallen was imminent.

Chapter Two

# Infirmary — The Revival

Consciousness came gradually and gently to Beatrix, like waking up on a lazy Sunday morning, snuggled under the covers. She felt content and didn't want to let go of sleep. With her eyes still closed she gave a long, slow stretch, extending her fingertips above her head and her wiggling toes. It felt so good.

The thought jolted Beatrix's brain to full wakefulness. There was no pain. She wasn't struggling to breathe deeply. With trepidation, Beatrix felt for the hard lumps that caused her so much suffering. She found...nothing. Confused, Beatrix lay still, her mind trying to piece together what had happened. She remembered going to bed last night. She had been in such misery, panting to breathe, her chest aching. She took a deep, slow breath.

She felt wonderful, better than she had in a very long time; in fact, she was feeling so good she was afraid to open her eyes. Perhaps it wasn't so much that a miracle had taken place while she slept, but that she had died? Surely this was the only answer to her miraculous recovery.

As Beatrix lay pondering the possibility of her own demise, the murmur of voices in the room finally penetrated her consciousness. Panic caused her eyes to fly open. Her gaze settled on an attendant helping another woman to sip from a cup. Releasing a pent-up breath, she calmed herself: now everything made sense. She must have been so sick she had been taken to hospital.

Beatrix turned her head, observing several other patients receiving attention from the attendants. Surely this was the women's ward at the London Hospital in Whitechapel, but she had no memory of her journey here.

Adrenaline from her moment of panic had dispelled any remaining grogginess left from her deep sleep. Focusing further, Beatrix noticed odd things about the hospital ward. The bed frames were constructed from a shiny material she couldn't immediately name, and those light bulbs tucked into grooves along the wall. ... *Light bulbs? Where did I come up with that name?*

Just as panic began to tinge her thoughts again, the monitor above her gave a sharp beep. Startled, Beatrix catapulted into a sitting position and swiveled sharply, looking for the source of the noise. When she saw the monitor she paused to wonder, *How on earth do I know what a monitor is?* She had certainly never seen anything like it before, yet somehow, her brain supplied a name.

Just as confusion threatened to overwhelm Beatrix,

one of the attendants approached her bed. Her name tag read *Joan*.

"Hello Beatrix," Joan said in a soft and soothing voice. "How are you feeling? Parched, I imagine. You've been with us for quite some time."

Beatrix was reassured by the familiar speech pattern and lilting accent of the attendant's voice. Shay had correctly judged that this small detail in Joan's programming would make Beatrix feel more at ease when she woke. It reminded her of home.

Beatrix had begun life as the fourth daughter of a yeoman. Beatrix's mother, just like her mother before her, had married a farmer. Not that being the daughter of a farmer was bad — Beatrix still missed the fresh scent of country air, but air, fresh or otherwise, doesn't feed twelve mouths.

At eight years old, Beatrix was sent to live with her Aunt Constance and Uncle Arnot. Uncle Arnot was a clergyman with a decent living, whose own son was already grown and gainfully employed. Denied a house full of children as they'd wished, her aunt and uncle had showered Beatrix with affection, and she'd never gone hungry.

Aunt Connie had done her the additional kindness of teaching her to speak properly, also instructing her on how to read and write. Her most precious possession was a small volume on letter writing, a gift her aunt gave her when Beatrix left the parsonage to enter service.

Aunt Connie's insistence that Beatrix learn to speak civilly had served her well over the years. Beatrix secured a position as an upstairs maid when she was barely fifteen.

Later, when she decided to move to London, her aunt's tutelage allowed Beatrix to correspond with an employment agency, thus securing herself a job as a ladies' maid. The gentry valued manners as an indicator of virtue. Beatrix's ability to write and speak civilly implied she possessed manners, and thus virtue. She was aware that Aunt Connie's lessons allowed her more advantages in life than her siblings and had always been grateful.

Beatrix realized with a start that Joan was still waiting patiently for a reply to her query. She hadn't yet tried to speak. Finding her voice little more than a croak, Beatrix gave a slight smile and a nod instead.

Joan picked up a pair of slippers left ready at Beatrix's bedside. "Let's swing your legs over the edge of the bed and sit you up properly." She instructed, reaching out to steady Beatrix by the shoulders. Joan bent to slide the slippers onto her feet with a smooth motion. "Now sip slowly," she advised, bringing a cup of water to Beatrix's lips.

The cool liquid eased Beatrix's throat. After several sips she was able to offer, "Thank you."

"You are most welcome."

Joan settled herself next to Beatrix on the edge of the bed. She dipped her head to catch Beatrix's eye, then reached out to clasp Beatrix's hands in her own.

"I know you must have lots of questions at this point. Where am I? How did I get here? For now, know that you are safe. No one here intends you any harm, in fact we've all worked very hard to ensure your return to good health.

Let's get you up and around, and soon enough any questions will be answered."

Joan gently squeezed Beatrix's hands and made to stand. Beatrix's fingers slide around Joan's wrists, loosely enclosing them, silently encouraging her to stay seated. "May I ask one question, please? That is, will you answer just one question right now?" Beatrix pleaded with her eyes if not with her tone. "Did I die?"

That the question amused Joan could only be discerned by the slight twitch of her lips. "No, my dear, you most assuredly did not die, and aren't likely to any time soon." So saying, Joan patted Beatrix's hands and rose briskly from the bed. She tapped rapidly at a device encircling her wrist, and walls formed, extending from the ceiling and floor, meeting in the middle to create privacy for Beatrix. "When you feel up to it, there are fresh clothes here," Joan said, indicating a neatly folded bundle resting on a chest next to the bed. "After you've changed, please come to the common area and get something solid to eat. You can also meet some of the other ladies from the ward."

Beatrix drug her stupefied gaze from the newly formed walls, giving Joan a nod in the affirmative. *Nanites*, her brain supplied the answer to her unvoiced question. Beatrix struggled to comprehend information beyond her experience.

Without warning, a piercing shriek-turned-giggle cut off the murmured conversations filtering in through the open doorway, startling Beatrix. The noise didn't seem to concern Joan. She didn't so much as flinch. "I'll leave you now, but I'll check back if we don't see you soon." With one last soothing smile Joan stepped through the opening left by the newly formed walls, the door closed behind her.

Left alone, Beatrix slid forward off the bed, putting some weight on her slippered feet. She stood up and felt strong, which seemed wrong. She hadn't felt this vigorous for some time. In the last twelve months Beatrix had sickened with an illness that sapped her strength and caused her a great deal of pain. *Cancer*, the answer floated into her consciousness. She found the unbidden knowledge unsettling.

Beatrix reached for the bundle of clothing on the chest, finding a pair of loose-fitting oatmeal-colored pants that gathered at the waist and ankles. She pulled them on, followed by a short sleeve, knee length tunic with slits on the sides. Lastly, there was a hooded robe with loose sleeves and a single button at the throat. The clothes were certainly of better fabric than anything she had ever owned. Beatrix ran her hands over the cloud-soft material with appreciation.

She folded the nightdress she had woken in and laid it neatly on top of the chest. Looking around the enclosed space, Beatrix spotted another door. There was no handle. She approached hesitantly, and the door slid into the wall, revealing the necessary room. A brush and comb set, along with a toothbrush and paste, had been left near the sink for her use. It was the mirror, however, that grabbed her immediate attention.

A strangled sound escaped her throat, and she leaned in, peering closely at the reflection that greeted her. The person staring back couldn't possibly be her. Gone was the loose ashen skin of her sunken cheeks. Gone were the dark circles under her eyes, the wrinkles that lined her face. Gone, just like her aches, pains, and lumps. She looked, and felt like a young woman again, her strawberry blonde hair restored so that it shone far more strawberry than gray.

Staring into the mirror, she suspected she knew the reason for the strange cries she'd heard emanating from her fellow patients. Had others also gone to bed old and sick, only to awaken young and hale? Beatrix smiled; Joan was right, she did have a lot of questions.

She employed both comb and toothbrush. Upon completion she felt ready to brave the common area. Leaving her room, she stepped through the sliding door into the aisle, which was no longer so much an aisle as it was a corridor, walls having been erected for each person's privacy. Beatrix could hear quiet conversations coming from open doorways as she passed by on her way to the common area.

The smell of food wafted along the corridor. Beatrix's stomach gave a very loud growl. She clutched her midriff in embarrassment, looking around to see if anyone had heard such an unladylike noise issuing from her person. Spotting Joan beside one of the dining tables, Beatrix hurried forward.

Joan looked up as Beatrix approached, precisely placing a tray in front of the young woman already seated at the table as she did so. "Splendid, you're feeling well enough to dress and join us. Can I get you some breakfast?"

Beatrix tried her voice again. "That would be lovely,

thank you." Her reply to Joan's query was husky, her throat and vocal cords still rusty.

Joan pulled out a chair, indicating that Beatrix should sit. "Beatrix, this is Npheba. You may find you two have some things in common." Joan threw the comment over her shoulder as she left to retrieve a tray for Beatrix.

Beatrix gave a smile and a nod to her table companion, who returned the gestures with a nod of her own. Just when Beatrix thought Npheba would commence eating without saying a word, she blurted out, "Did you die last night also?"

"Joan assured me that I did not die, but I'm not quite sure I believe her. I was very ill when I went to bed."

Npheba stared at Beatrix with a dazed look. "I was quite sure that I took my own life last night," she said. Then, continuing with a slight hitch in her voice, "However, as my throat seems intact, I must conclude either I was in error as to the depth of my cut, or — this is the afterlife." She shrugged off her momentary melancholy, blew vigorously at a forkful of golden flaky pastry, and grinned at Beatrix over the rising steam, "I've never been so well-dressed," she indicated her identical outfit, "nor so well-fed." Still smiling, she took the fork into her mouth. As the food passed her lips, Npheba closed her eyes and gave a small groan. A heavenly expression lit up her face.

Beatrix's stomach gave another embarrassing growl just as Joan returned with a tray. "Sounds like you're ready for a hearty meal," Joan teased gently, sliding the food in front of Beatrix. Then, with a quick grin, she headed back toward the patients' rooms.

Beatrix examined her tray. It was identical to Npheba's fare, a thick slice of quiche, a single sausage, a bowl of fresh fruit, a glass of milk, and a small pot of tea. Hunger had Beatrix tucking in quickly. Just like Npheba, she closed her eyes in bliss as she chewed her first bite of the delicious quiche.

As Beatrix ate, more women began to find their way out of their cubicles, filling up seats at the other tables. There were ten tables total spread around the dining area. Every table had five or six chairs, and a single attendant seemed to be assigned to each table.

While savoring her last bite of quiche, Beatrix observed Joan and another young woman walking slowly toward their table. Joan guided the woman, seating her alongside Npheba; a fourth woman followed behind the attendant, also seating herself at their table. Joan introduced the two as Sophia and Regina before hurrying away to collect their food.

Npheba had pushed back her tray and was sipping her tea at leisure, a replete expression on her face. She offered the two a shy, "Good morning." The newcomers sat quietly, still looking a little shell-shocked. Both nodded absent-mindedly at Npheba's greeting.

Joan returned moments later with food, which she placed in front of Sophia and Regina. Pausing only long enough to ensure the women registered delivery of their trays, Joan spun away and headed toward the curtained corridor once more. A single open chair remained at the table, and Beatrix assumed Joan would bring a fifth patient to fill it. Her assumption proved correct. Joan arrived arm-in-arm with another young woman, a curvy brunette who walked head down, staring at her legs. After assisting her to a seat and introducing her as Gertrude, Joan left to retrieve one last tray.

Gertrude peered around the table, the goofiest grin on her face. Her glance rested on Npheba for several moments before she looked away. "I walked. Did ya see?" Her question was addressed to no one in particular. "I haven't walked since I was fifteen. They must employ miraculous doctors at this here hospital. I'm Trudy, by the way," she finished breathily, in her southern colony accent.

The need to reply to Trudy's rush of comments was curtailed by Joan's arrival. Beatrix followed Joan's movement with her eyes. The attendant delivered the last tray, then collected the remains of Npheba and Beatrix's meal. It did not escape Beatrix's notice that Joan never stayed still long enough for any of them to ask questions. She flitted away with the empty trays, Beatrix following her progress through a doorway at the far end of the room.

Judging by the steadily rising noise, conversation at other tables was flowing, while silence filled the space among the women at Beatrix's table. Trudy continued to eye Npheba from under her lashes. Regina never took her eyes off her companions, not even to glance at her tray. She stabbed blindly at her food, bringing whatever her fork found to her mouth. Finally, Sophia broke the spell, speaking for the first time; her voice wavered, her smile shy and timid.

"I'm Sophia." She pronounced her name in the British fashion, with a long O and a long I. "I'm not sure how I ended up here. The last thing I remember was my husband locking me in the cellar. He always threatened to send me to Bedlam. Is this Bedlam?"

"I visited Bedlam once when I was a novitiate," Regina said, speaking with authority. "This is not it, be thankful. Nor is it any other hospital on the continent."

Regina's appearance was the opposite of Sophia's. Where Sophia was shades of winter — ice-blue eyes, snowy blonde hair — Regina was summer warmth. Her lustrous ebony hair fell in a loose plait, glinting purple and green in the light; her eyes were the color of cinnamon, gaze alive and wary, while her skin was the exact shade of the caramels which Beatrix treated herself to each year on her birthday.

Caught up in her own observations, Beatrix missed part of the conversation as Regina continued to speak. "...circumstances appear to have changed drastically, so I suppose Sister Theodora is no longer appropriate. My given name was originally Regina, but please call me Gina."

"If this isn't a hospital," Sophia's voice was still barely a whisper, "where do you think we are, Gina? Have any of you had an opportunity to question Joan?"

"I cannot say where we are, only that something very odd is happening. I've seen many places for healing the sick, but here is equipped like no other I've encountered. I can put names to things I've never seen before, and, well...

my reflection in the mirror is a me I haven't been for some decades."

A simultaneous gasp of, "Me too!" from the other four women drew glances from some of the nearby tables. As if given permission, the noise of conversation in the room ratcheted up.

Beatrix hadn't noticed when all the attendants melted away, leaving the women to eat and chat by themselves; she only noticed their return. All ten attendants came streaming back into the room from the kitchen, as if the rising voices signaled a need to intervene in the collective conversation.

Joan approached and began gathering empty trays. She moved quickly and efficiently around the table, smiling but never looking anyone in the eye. Before Joan could rush away again, Regina boldly grabbed the attendant by the wrist.

"You promised answers to our questions. We are ready for those answers."

Joan cocked her head to one side for a brief second. "You have been patient. After I remove these trays I will escort you to the auditorium. There, the pilot will answer any questions you have."

# Chapter Three

# Command Deck— The Revival

"Lanaq, all fifty-three candidates are awake and lucid."

"I'm relieved to hear it."

"I've re-equipped the starboard side of deck ten. I've created leisure and interaction zones for the Vashallen's use."

"As usual, you've thought of every detail. Thank you."

"You sound nervous. You have no reason to be. You will handle the explanations with your usual deftness. It's why you were chosen."

"You and I both know deftness was not the main reason I was chosen to pilot this mission."

"No, your mother's faith in your integrity is the reason you are here, Lanaq. You've proven her trust was well-placed. You have adhered strictly to the Quorum's mandates. You really ought not be nervous."

"You're right; nothing at all about which to be nervous. Just the fate of my entire species resting on my ability to explain an impossible situation to possibly traumatized individuals."

Lanaq rose from his console, straightening his tunic and robe as he headed for the door. Shay called out a soft, "Good luck!" as he strode down the hallway and entered the lift.

While Lanaq waited for the lift to complete its descent, his mother's parting words came to him again, calm settling over his mind. He was ready. Still, his pulse raced as he neared his destination, and no amount of training or dedication to duty could make it slow. He wasn't nervous; rather, his pulse quickened with excitement. He was about to meet the Vashallen. He had watched over their lives from the moment he'd verified each of them as Vashallen, but he'd never spoken to one of them.

The doors opened, and Lanaq straightened his tunic one last time. He stepped out of the lift and made the short walk to the auditorium. The double doors parted with a whoosh; fifty-three heads swiveled in his direction.

As his gaze swept over the seated women, seeking Beatrix, Lanaq offered a slight smile. Then, placing his palms on his thighs, he gave a long, low bow to those in the room. He held the pose long enough for the women to adjust to his presence, then he straightened and crossed the threshold.

The Vashallen sat in a semicircle on sunken risers, like an amphitheater. Lanaq navigated the steps down to the center, feeling fifty-three pairs of eyes silently following his movements. He continued to search for Beatrix, finally spying her sitting next to Sophia three rows up. He gave a sigh of relief. It wasn't that he hadn't believed Shay's reports regarding her good health, but seeing her awake with his own eyes was comforting.

"Greetings," he began, "my name is Lanaq. On behalf of the Devetian people, allow me to welcome you aboard the Starship Revival."

Silence met his statement. No one spoke. Lanaq noted skepticism on many Vashallen faces. "While you have been in our care, we have utilized our advanced healing techniques to restore you to optimal health," he continued, speaking into the stillness.

"Your healing techniques made us young again?"

"I think a better question is, who are the Devetians?"

"How did we come to be in your care?"

"Start with, where are we?"

Once the floodgates opened the Vashallen had many questions. Unable to keep track of who asked specific questions, Lanaq addressed his answers to the group. "The short answer is yes; the healing process has returned your youth."

A stool rose out of the floor behind him. Lanaq took a step back and seated himself, hoping to make his height less intimidating. The women followed his every movement with wide tense eyes, but relaxed perceptibly once he was seated. He began to address the questions already asked in a logical order.

Beatrix was fascinated by the seat which materialized

as if from nothing. She understood the seemingly amorphous material was really nanites flowing from one form to another; it was strange to know something but not know how she knew. The knowledge confused her more than it frightened her; occasionally it left her slightly dizzy.

Beatrix might not be frightened by all the new things around her, but Sophia's grip on her hand indicated she wasn't so comfortable. Beatrix gave Sophia a quick squeeze of reassurance, then returned her attention to Lanaq.

"Each of you came to be in our care because you would have expired but for our intervention. You were brought aboard, and your injuries or illnesses treated."

A hand in the middle flew up, Lanaq recognizing the doctor he'd rescued from a war-torn area in the late twenty-first century. He acknowledged her with a nod and said, "Yes, Mirabel?"

"I've never heard of a people called Devetians. Who are you? Why did you help us, and what do you want in return?" A chorus of agreement met Mirabel's inquiries.

A restlessness entered the group's demeanor. Lanaq strove to maintain calm. "Devetians are a people very similar to yourselves, as you can see." He stood, rotating slowly in a circle. "I am a typical Devetian male. I heard someone ask which region we're from; we are not from Earth. We come from a very similar planet, called Devet."

"Let me get this straight. You claim to be an alien from another planet who came here to...what? To heal us?" Mirabel's voice was incredulous.

"Not possible!" The interjection came from Zhilan, an

astrophysicist from China. "What form of propulsion do you claim can traverse galaxies in one human's lifetime?"

"This starship utilizes folded space technology," Lanaq responded as a matter of course.

"Folded space?" Zhilan was incredulous, "As in wormholes? Impossible! Even if you could create a stable wormhole, the forces inside would tear a body apart, to make no mention of the time distortion."

"Yes, wormhole technology is still merely theoretical for your scientists. Mainly because the element required to power a stable wormhole isn't present in the Milky Way galaxy. But rest assured, when correctly powered FST is not only possible, but safe."

"Truly?" a note of hope and curiosity colored Zhilan's query.

"Truly," Lanaq smiled his reply.

"Even if we accept all you've said thus far as truth," Mirabel interjected, reasserting herself in the conversation, "I'm still waiting to hear what you want in return for healing us."

"I will not lie to you and say we want nothing. If you'll bear with me a little longer, I'll explain."

Mirabel leaned back, crossing her arms; Lanaq knew he needed to handle this with careful grace.

"Devetians are an old species," he began. "Our history dates back far longer than Earth's. We are also a long-lived species. Our natural life span is around a thousand years on our world. Unfortunately, all our longevity and history hasn't made us less prone to mistakes. Some generations ago my ancestors became dissatisfied with a mere thousand-year existence. They sought to extend our life span by halting the degeneration of our cells. They eventually succeeded, but at the expense of our species' fertility."

"Forgive me if I'm being obtuse," Mirabel interrupted, "are you suggesting that your race has somehow perfected a technique to make yourselves immortal?"

"I wouldn't say we perfected the technique, considering the result. Each successive generation of female Devetians have been less fertile. It's led to the near-extinction of our species."

"But it has made you immortal."

"We are not immortal in the sense that we can't die. We can still be killed by violence or disease. While more advanced than your own, our medical abilities aren't without limits. But Devetians do not die of old age."

"Essentially, barring illness or accident, Devetians live indefinitely?"

"You have the gist of it," Lanaq affirmed

"I can only assume you have undergone this procedure."

"Yes," Lanaq confirmed without interrupting the Vashallen's verbal train of thought."

"So how old are you exactly?"

Lanaq hesitated. He'd prepared an answer; had known the question would arise, but were the Vashallen ready for the answer? He wasn't sure, but he didn't want to discourage questions. He answered truthfully, if obliquely. "Age is relative to how people measure time. On Earth you measure days and years based on the Earth's orbit around its star. We do the same on Devet, but our days and years are longer."

Mirabel's eyes narrowed. "I assume you know your age measured in Earth years?"

Cornered, Lanaq knew honesty was the best policy. "I'm roughly thirty thousand years old by Earth measure." The stunned silence that followed was worse than his imagined outcry. Awkwardness forced him to attempt some humor. "On the bright side, I'm not even close to one, if measured in galactic years." Zhilan was the only one who chuckled at his weak attempt.

Mirabel closed her mouth, which had fallen open in astonishment. She wetted dry lips before asking hesitantly, "Was this cellular procedure part of the medical treatments you applied to us, and are there other treatments of which we should be made aware?"

The magnitude of the possibility, the ramifications of the actuality, froze some Vashallen in place. It took others a minute longer to work out the implied consequences, but Lanaq noted the women's shock and proceeded with sympathy.

"The medical units which cured your ailments also rejuvenated your cells. Due to the process, you now possess a natural Devetian life span."

They remained deafeningly silent as the women digested this revelation. Lanaq's chest tightened as he waited for their response. The tension was finally broken when someone to his right asked timidly, "Will we live as long as you now?"

Lanaq lowered his chin for a moment before responding. "You will live a natural Devetian life span," he answered, stressing the word *natural*, "of roughly a thousand years." His statement caused a wide range of emotions to pass across the Vashallen's faces. "Mirabel asked about other procedures. You may be experiencing side effects of the subliminal teaching program utilized during stasis. A dizzy sensation that should pass within a few weeks, as your mind assimilates the given information. While the body is inactive, the mind is capable of great retention; needs it in fact to avoid psychosis. Subliminal study is the method Devet uses to teach," Lanaq paused, correcting himself, "or rather, how Devet once taught its children."

Gina stood. She held herself with authority, shoulders back, hands upon her hips. "Does this explain how all my groupmates speak perfect Italian?"

"You have the right idea, but I think you'll find that you are all speaking perfect Devetian." Confusion and consternation, followed by understanding, swept over the group. Lanaq continued, "Teaching you all to speak Devetian was deemed the most efficient use of the process. Your brain is translating the language without you even realizing."

"You offer many well-prepared answers," Gina gave an indignant sniff that spoke volumes about her doubts, "but so far, you've avoided answering one question in particular: What do you want in return for your generosity? Are we your prisoners?"

"Most assuredly not. You were brought here without your express permission, so I understand your trepidation, but whatever happens from this moment forward will be your choice. My goal is to persuade you to make Devet your new home."

This statement seemed to relieve some of the tension in the room. Lanaq elaborated, "Many of you came from difficult situations — not all, but many. It is our belief we can offer you a better life on Devet."

Gina wasn't completely satisfied. She remained standing. "What if we don't want your better life?"

"If it is your desire, you will be returned to Earth."

"Returned to Earth? As in, we aren't currently located on Earth?"

"That is correct. As I said, you are currently aboard the Starship Revival." Lanaq still saw disbelief on some faces, and judged the moment was right. "Shay, would you be so kind as to open a viewport in the auditorium?"

Behind him, a section of wall lost its opacity. Drifting in front of the viewport was pockmarked Callisto. Beyond loomed Jupiter's massive curve, showing the planet's striated bands of color and ever-present Great Red Spot. Shocked gasps greeted the majestic sight, and Lanaq gave the women a few heartbeats to stare. "As you can see, we are currently in orbit around Callisto, a satellite of the world known as Jupiter. We will remain here for the next thirty days, at the end of which I will ask you to decide: Either be returned to Earth, or make the journey to my home planet, Devet IV."

The women seemed subdued now — Lanaq suspected

information overload. He was about to suggest a break when Beatrix rose from her seat.

"Hello Lanaq, I'm Beatrix. It's a pleasure to meet you." She gave a quick curtsy. "My last days on Earth were filled with a great deal of pain. I was sick with a malady, from which I suspect one doesn't normally recover. I suppose you know that already," her face twitched into an apologetic grimace. "For my renewed health, I offer my gratitude, sir." She gave him a radiant smile and another curtsy before quickly reclaiming her seat.

He heard her lilting voice for the first time. The sound was music to his ears. It warmed him, and he had to work hard to keep the smile off his face. "You are most welcome, Beatrix," Lanaq replied. Returning his attention to the group, he said, "Enough new information for one day, I think. I will be available during the next thirty days to answer questions about life on Devet, or whatever else your curiosity suggests. You may ask me anything that will help make your decision."

The doors parted at that exact moment, admitting the attendants. Lanaq mounted the steps, turning at the door to offer another respectful bow before leaving the room. He caught Beatrix following him with her eyes, and just for a second his pulse flared. Then, a little embarrassed, he realized that most of the Vashallen followed him with their eyes. Annoyed with himself for making something out of nothing, he passed through the doorway and made for the lift.

# Chapter Four

# Starship Revival

Silence held for a full ten seconds following the closing of the doors. Then, as if by invisible signal, pandemonium ensued. For several minutes sound and fury filled the space. Eventually, everyone wound down and began to discuss the situation quietly, each cadre huddling together

Beatrix sat with her hands folded in her lap, bemused air lighting her face. Despite the confusing situation, she found herself attracted to Lanaq. He was calm and centered. His deep voice was comforting, like a thick warm blanket on a cold winter night. Beatrix acknowledged to herself that now was perhaps an inappropriate time to be focused on her romantic feelings. She could see by the stunned expressions of her fellow groupmates they were struggling to come to terms with the information presented by Lanaq. She felt slightly ashamed of her own frivolous thoughts. She put aside her musings to focus on the others.

Gina sat gnawing at her lower lip, a scowl marring her brow. Npheba's brow was also drawn in, her lips pursed tightly. Beatrix saw her head twitch with barely perceptible nods. Both were deep in thought, possibly even shock, and neither appeared open to discussion.

Beside her, Sophia was quiet. Her head hung down, hair hiding her expression. Beatrix turned to her right. Trudy sat with her hands grasping her legs. Tears spilled unheeded from her eyes, running down her cheeks in twin torrents. Beatrix reached out, placing a hand atop one of Trudy's, offering what little comfort she could.

At her touch, Trudy turned her head, meeting Beatrix's concerned gaze. She blinked, causing another deluge to slide down her cheeks. She raised a single digit, swiping haphazardly at the tears. "I'm cured. This isn't me having one of my dreams. I can truly walk again." Trudy's voice petered out for a moment, overwhelmed by her changed circumstances. Her hands and eyes kept returning to her legs, as if she couldn't quite believe her own senses.

"As fantastic as it seems, I believe it's true. How are you feeling?"

"I feel amazing. But part of me still thinks this must be a dream, and sooner or later I'll wake up."

"I have those moments too. Then, I realize my imagination just isn't that good," Beatrix indicated Callisto, still visible through the transparent portion of the hull. The two women stared at the staggering sight for several minutes before Beatrix ventured, "I really meant, how are you feeling about being here? Scared? Angry?"

"I'm not sure...there hasn't really been time to examine how I feel. I'm not scared. I'm more grateful than anything else. I guess I'm not completely opposed to the idea of living on Devet."

"I feel the same way — certainly, I'm grateful to be well again. As for Devet, I'm willing to hear him out."

Gina abandoned contemplation to join the conversation, saying, "It's too soon to decide all is well. We must be cautious, ask many more questions. Did your mothers never warn you of gift horses?"

"Of course, we should ask more questions," Beatrix replied, her tone that of reason. "That shouldn't stop us from being grateful for the physical gifts the Devetians have granted us. Personally..."

"Bah," Gina hissed, interrupting anything else Beatrix might have added. "You are foolish if you think they give us something without expecting something in return."

"I'm far from foolish, Gina. I am merely willing to hear the man out, considering what he's done for me thus far."

"I'm not going back," Sophia gasped out suddenly, her quavering voice rising above their conversation. "I'm not going back; I'm not going back." She repeated the words over and over until they became a chant, shaking her head back and forth in time to her statement.

Until now, the petite blonde had been in a daze. Hearing the rising panic in her voice, Beatrix wrapped her in an embrace. She swayed back and forth with Sophia, whispering comforting noises as one would to an upset child. The commotion drew attention from some of the other women, and the others moved to huddle around their groupmate, offering her a modicum of privacy from prying eyes.

Npheba spoke up then. "Like Sophia, I'm leaning toward accepting Lanaq's offer of living on Devet. I have no desire to return to a life of cutting sugarcane under the overseer's lash."

"You were a slave?" Beatrix questioned, aghast.

"I reject the very idea. Men may have forced their will upon my body, but my head and heart have always been free."

"Where are you from?"

"I am of the Igbo people. Slavers took me from my home. They caught me as I gathered water from the river. They tossed my infant son into the water and laughed as they watched him sink."

"That's horrible."

"I don't need your pity, pretty English white lady."

Beatrix drew back from Npheba's vehemence.

"How did you end up here? What's the last thing you remember?" Gina's question distracted Npheba.

"A group of us escaped Jamaica, heading for freedom in Haiti. We outnumbered the plantation overseers ten to one. We killed them and seized a small trading vessel from the harbor, forcing the crew to set sail, but too many of us died or were injured in the fighting. Some miles out the ship's crew regained control. They would have returned us to the authorities. Rather than submit, I sliced my own throat and threw myself overboard. The last thing I remember is hitting the water, then I woke up here."

Npheba ground to a halt. With a sigh she continued softly, "I tell you this not for pity," she eyed Beatrix, "but so you will understand. I will entertain Lanaq's proposal because who would wish to return to such a life?" Having finished her speech, she caught Sophia's eye. The two shared a long look, deciding something without speaking. "We two shall stay and take our chances with these Devetians, I think." Sophia shared Phe's stare, agreeing with a nod of finality.

Sophia, previously so timid, surprised everyone when she spoke firmly. "I wasn't sold into slavery, but I also had no control over my life. My father, the honorable Sir Trembley, inherited a knighthood of no importance whatsoever; Trembley Hall is as unimportant and forgotten as the ancestor and the battle which earned the family its title. To put it plainly, my father is a puffed-up country bumpkin, a fact my husband never lets me forget. Nothing delights him more than ridiculing me with my father's absurdity.

"Not that absurdity was Father's only fault. He was also a drunk and a gambler, who squandered what little we had and ran up debts. It came as no surprise when Father informed me that he had accepted a proposal of marriage from a Mr. Potts on my behalf.

"I wish I could say that my husband's cruelty came on gradually, but it began on our wedding day. The moment we were behind closed doors, he took my virginity on the carpet in the foyer of his home." Sophia wept softly into her hands, remembering the many indignities she had been subjected to in her short life, the shame she had felt overwhelming her. The group sat quietly, patiently waiting for Sophia to continue.

"There were many rules under my husband's roof. If I so much as spoke without permission, he would backhand me. He enjoyed blacking my eye or cheek for flouting his rules."

Sophia gave the group a weak, watery smile, but soldiered on with her account. "On the last night I can remember, Mr. Potts came home, and we began our evening meal. He questioned me about my day, as he always did. I don't even remember what I said that set him off. He began screaming and yelling. I won't repeat the vile names he hurled my way that evening. His anger eventually turned to violence, as it always did. He punched me in the face till I was dizzy. He doubled me over with shots to the stomach. He kicked my legs out from under me, then dragged me to the coal cellar by my hair. He left me there in the dark. That's the last thing I remember before waking here." Sophia ended her tale with resignation. A sob escaped her lips, though she tried to hold it back.

Gradually Sophia's tears stopped, replaced by shallow hiccups that shook her rib cage. She wiped at the tears staining her cheeks. Her spine straightened, and she regarded her companions with renewed determination. "For my entire life I have existed as a leaf afloat on the water, with no control over my destination and no means to change my fate. I acknowledge Gina's concerns are valid," Sophia patted her companion's hand, "especially considering Lanaq has admitted to essentially kidnapping all of us. However, if I must choose between returning to a world where women are treated with such disregard or risking the unknown, I'll take the uncertainty over daily humiliation. The important point from my perspective is Lanaq has offered us a choice."

Compassion was written across Gina's face. "I don't condemn you for considering Lanaq's offer, but we need to know more before we decide. We don't know, for instance, whether or not Devetians condone slavery or wife beating."

Beatrix and Trudy stood watching on the sidelines with solemn expressions. Hesitantly, not wanting to draw further ire from Npheba, Beatrix ventured, "Would you tell us your story, Gina?"

Three other heads nodded along with Beatrix's inquiry. Gina sagged sadly, a sigh escaping her lips.

"Tell us," Sophia urged gently.

Gina nodded, deciding she would share her story. "We women know what it is to be without power. As Sophia said, we often have no agency in our own lives. This is very true for the daughters of Venice. We are bought and sold into marriage for the benefit of our families. You might expect this among the nobility, but even in merchant families the practice is the norm rather than the exception.

"My family has lived and traded in Venice for many generations. We can trace our history back to when Constantine reunited the Roman Empire. We came from Constantinople, a merchant family, eager to participate in the prosperity of the empire. Even after hundreds of years as Italians, those of us with Eastern heritage are still seen as outsiders. Unfit for marriage with the best families." Gina's voice was colored by bitterness. She pressed on: "My father was a practical man, with five daughters and only one son. My adolescent self thought him to be cruel. In retrospect, I know he struggled to settle us all. His options were limited, as were our dowries.

"When my father wanted to expand his import business he sought a partnership with a carting merchant, who just happened to have an unmarried son. He offered my eldest sister in marriage as part of the deal. He rid himself of one mouth while adding to his profit. I hated him.

"My second sister was admired by a merchant from the East. The merchant offered my father favorable prices on his goods for a term of five years in exchange for her, and so Donata," a hitch in her breath caused Gina to stumble over her sister's name. She took a determined inhale and continued, "Donata became his bride." Her voice reflected the sadness she still harbored at this loss.

"On the day after my mother gave birth to my fourth sister, my father woke me early. It was still dark outside. He threw a bag onto my bed and told me in harsh tones to pack, because I was leaving to be married." Sharp gasps from her companions followed Gina's words. She appreciated their sentiment, even as she hastened to finish the most painful part of her story.

"We rode through the countryside. I was numb with cold and fright, but we rode until we came to a convent. Thinking that I was to be married at the chapel within, I was surprised when my father handed the nun at the gate a small purse of coins. I remember vividly the moment he gave me into a life of servitude. The weak winter sun was just slipping below the tops of the trees when Father slapped his gloves into his hand and told me, matter-of-factly, that I was to be a bride of Christ. He plucked the reins from my chilled fingers, mounted his horse and rode away. The distinct sound the leather made when it slapped against his palm rings in my memory." Gina sighed heavily, "He never said goodbye, nor turned around as he abandoned me to my fate. I was thirteen."

Gina's voice finally broke. She raised fingers to her trembling lips, attempting to cover her emotions. She breathed slowly until she felt in control once more. "Because I had no other option, I became Sister Theodora. I had a roof over my head and meager food in my stomach, but my youth was spent on my knees in prayer, scrubbing pots and pans in the kitchen, toiling in the gardens, and learning to care for the sick. In later years I became Mother Superior's assistant, so I was taught to read and write, but I was never truly educated."

Glancing around, Gina found herself looking into the moist eyes of her group members and melted. She stretched out her arms, finding and grasping hands on either side of her. "Like Npheba and Sophia, I'm not telling you my story to earn your sympathy, but to emphasize the lack of choice in my life. I had no voice, no control. I use my voice now because I don't want us to be fooled into thinking these Devetians have only benevolent motives. They obviously want something in return. We shouldn't trust too quickly," she finished fiercely. Joan appeared then, cutting off further conversation. The attendant offered to show the group to their quarters. She led them down a hallway off the common room. With a couple touches on the device strapped to her wrist, Joan opened the last five doors along the corridor simultaneously. "Beatrix, Regina, Npheba, Sophia, and Gertrude, you have been assigned rooms one through five respectively. You should find everything you need at your disposal."

"Ugh. Please call me Trudy, Gertrude makes me sound like somebody's deaf old aunt."

"And I'm Gina, Joan."

"I'm simply Phe," Npheba added.

"As you wish, ladies. Now then, your rooms. Inside you should find all that you need, along with both a handheld personal screen and a wrist strap." She held up her wrist to display her own strap. "This self-tuned recording and activation pad will open all authorized doors aboard the ship. Both the strap and the personal screen will initiate at your touch. Let me know when you are ready for more instructions on their use.

"Second, you've all seen the auditorium. The remaining doors along the main corridor house leisure and activity areas for your use. Feel free to explore." Joan reached again for the device on her wrist. At her touch it emitted a soft gong. "Lastly, this sound will be heard throughout the ship thirty minutes before each meal is served." The attendant paused, ensuring everyone seemed satisfied with her instructions. "If you lack anything, just ask. I'll leave you to settle in and see you at the evening meal." Joan's brisk walk took her quickly down the hallway and out of sight.

Curiosity separated the women as they moved to inspect

their quarters. Beatrix entered her room and immediately felt at home. The bland space had been transformed. Gone was the sterile medical equipment, replaced by furniture in rich jewel tones of emerald and sapphire. A bed, a sofa and chairs, and a vanity all rested on thick, soft rugs.

Besides the door to the corridor and the door to the necessary room, there were two large doors on the left wall. Beatrix assumed they were wardrobes. Her fingers tingled with anticipation. Unable to contain her curiosity any longer, she pressed the button on the first of two wardrobe doors and the opaque door slid upward, disappearing.

She was a bit disappointed upon finding clothing much like what she was wearing. Tops, pants, skirts, robes, and nightwear, all very utilitarian. Everything was soft and loose, and in varying shades of blue or green. She chided herself for being disappointed; after all, these clothes were nicer than any she was used to wearing. Satisfied that everything she needed clothing-wise had been provided, Beatrix wondered what could possibly be in the second wardrobe. She pressed the button to open the second door; her jaw fell open when the contents were revealed. Any disappointment she'd felt upon opening the first wardrobe was replaced by sheer joy.

The dress, a single magnificent dress, was the opposite of the utilitarian fare housed in the first. The garment sparkled and gleamed, even in the diffuse lighting. Beatrix fingered the silky material, watching the sheen catch the light as it slipped between her fingers.

Still a bit stunned by her find in the second wardrobe,

Beatrix drifted over to examine the vanity. A small stool rose out of the floor at her approach. Beatrix sat, examining the two items that awaited her attention. The personal screen was the size of a large book. Like a blank manuscript it awaited her input. When she lifted the device, much lighter than a book, words appeared as if an unseen hand wielded an invisible pen. The message read: Welcome Beatrix. How may I assist you? She stared at the device, waiting for further information to surface from her brain. When no revelations were forthcoming, she replaced the screen and picked up the wristband of her strap. She placed the screen across her wrist as Joan's had been and drew the two ends of the strap together, wondering how they fastened.

She didn't have to wonder for long. The two ends made contact and melded together, sizing perfectly to fit her wrist. Once secured to her arm, the strap device also displayed a welcome message, and behind her the door to her room slid closed, startling her.

Beatrix stood and approached the door; it slid open as she drew near. Her brow wrinkled for a moment in thought. She stepped back, and the door slid closed. With a full-blown giggle and newfound understanding, she stepped forward again, passing through the door as it glided open. Once in the hallway she turned without thinking, heading for Trudy in room five.

Trudy's door was still open, her wrist device lying untouched on her vanity. Beatrix paused on the threshold, rapping on the doorframe to draw Trudy's attention.

Trudy's room was identical in layout to Beatrix's own, the lush pink-and-white ruffles and lace reflecting the occupant's taste. Trudy closed her wardrobe at Beatrix's knock, motioning her to enter. "Can you show me how to close my door?" she asked.

"Just put on your strap." Beatrix pointed to the device lying on Trudy's vanity.

Figuring out the mechanism, Trudy settled into the seat opposite Beatrix. "Did you like your room?"

"I did. It's identical to yours only dressed in different colors."

The conversation lapsed for a moment, until Trudy asked somewhat hesitantly, "Why do you think Npheba snapped at you earlier?"

"I admit I was taken aback at first by Phe's reaction. Now that I've had time to think about it, I'm not taking it personally. She was recounting a horrific story, opening deep wounds. Jamaica, where she was taken as a slave, is a British colony. I'm British. I was a proxy for her understandable anger."

"But it isn't your fault she was made a slave."

"No, not directly, but I do look and sound like every person who made her life a misery."

"Yeah, I guess," Trudy replied, her voice wan.

# Chapter Five

# Starship Revival

Over the next few days the women explored the ship, making use of the gardens and the pool. They began to acclimatize to their environment, the technological wonders of the Revival becoming their new normal. The dizziness that indicated implanted knowledge swimming to the surface of their minds receded as strange became familiar.

Lanaq continued to make himself available. Beatrix had seen him at a distance talking to others but the strong feelings his nearness evoked had Beatrix avoiding those conversations. She felt a pull toward the man that was undeniable and, in her opinion, highly inappropriate for the situation. She didn't want to make herself foolish by mooning over their pilot, well, she couldn't help mooning, but she would rather do it in private than be the object of ridicule by others. After breakfast she intended to make her way to the auditorium. Lanaq was often there answering questions in the morning. *"I can do this. I'm a grown woman. I will control my reactions,"* she told herself firmly.

Joan approached, breaking Bea's reverie. She didn't feel too guilty at ignoring her social graces; none of her table companions were very talkative this morning either. Each seemed distracted by their own internal struggles and startled by Joan's arrival.

The attendant was pushing a cart filled with food and drink options, a pleasant smile pinned in place.

"Good morning, Joan," Bea intoned as the attendant arrived at the table.

"Good morning, Beatrix. What would you like to eat this morning?"

"Whatever you have on the cart will be fine, Joan. I'm not fussy."

Bea studied the other woman as she retrieved a prepared plate from the cart. "Joan," she began, curiosity lilting her tone, "are you a typical Devetian female?"

"That's an interesting question, Beatrix. I have been given all the relevant features of a Devetian female, but I am an android. I have a biosynthetic shell coupled with artificial intelligence. Devetians refer to us as synthetic workers, or synths."

"You aren't alive?"

"Not in the way you mean."

"Do y'all have feelings?" Trudy asked.

"A complicated question, Trudy. My programming gives me purpose. When I fulfill my purpose, I am...satisfied. I believe you would call that happy."

"What is your programmed purpose?" Gina's tone was rather aggressive, but Joan answered calmly.

"My primary directive is to ensure the health, welfare, and safety of the first five Vashallen during your time aboard the Revival."

"Vashallen?" Beatrix sounded perplexed.

"Maybe, if you showed up to Lanaq's sessions you'd already know that Vashallen are the blessed women who can save the Devetian species."

"Don't scold Beatrix, I didn't know either," Trudy defended.

"Then maybe you should pay better attention when you do show up, Gertrude." Sophia used Trudy's full name knowing it would get her goat.

"Ladies, please!" Joan cut in, curtailing the rising tensions. "You are the first five blessed women chosen by Pilot Lanaq. As such, it is important you understand that when we reach our destination all eyes will be examining and judging your integration into Devetian society. I was programmed with you in mind to better assist in your preparedness. I speak each of your native languages, with regional dialect and idiomatic expressions. I also have extensive knowledge of the eras from which you all come."

"We come from different eras? How is that possible, Joan? I'm loath to ask in case I get another lecture from Sophia, but this seems like something I should know." Bea flashed a look at Sophia without moving her head, trying to judge her reaction. A hint of a grin tugged at her fellow Vashallen's lips; Bea allowed her own to climb upward. The two women put their annoyance behind them with a mutual shrug.

Joan continued speaking, pretending not to have noted the interaction. "I'm pleased to explain. Beatrix, you were forty-seven in the year 1780, when you would have died of breast cancer had Lanaq not intervened. Regina, you would have been eighty-four in 1798. A heart attack in the apple orchard prevented you from making that birthday. Lanaq arranged your disappearance, leaving a letter of explanation and a healthy donation to the convent."

"My explanation! What explanation?" Gina sputtered, anger evident in her posture and rising color.

"A message from your long-lost sister, Donata. An invitation to join her in the East and funds to make it possible."

"Lanaq fabricated a story?"

The android attendant nodded. "It was necessary to meet Quorum mandates during your retrieval," she added for clarity.

Gina was stunned into silence, which Joan took as an end to the inquiry. The synth returned to her earlier list as if the conversation in between had never taken place.

"Npheba, you were a relatively young woman, only thirty-two, when you threw yourself overboard in 1807. Though the cut to your throat was shallow enough not to kill you too quickly, the water rescue was tricky. Sophia, your brutish spouse left you with internal bleeding. It would have resulted in your death had Lanaq not brought you aboard the Revival. What age were you in the year 1821?" Joan asked the question not because she didn't know the answer but to break the stunned reaction of her charges.

"I was twenty-nine," Sophia responded automatically.

"Last but not least," Joan continued, "Trudy, you joined us in 1844."

"I was forty-five," Trudy offered unbidden before Joan could add anything further, greatly relieved when the synth moved on with her explanation.

"When Lanaq intervened in your lives, he took you from your timeline. You slept in stasis, but your world continued without you, time passing, things changing."

As Joan spoke, Beatrix knew she spoke truthfully. Flashes of subliminal knowledge showed her moments of Earth's history. A future she would have been part of, if she hadn't died. And much more she would never have lived to see, no matter how healthy. It was still confusing having knowledge of a future you didn't live which was now the past. She struggled to imagine ever keeping it all straight in her head. The implanted knowledge worked best when she accepted rather than fought to understand. She stopped fighting her own brain and listened.

"The last Vashallen selected are from the current year, 2130. The world they know is very different from yours. Cultural norms have shifted over the eras. Trust me, when you've had more contact with the different Vashallen cadres, the differences will become evident. I can help you navigate these differences; you need only ask. My programming was designed to put you at ease, to make this transitional time as stress-free as possible."

Gina harrumphed, "In one breath you ask for our trust, and in the next admit that you are designed to lull us into compliance."

"I don't believe that is at all what I said, Gina. I'm disappointed you choose to hear it that way."

Beatrix would have said that Joan appeared crestfallen, though somehow she knew a synth was only programmed to mimic emotion. Nevertheless, she offered Joan an apologetic look. The subdued synth spread her hands in apology and left.

A heavy silence followed Joan's departure. Beatrix felt rather annoyed with Gina, and apparently she wasn't the only one. Four pained stares pinned Gina in place, but Beatrix spoke first: "Why must you be so aggressive and confrontational with your questions?"

"Please pardon my manners. Already you four begin to feel like sisters. I do not wish us to be duped into a life of servitude," she finished, with a hitch in her voice.

Gina's words must have affected Trudy. She began to sob quietly.

"Trudy? What's wrong?" The concern in Sophia's voice was reflected in the expressions of the others.

"How...can y'all...even look at me?" Trudy asked between sobs. "I'm...a disgusting...human being!"

Sophia exchanged a questioning look with the others over Trudy's bent head. Shrugs all round answered her unspoken inquiry. "What's happened?" she pressed.

Trudy sat a little straighter, leveling blotchy red eyes at Npheba. "I'm so sorry," she wailed, returning to sniffling quietly into her hands.

Npheba shrugged once again at the looks from her

groupmates. "I do not know why Trudy is upset. She and I have not had words."

Sophia tried again. "Trudy, did someone upset you?"

"Cashondra, from group seven, said I should be ashamed of myself. That I didn't deserve to be here. She said..." Trudy gulped, and tears pooled on her lower lids. "She said I should throw myself out an airlock."

Shock ran through the group. "What! Why on Earth would she say such a horrible thing?"

"Because my family owned slaves." Trudy looked defeated. "I really am sorry for everything that happened to you, Npheba."

"You have done nothing to me.I don't need your apology. I understand Cashondra's anger, but her solution is untenable."

"I didn't try to stop it. I didn't try to stop my father or my husband from buying people. My whole life was made possible by the forced labor of others. And I admit, I thought I *was* better than the slaves we owned. I thought the color of my skin meant something." Her cheeks flushed with shame as she spoke, knowledge acquired during her long stasis rising to the surface, revealing the ugliness of her past virulent prejudices.

Npheba closed her eyes for a moment, then opened them. "In this new environment, we all must face what we once were while growing toward what we are becoming. It is good for you to understand, to see the injustice of the system you lived with, and understand how you were a part of it. But... kill yourself? That would serve no purpose.

Coming to new understandings should be welcomed, not punished. Be remorseful, Trudy, but use that to create some good in the world around you." She paused. "It was Cashondra who put the idea of suicide into your head?"

Trudy's head bobbed up and down. "She poi...nted out my cul...pabil...ity," she managed through a plague of hiccups. "And I kn...ew she was r...ight."

Npheba glanced around the common room. Her lids narrowed, seeking the woman who had upset her groupmate. She drew herself to her feet. "Let us find Cashondra and clear up this matter." She strode toward the door, head high, back straight. The others followed in her wake, Sophia pulling Trudy to her feet to trail after the others.

Npheba found Cashondra in the auditorium. Small groups were gathered here and there about the room, the sound of conversation providing a constant buzz. Npheba boldly gained the center of the room and raised a hand for quiet. "I would like to speak with Cashondra of cadre seven," she said with authority, "I would like to discuss your suggestion that my groupmate kill herself."

Silence rocked the auditorium. "I'm Cashondra." A petite, curvy woman stood, joining Npheba at the center of the room. "Why do you care what I say to her?" Cash jabbed a finger in Trudy's general direction.

"She's my groupmate. Why would you say such a spiteful thing to someone you don't even know?"

"Why do you feel the need to stand up for her? Is she incapable of speaking for herself?"

"Though I've only known Trudy for a few days, it's clear

there's not an evil bone in her body. Besides, whatever any of us were or did in the past, things are different now."

Cashondra wrinkled her nose. "Trudy was a slave-owner, nothing you can say will make that less disgusting. I'm shocked it isn't worse for you, being a former slave — and her groupmate, to boot."

"She understands now how horrific slavery was and regrets the part she played in its furtherance. I don't hold her personally responsible for my experiences. Regardless, it seems unnecessary to suggest that someone take their life."

Cashondra paused, her lips coming together, her head bobbing slightly. "You're right. That was a step too far, but I stand behind my statement that owning people is a disgusting practice."

"We can both agree on that, and Trudy would agree with you if you would give her a chance."

"I don't owe her a chance. I don't owe her anything."

"Is there a problem?" Lanaq's voice startled the women, the majority of whom had been focused on the discussion at the center of the room. The two Vashallen turned to watch Lanaq trip lightly down the stairs. "If there is a problem, how can I help?"

"The problem is, you chose a former slave owner as one of our number," Cashondra spoke to Lanaq but leveled her gaze at Trudy.

"Cashondra suggested Trudy should kill herself," Npheba appealed to Lanaq.

Lanaq nodded, his expression growing solemn. "I see. Let's all sit down and discuss this calmly."

Npheba's shoulders relaxed slightly, and Beatrix let out the breath she'd been holding. The tension didn't leave the room completely, but it did ratchet down a few notches. Trudy was still hovering just inside the door. She looked sad. Beatrix took her hand, leading her to a seat as the others in the room did the same. Sophia took a seat on Trudy's other side. She offered an encouraging smile.

"Now then," Lanaq addressed the room, "let me see if I understand the situation correctly. Cashondra, you are upset because Trudy comes from a slave-holding family?"

"Yes. Owning another person is just evil. She doesn't deserve to be here."

"I have the gist of your position. Npheba, you are upset because Cashondra suggested that Trudy should commit suicide?"

"The suggestion was reprehensible. Though I can sympathize with Cashondra's feelings on the matter of slavery, I think it's more important right now to stick together, not turn on each other."

"How can you defend her?" Cashondra said, shaking her head.

"I can defend her without defending slavery." Phe offered an open hand to Cashondra, who took the proffered member hesitantly. "Remember, I killed myself rather than return to it. But Trudy, like us, has been taken far from her place and time. As she has shown nothing but kindness to me, I am willing to overlook her past and deal with her as a sister in this otherworldly scenario in which we find ourselves. Above all else, I think we should support one another which would include not urging each other to self-harm."

Cashondra rolled her eyes and blew out a breath. "Assholes like her owned people that look like you and me. They got rich trading in our flesh, blood, and bones. How can you just 'overlook' that?"

Beside her, Beatrix could feel Trudy trying to make herself smaller. She shrank in on herself with each barb from Cashondra. Her haunted eyes had run dry.

Npheba bowed her head for a moment before speaking. "You have the right to feel the way you feel. Take it from someone whose flesh, blood, and bones *were* traded, anger doesn't heal. Now we are all in the same boat, taken by an alien civilization. We can see by the assortment of women Lanaq has gathered from all over the world that no race is better than any other. Can we put the past behind us and start with a clean slate?" Phe asked with hope evident in her voice.

"She should be held accountable for accepting the wealth and position that came from slavery," Cashondra countered. "I can't help but feel that, despite how much everything else has changed. As you said, it's my right."

Npheba sighed, nodding, "I understand," she said with resignation.

While the others spoke, Trudy crept forward, her eyes downcast. She bowed toward Cashondra, fresh tears still glistening in her eyes. "I accept how you feel about me," she said through a sniffle. "I understand why you do," she blinked, swaying with dizziness, reaching up to hold her forehead. "All this new knowledge," she said, speaking in an undertone, "it can be overwhelming." She raised her eyes to Cashondra, "I understand now, how awful slavery was. I will strive to be a better person going forward and I hope someday you will forgive me my past. But I'm not going to throw myself out of an air lock!" Trudy finished with more spunk than anyone had seen from her in days. The declaration produced a ripple of mirth. Even Cashondra cocked an appraising eyebrow.

Lanaq, who had maintained a studious silence, finally spoke up. "Now that you have expressed your feelings to Trudy, and know she accepts those feelings and her own responsibility, do you feel any better?"

Cashondra scowled again, then released a sigh. "Whatever. I spent so much of my life dealing with clueless white people, meeting someone who actually owned people who look like me is a little hard for me to handle. But, as long as Trudy stays out of my way, I suppose I can refrain from thinking up other creative ways for her to kill herself."

A further chuckle rose from the crowd.

Npheba smiled, squeezing the hand still grasped in her own. "Sisters," she asked hopefully, pleased when Cashondra echoed her sentiment despite their difference of opinion. Trudy looked like she would step forward, offering her hand too, but instead she fell back and sat down in a plush chair, an expression of thoughtful relief slowly spreading over her face.

Lanaq smiled, glad to see the Vashallen could resolve such complex differences themselves. "'Hatred does not cease by hatred, but only by love; this is the eternal rule,'" he quoted. "So says your Siddhārtha Gautama, also called the Buddha."

"You've read the religious texts of Earth?" It was a Vashallen from another group who spoke, a dark-eyed brunette named Tanya. Lanaq turned to her with a smile, gratefully feeling the tension in the room dissolve.

"I've been blessed with an abundance of time on my hands. I've read all the pivotal texts of your civilization."

"What do Devetians believe? Do you have a religion?" Clearly, the question had been weighing on Tanya.

"I would call Devetians spiritual, not religious. We strive for balance with the universe in our actions and thoughts. We believe harmony will beget happiness. Our deity is Mother Balance, or The Mother."

"Sounds more like philosophy than religion."

"I'd say they are one and the same."

"Do Devetians attend worship services?"

"We don't gather weekly in sacred places, no. House Ukanii sees to our spiritual health. Their House maintains our sacred sites and offers guidance when one feels the need. When we had young ones, Ukanii was responsible for teaching them about Universal Balance and The Mother."

"What does your spiritual philosophy have to say on the subject of enslaving others?" Tanya's background in investigative reporting was apparent, her question relevant to the previous topic.

"Our spiritual teachings? Not much. Our laws, however,

are explicit. No sentient being may be held or forced to labor against their will, except as punishment for a crime"

"Your religion doesn't teach that slavery is wrong?"

"I would say our religion doesn't need to teach that such an act is wrong. One knows instinctively when an act is amoral. Imbalance with the universe is uncomfortable, as is The Mother's disappointment. It's up to the individual to make better choices if they wish for a harmonic life."

"That is similar to the principle of karma," Mehika, a member of the final five Vashallen, said. She was one of three Vashallen Lanaq had rescued on the night of Earth's largest to date earthquake and tsunami event.

"Earth and Devet share many similar tenets," Lanaq agreed.

"Do your laws protect women?" The voice was timid.

"Our laws make no distinction between individuals, Sophia. It applies equally to all sentient beings."

"You keep stressing the term 'sentient being.'"

"Indeed. There are a vast number of species in the universe, many possess sentience. Should those species visit Devet, they would enjoy the protection of our law."

"Do you have a law against men hitting their wives?"

"First, and let me be clear, Devetians don't strike one another. Devetians have decried violence for as long as our historians have been keeping records. That being said, our society is matriarchal. Women are held in high esteem. To answer your question, we do have a law specific to the point. No sentient being may touch another sentient being in violence without their permission."

"Lanaq, I'd like to switch topics if I may."

"By all means, Mirabel. I'm here to answer your questions."

"On our first day here, you said that your species was experiencing fertility issues, nearing the point of extinction. We've asked all manner of questions in the intervening days and you've answered, but we've been dancing around the one question that matters most. Did you heal us so we can make babies for you?"

"It is as I expected, they wish us to be broodmares." Gina thrust herself to her feet, balled fists landed on her hips, fury flashed in her eyes. Angry grumbling arose from the assembled women.

This was the first real instance of strong emotion exhibited by the Vashallen as a group. Lanaq knew he needed to answer their concerns with care or the situation could escalate. "Ladies, in no way are the Vashallen seen as broodmares. We are offering what we hope will be a rich life on Devet. Do we also hope that your lives might eventually include children? Yes, because the Vashallen are the last hope to save our species. I assure you, your value to our society doesn't rest solely in your ability to reproduce."

Lanaq stood, straightening his tunic. "We've tackled weighty topics today. I suggest we take the day to think. I'm available should you need me."

Lanaq's bow was nearly perfunctory; his retreat less formal than was usual. He was preoccupied, already drafting his report in his head. "Of all the details to overlook," he grumbled under his breath, stepping into the lift. He was angry with himself for letting the Vashallen down. He could put procedures in place that would prevent a similar occurrence in the future, but that wouldn't be much solace to Cashondra or Trudy today.

# Chapter Six

# Starship Revival

Lanaq's office was located near the command deck. The room, like all the others aboard the Revival, could be shifted and changed to match the occupant's taste. Unlike the minimalistic functionality of his sleeping quarters, his office resembled a study found in any respectable English manor: wood paneling, bookcases, and an impressive marble fireplace. Tufted leather chairs with tall backs and ornately carved legs occupied pride of place in front of the fireplace. A heavy desk of gleaming burled wood anchored another wall.

The wall was graced from floor-to-ceiling with museum-quality replicas by some of Lanaq's favorite Earth painters: Michelangelo, Vermeer, Degas, Durer, and Botticelli. Like most Devetians he was drawn to art, and his study reflected his taste.

The decor and furniture were like most everything aboard the Revival, composed of nanites. All could be reassembled at Shay's direction. The exception in Lanaq's study was a small watercolor which hung above the fireplace, an

Albrecht Durer, painted during his journey from Germany to Italy. Like many of the watercolors inspired by Durer's trip through the Swiss Alps, the subject of the painting was a single plant. The canvas was cream-colored with age, but even so the delicately depicted leaves and stems seemed ready to sway in a breeze. It bore Durer's ubiquitous ini-tialed signature alongside the year of composition, 1512.

Lanaq had bought the watercolor from the artist as a gift for his mother; after all these years he could still get lost in the perfection of the details. He knew his mother would love this little depiction of Earth as much as he did.

A chirp from his strap alerted him to an arrival at his door. He thumbed the control from his strap, went to the door and escorted his visitor to a chair, offering her refreshments before they sat.

"I'm glad you decided to visit with me, Trudy. The last couple of days can't have been easy for you."

Trudy sipped at the water Lanaq had provided, more to give her hands something to occupy them than out of thirst. "No, they haven't been. I can hardly look at Phe without being wracked by guilt." Trudy's voice was thick with emotion. She paused, trying to hold back sobs. "Phe has been so kind and generous toward me, considering all that she endured."

"I agree. Npheba is an impressive woman."

"Her kindness makes it worse. Cashondra's anger feels like what I deserve."

"Why do you think you deserve anger?"

"While I lived on Earth, I never even thought to

question the idea of owning," Trudy hesitated, "slaves." She forced herself to say the word. "It feels awful to know I failed at being a human being."

"It is a sign of progress that you understand the intrinsic wrongness of owning other sentient life. As for Cashondra, she seems willing to at least forgive, if not forget. Guilt is only healthy when it leads us to remorse, which certainly seems to be the case with you."

"Par...don," Trudy hiccuped through tears.

A square of fabric materialized on the table next to Lanaq. He took Shay's hint, offering the square to Trudy. She accepted the fabric and dabbed at her wet eyes and runny nose.

"We feel guilt when our psyche acknowledges that we have caused harm. It's an uncomfortable feeling, as it should be. But remorse, when we accept full responsibility for the harm we caused, is the stage where true change occurs. Our hearts and minds shift."

"How do I get past guilt to remorse?"

"Everyone carries shame or regret. Let the feeling push you toward better actions." He offered a gentle smile. "As to the other Vashallen, you can't change the past, so show them who you intend to be going forward. You can't control how they think or feel, only how you respond. Be kind. Be patient."

"Thank you, Lanaq. I feel better after talking to you. You seem to know the perfect thing to say in any situation." Trudy dried her eyes one last time, offering the now damp square with a gesture.

He declined. Trudy rose to take her leave. She stopped at the door to ask, "Did Devet ever experience the same issues, Lanaq?"

"You mean slavery? No. Though Devetian history is full of its own tumultuous, sometimes shameful, periods. Every culture has challenges. We aren't perfect either."

"That's comforting. Thanks, Lanaq."

Lanaq tidied away the cups from Trudy's visit while he waited for his next appointment. The Vashallen Noa, a lawyer from Rehovot, Israel, had requested the meeting. He had no idea why. He was still reviewing his selection notes when Noa arrived at his door.

He rose from his seat in front of the fireplace, opening the door. He bade Noa enter and to make herself comfortable, gesturing to one of the large chairs. He offered refreshments, then asked after her health. Observing the niceties gave the Vashallen several minutes to become comfortable in Lanaq's domain.

Lanaq resettled himself in his chair, hands resting lightly on the arms. Crossing one leg casually over the other, he gave Noa a gentle look. "What can I do for you, Noa?"

Noa swallowed past the lump in her throat. Her blood was pounding in her ears, and she felt hot nausea for a few seconds. Lanaq sat in silence, passively observing her struggle. He applied no pressure, allowing her to answer in her own time.

Finally, Noa summoned up her courage to say, "I don't like men." There, she'd spoken it aloud for the first time ever. She felt another wave of nausea sweep over her body.

This time she was left feeling cold and clammy. She swallowed hard again, willing the nausea to pass. She waited on tenterhooks for Lanaq's response.

Lanaq schooled his features carefully, not allowing the surprise he felt to be reflected in his expression. His surprise came not from any judgment regarding Noa's statement, but from the fact that extensive observation and assessment had shown no indication of homosexuality. However, Noa's statement was open to interpretation, and he didn't want to jump to conclusions. With careful neutrality he asked, "Do you mean that you aren't romantically interested in men?"

Noa's head dipped, hanging low between her shoulders, making it difficult for Lanaq to ascertain her tiny nod of affirmation. Her riotous curls flopped forward to cover her face, but he could hear her sniffles.

Lanaq was on shaky ground here; this was not a scenario that he had anticipated. While his brain processed solutions, he offered words of comfort. "Please do not distress yourself, Noa. While this development is unforeseen, it's definitely not insurmountable." Lanaq reached for another handkerchief, which Shay manifested at his side. He proffered it to Noa for her tears.

She dabbed at her eyes. Then, gathering her composure, she tucked her hair behind her ears and sat up straighter. "I'm sorry," she offered meekly.

"You have nothing for which you need to apologize."

"I think I do. You've wasted a great deal of time and energy on me. The Vashallen are intended as mates for your masculine population." Lanaq began to shake his head in the negative, but she cut off his response. "Say what you like, but you know I'm right. You need women who can help regrow your population. That just isn't me."

Lanaq considered her words before replying. "I'd like to clarify my understanding of the difficulty," he began. "A physical or emotional relationship with a male is unappealing to you, therefore you believe you won't be made welcome on Devet?"

Noa gave him a wry twist of her lips, accompanied by a resigned bobbing of her head. "That's part of it."

"Okay," he said, feeling on more familiar ground. "Two things I'd like you to consider. One, a physical relationship isn't necessary to produce offspring. Devetian medical care has several methods that can be employed. Two, ours is a patient race. The men will be disappointed that you aren't open to a relationship with them, but they'll be hopeful your future daughters will be."

Lanaq realized as soon as the words left his mouth just how selfish and dismissive they sounded. Noa stiffened and crossed her arms over her chest, mentally withdrawing from the conversation. He decided to take a different tact. "That was insensitive and selfish. Let me try again, and instead of trying to refute your objections, why don't I just listen?" This last was accompanied by a rueful smile.

Noa responded with a smile of her own. Lanaq could see her visibly relax. "Well, that's a refreshing attitude," she said, amusement lacing her words. Slipping off her flats, Noa drew her legs up, crossing them akimbo in front of herself. A more serious expression settled across her features as she leaned forward, resting her forearms across her knees.

"I wasn't really worried about the physicality involved in producing a child. I assumed you would have some sort of artificial insemination technology, because..." Noa paused, using both arms and hands to indict everything. "Because, well...you know, spaceship, outer space. In fact, I don't really understand why you need us at all. Surely with all your technology you should have a way to artificially incubate your offspring?" Noa waited, her question was not rhetorical.

It took Lanaq a heartbeat to respond; this was not his anticipated direction of the conversation, his reply was heavy with melancholy, "We did try. Our medical researchers did everything they could, but all attempts at artificial incubation ended badly. No fetus survived till birth. Failure after failure sapped the will and desire of our people. Some called our failures the condemnation of Mother Balance. Eventually that avenue of research became an anathema to Devetians."

"I see," Noa responded, but said no more.

Lanaq attempted to refocus the conversation, "You said you weren't worried about the physicality of a relationship. What worries you, Noa?"

She shrugged. Her reluctance to speak manifest in her averted gaze. Her voice, when she finally spoke, dipped to a whisper as she said, "The problem is, I'm a lesbian." She looked up at Lanaq, almost daring him to condemn her.

"I've promised to listen rather than talk, but lesbian

isn't a dirty word. There's no need to whisper." Lanaq's comments were offered lightheartedly: designed to put Noa at ease, lift the mood, and perhaps elicit a smile.

A wry twist lifted one side of Noa's lips, letting Lanaq know he had at least partially succeeded. Her next words came easier, with less hesitation. "As you know, I grew up in mid 20th century Israel. Admitting my sexuality was unthinkable. I avoided admitting it to myself, for my entire life. I've never been free to find someone. I'm lonely. I want someone with whom I can make a family. I want to experience that close emotional connection. Are there gay people on Devet?"

Having been asked a direct question, Lanaq felt free to offer, "Devetians have a less rigid relationship with sexuality. At one time there were many Devetians who preferred same-sex relationships. House Eschenwell is home to most males who prefer male partners."

"Most males?"

"Homosexual males aren't required to adopt House Eschenwell. Some opt to stay with their birth Houses, some choose a House based on shared interests. We digress. What you really want to know is, are there Devetian lesbians? There are currently thirty-two living Devetian females. They all have male partners. House Ibinaya was at one time populated by lesbian females. Unfortunately, as our population has dwindled some of our Houses have become dormant. Ibinaya was one such House. You could revive House Ibinaya, though I cannot say when or if you might find a partner on Devet," he admitted honestly.

Noa inclined her head in understanding. "Thank you for recognizing my dilemma," she said softly. "I've been using my personal screen to find out how things were on Earth after my death."

Lanaq's chest sagged with frustration. *Why won't the Vashallen understand that they did not die?* he wondered to himself.

Noa continued to speak. "...been legal since the early twenty-first century. All the articles I've read suggest that in 2130 being gay isn't an issue." Noa's face was alive with hope. She uncrossed her legs. Unconsciously mirroring Lanaq's body language, she dropped her elbows to her knees, leaning forward as she asked, "So, if I choose to go home, do I get to pick where I return? And," she added with growing enthusiasm, "do I get to pick when?"

Lanaq chuckled briefly, answering with amusement in his tone, "Our technology is quite advanced, I admit, but we haven't gotten around to inventing a time machine. You would be returned to Earth in its current year. As to where, well, anywhere you'd like, really. Shay could help you choose the right place."

"And I get to keep the health and youth you've bestowed upon me?"

The fact that Noa had been a lawyer during her Earth life was apparent in the questions she asked, like she was nailing down the conditions of a contract.

"Yes, you keep your renewed youth and health. However, your cell degeneration rate must be returned to Earth norm. You would live an average Earth life span."

"How much of my memory do I get to keep?" Noa's question was pointed, almost aggressive. She stabbed him with a fiery gaze, but quickly deflated, expelling a breath that blew curls away from her temples. "I'm not naive. I know you aren't going to let me remember aliens coming to Earth. How much of my old life will I remember?"

"You'll remember the people from your life. The details will be adjusted. You won't remember this experience at all."

Noa was once again looking at the floor between her feet, so Lanaq couldn't judge her reaction from her expression. She said nothing for several very long moments; then her head bobbed in acknowledgment, accompanied by a terse, "Okay."

The conversation appeared to have reached a natural conclusion. Lanaq and Noa stood simultaneously. "Let me know when you make your decision," he said to her.

"No need to wait. I've made my decision. I want to go back to Earth."

"You're sure?"

"I am."

"Very well. Shay?" Lanaq paused, then said, "Would you please ask the Vashallen to assemble in the auditorium?"

* * *

Speculative chatter about the unusual summons they'd received created a constant hum as the Vashallen filled the auditorium. The noise ceased abruptly when the doors slid open, admitting Lanaq and Noa. Lanaq gave his usual low bow before proceeding to the center of the chamber. Noa followed in his wake, conscious of the curious stares tracking their movement.

"Thank you all for coming this morning. I've asked you here because one of your number has decided to return to Earth. I thought it best to explain the process rather than leave it to conjecture.

"Noa's reasons for returning are her own. I'll let her decide how much to share, and with whom. What I need to impart are the consequences and the limitations that such a decision brings. Noa and I have had these discussions privately; however, in order to make a fully informed decision regarding your futures, you must be apprised of the conditions a return to Earth would entail."

Lanaq paused. He offered Noa refreshments and a seat to his left. He poured himself a glass of water and took his own seat, drawing out the moment, letting what he'd said thus far sink in.

"Okay then, I'll detail the process as succinctly as possible, then open the floor to questions. I appreciate your patience." Lanaq paused once more, watching as heads bobbed around the room, acknowledging his request. He felt this would be one of the more difficult discussions to have with these women. The Quorum had mandated strict protocols in order to protect the knowledge of Devetian existence. Those protocols were bound to feel harsh for some.

"First, regardless of the year you left Earth you will be returned to its current calendar year, which is 2130.

With all our technology, Devet still hasn't gotten around to inventing a time machine." Lanaq used the same joke to bring forth a few chuckles. He noticed that Beatrix was one of the few who laughed, and they exchanged a quick smile.

"Second, you will get to keep your renewed youth and good health. However, your rate of cell degeneration would be returned to Earth norm in order to keep Devet's existence a secret.

"Third, Shay will help you decide where on Earth you'd like to begin your new life. Monetary support for your lifetime will be provided, alongside all relevant documents. Electronic records will be adjusted accordingly.

"Lastly, I must discuss your memories. I'm sorry, but should you return to Earth you will not be allowed to retain any recollections of the Revival or your fellow Vashallen. Your memory will be altered to incorporate your former life with the current time period."

Lanaq took this moment to look over at Noa. He felt every eye in the room follow his own. He wanted the Vashallen to feel the weight of their decision — what better way to emphasize the importance than with a living example? He waited for the explosion but was surprised by the non-reaction his statement produced. He had not expected calm acceptance. Noa then further surprised him by standing to speak.

"No doubt there are downsides to my decision, such as a reduced life span and altered memories, not to mention everyone I once knew being long dead. The upside is you can choose a whole new life. I've decided on a new career in a new city, and I'm excited by the opportunity I've been given." Noa's expression turned serious. "What you need to keep in mind is the old adage: 'You can't get something for nothing,' you have to accept compromise." With a deep shrug of her shoulders, she sat back down.

Lanaq attempted to pick up where she had left off. "Noa is correct. In the long run, whatever decision you make will have pros and cons. I encourage you to consider carefully." He paused, struck once again by the self-possession of the Vashallen. "Those are the conditions placed upon your return to Earth. Any questions?"

Lanaq answered a few subdued follow-up queries. When no further questions seemed forthcoming, he rose and offered his hand to Noa in an antiqued Earth custom. She returned the gesture, shaking his hand.

"I wish you a fulfilled life on Earth, Noa. Take the day to say your goodbyes."

Lanaq stepped back and dropped into an exceptionally low bow, holding the position for a few extra beats to show his sincere respect. Straightening, he adjusted his tunic, nodded toward the other Vashallen and excused himself.

# Chapter Seven

# Starship Revival

At the end of the prescribed thirty days Noa was the only Vashallen who had requested a return to Earth. Fifty-two decided to make Devet their new home. The Revival broke orbit, setting out for the first of three FST jumps required to reach the Devetian solar system.

On this day, the last day of their journey before reaching Devet, Lanaq and Shay had arranged a celebration lunch. Shay suggested the women might like to sample the tastes of Devet. In fact, Shay had many suggestions regarding the luncheon. Lanaq deferred to her superior wisdom in this department. It was fairer to say that Shay had arranged the celebration.

"Do I have time for a run and a shower before lunch?"

"You sound tense, Lanaq. Anything you'd like to share?" Shay's programming responded to the anxiety in Lanaq's voice.

"Admittedly, I am a little on edge. There's pressure to deliver for Devet, while simultaneously doing right by these women. Soon I'll see my family, my home, for the first time in more than three millennia. There's plenty on my mind, Shay, but nothing unexpected."

"Fair enough." Shay deduced Lanaq's anxiety was normal. "I've arranged with the attendants to serve lunch in the garden. I designed a gazebo."

Lanaq laughed, relieving some of the tightness from his shoulders. "Ah, Shay, you're a born party planner at heart."

"I prefer to think of myself as a creative architect, thank you very much. Would an hour suffice for a run?"

"Perfect. Thank you." Lanaq removed his tunic and stepped into his exercise pod. The pod could be programmed to simulate a preferred exercise. He could scull the lakes of his mountain home, surf the shores of Hawaii, or practice hand-to-hand combat. Today he chose to jog the winding rocky paths of his mountain home.

Precisely an hour later, Lanaq left his quarters feeling loose-limbed and refreshed. A run had been just the medicine he needed. When he entered the garden, he was impressed with the amount of detail Shay and the attendants had managed. A woodland scene straight out of a Hollywood set greeted him. "We watched way too many Earth movies," he chuckled under his breath.

The plaited branches that formed the gazebo grew directly from the lawn, twining together overhead, leafy vines provided shade. Here and there, lantern-like blooms offered soft illumination. Bell-shaped blossoms hung in graduated clusters, adding an intoxicating scent. The details reminded Lanaq of Hekaria Square in the capital city of

Devet, and a wave of home sickness unexpectedly washed over him. He ignored the uncomfortable feeling, pushing it aside to attend the waiting Vashallen.

Under the canopy, buffet tables offered a variety of uniquely Devetian food and drink. Random seating created a casual atmosphere.

"Good afternoon, ladies," Lanaq said, giving a hearty wave as he approached. "I thought you might like a taste of Devet before we arrive."

Lanaq spent a pleasant couple of hours introducing the Vashallen to the flavors of his home. The women sampled savory, sweet, non-alcoholic, and alcoholic, but Lanaq suggested they finish the tasting with the Devetian version of coffee.

"The beverage is brewed from the bark of fossmore trees. Much like Earth's coffee it is served warm, sweetened to taste. The mood-altering effect of fosh is stronger than caffeine, so you might want to sip with restraint until you become accustomed."

Mehika had been the most adventurous of the Vashallen today. She stepped forward eagerly to try each new flavor, and fosh was no exception. She declined Lanaq's offer of sweetener and sipped the hot liquid carefully. With the first sip her eyes slipped shut in delight.

"Mmmmm. It's slightly spicy, with a hint of molasses flavor."

"You are tasting the caramelization that occurs during the roasting process. You have a fine palate, Mehika. House Rafeen specializes in all things edible. It might make a good fit for you." Mehika beamed, both pleased by Lanaq's compliment and reassured she would find a place for herself in this new life.

Once everyone was settled with a cup of fosh, sipping away, Lanaq addressed the elephant in the room. "Late tonight we will arrive in Devetian space. Tomorrow, the planet will hold a welcome ceremony in your honor. A great deal of Devetian culture revolves around social events, something you will discover for yourselves soon enough. I wanted to take a moment to thank each of you for keeping an open mind during the time we've spent together. I'd also like to thank you for the decision you've made. It is Devet's great hope the Vashallen will be instrumental in saving our species. Let me be the first to say, 'Welcome home.'"

The celebration broke up soon afterward, the Vashallen leaving to pursue their own interests. Lanaq watched Beatrix cross the pond and disappear into the tropical foliage. He shouldn't follow her, but he couldn't help himself.

He found her sitting in a honeysuckle-draped arbor. He smiled and strode forward, letting the giant palm frond that covered the path drop behind him like a curtain. "May I?" he requested, indicating his intention to occupy the seat across from her.

"Please do."

Beatrix watched Lanaq closely as he settled himself opposite. They sat quietly for several minutes, until Beatrix broke the silence. "You might not have realized, you called me Bea earlier."

Embarrassment showed on Lanaq's face. "Did I? My apologies. It's how I think of you."

"No need to apologize. I like it." The corners of Beatrix's mouth lifted slightly. Her eyelids drifted closed and she tilted her head back, as if seeking the sun. With eyes still shut, heart fluttering, she asked, "Do you have a nickname for any of the others?"

"No." He kept his answer short and simple. Beatrix, in this moment, was like an exotic bird caught preening. He was afraid to disturb her and have the moment fly away.

"I like that too." Her voice was a lazy whisper. With a deep breath Beatrix opened her eyes. Standing, she said, "I think I'd better return to my quarters before I fall asleep right here."

Lanaq stood also, falling into step beside her.

"This really is a lovely spot. Did you design it?"

"As much as I'd like to take credit, this is all Shay."

"Is Shay your shipmate?"

"Yes," Lanaq affirmed, "Shay is my shipmate, but she is also the ship itself. She is an artificial intelligence. This ship is Shay's body, and its memory core is her brain."

Beatrix wore an unreadable expression for a moment before she offered, "Please tell Shay that I liked the gardens very much."

Lanaq gave a low chuckle. "You just did. You can talk to Shay from anywhere on the ship. She won't answer unless you address her directly."

Beatrix realized their conversation had carried them to the corridor. She also noticed her fingers were entwined with Lanaq's. Somewhere along the path he had reached out to help her under one of the giant leaves and never let go. It felt natural to hold his hand. She looked up, meeting his eyes. Raising their hands, she told him, "I like this, too."

As their eyes met over their entwined hands a sensation like pins and needles ran up and down her body. Pops and prickles floated across her skin, and the hair rose on the back of her arms and neck. Beatrix swooned toward Lanaq; her vision swam, darkness bleeding in at the edges. His expression told her he was experiencing it too. She opened her mouth to ask a question, but he silenced her with a slight shake of his head, steadying her on her feet.

"It's called frisson. Will you trust me if I tell you this is a good thing, but a question for another day?"

She agreed with a short nod, but confusion was in her eyes.

Lanaq cupped Bea's cheeks in his palms, pressing a kiss to her forehead. They remained that way for several long seconds before Lanaq stepped back, putting a little distance between them but drawing her fingertips into his own, as if he couldn't bear to lose contact completely.

"Bea, I've struggled with allowing us to become too connected during this time. I wanted to be fair to you, and to all the single males waiting back on Devet to meet the Vashallen. But now that the moment has come for fate to take over, I find I don't want to be fair."

Lanaq's face was grim, a frown pressing his lips downward, drawing deep lines across his forehead. With a great sigh he scrubbed his free hand across his brow, as if to wipe away the furrows.

"Why does this feel like goodbye?" she breathed.

"It feels that way for me, too. It's not forever, though we may not see each other for some time. I look forward to showing you the man I am when I'm not bound by restrictions and mandates."

Beatrix nodded mutely; afraid her emotions would get the better of her if she tried to speak. She hoped Lanaq knew she meant, "Me too."

They stood in front of the lift door. It opened, and Lanaq stepped backward, their fingers parting reluctantly. Then the doors slid shut, leaving Beatrix alone in the corridor.

* * *

THE SHORT LIFT RIDE was lost on Lanaq; his thoughts careened inside his head. By the time he approached his personal quarters the shock was wearing off. The statistical probability of his sharing frisson with Bea had been quite low, but there was no denying they had it. He wanted to waltz along the corridor toward his room. Of course he didn't, instead walking sedately, but inside he was dancing.

"Shay," he called out, entering his quarters. He stretched out on his bed, arms crossed behind his head, a satisfied grin crooking his mouth.

"You enjoyed your interlude with Beatrix." Shay stated this as fact rather than asking.

"I did. Thank you. Do me a favor, run a bio scan."

"Okay." Shay was silent while processing his request. "Interesting, elevated pheromone levels." She lapsed into another short silence. "Ooooh, Beatrix too! How long since the surge?"

"Ten minutes at most. Why?"

"Your hormone levels are still considerably elevated. Given the amount of time between the event and the measurement, frisson must be quite strong between you and Beatrix. Why didn't you measure the event yourself?"

"Didn't want to leave a permanent record, did I?"

"Wise. This could complicate matters for your mother."

"No 'could' about it. Matters will most definitely become complicated if anyone finds out." Lanaq's frown inverted, the deep furrows relaxing across his brow. "Still, I can't help but be thrilled. Beatrix and I share frisson. We're compatible." Lanaq tried to keep the gloat out of his tone but failed.

"Lanaq," Shay's tone was sharp, all business. "The Vashallen Cashondra has entered the lift. She is requesting your office level."

Romantic thoughts fled. He sat up and swung his legs over the edge of the bed, his movements crisp with renewed tension. His voice was rendered hard by his apprehension, "I'm on my way." He gave a short prayer to The Mother that he would not lose this Vashallen, before snapping the hem of his tunic into place and hurrying to reach his office.

He strode down the corridor, arriving just ahead of Cashondra. At her approach he dropped into a bow and was pleased when she reciprocated the gesture.

"You honor me," his voice smiled at her while his hands gestured she should enter through the open doorway.

"I've been practicing," she supplied with a lift of her lips. "No harm in trying to fit in when we arrive on Devet."

Lanaq was reassured by Cashondra's comment. "I'm pleased to hear it is still your intention to make the journey to Devet. To what do I owe the pleasure of your visit?"

"I wanted to talk," she supplied, sinking into a chair.

"Then I shall listen. Can I offer you a refreshment?"

"Banga would be nice." Her answer was distracted, her eyes moving about the room, taking in his possessions. "You like these old paintings?"

"I do," he replied from the direction of the food dispenser. In short order, Lanaq handed Cashondra a cup of steaming banga and found his own seat facing his guest. "Each is a replica of a work that appeals to me in one aspect or another," he added, keeping the conversation moving.

"Not my taste at all. I need more color, more movement, more texture. Sculpture is my favorite art form. Place your hand on the face of a statue and you can feel the artist's emotion in the expression of the figure, not just imagine it." Her eyes landed on the Durer above the fireplace. "That's the only thing in here with any life in it."

Lanaq smiled. "That's my favorite." He took a sip from his cup. He knew that Cashondra hadn't come to discuss his art collection. He was reluctant to push her for the reason for her visit. He felt sure she would come to it in her own time. It wasn't long before his patience was rewarded.

"I wanted you to know that I understand. Why you

included Trudy, that is. After your explanations about strict criteria and all, I get it. I don't have to like it, or her, but I can accept the necessity from your point of view."

"I appreciate that. I regret the distress the situation caused you. In retrospect, I should have anticipated the situation and handled better how you received the information. You have my apologies."

"And you have mine for the self-harm comments. Phe was right about that; I crossed the line."

"You and she have resolved your differences?" The tone of his question was buoyant, but the lift of his eyebrow questioned the sincerity.

"She and I have become friends. We help each other see things through a different lens."

"And Trudy?"

"She stays out of my way, and I stay out of hers." Cash rolled her eyes and huffed a frustrated sigh. "Look, she isn't the devil incarnate. I admit that. I can see she's trying, probably a little too hard, but that's better than not at all. Phe's also right about supporting rather than tearing each other down, so I don't wish Trudy ill, I just don't want her in my face."

"I understand. I know the ship is a close environment. It should be easier to give each other a wider berth once we reach the planet."

Cashondra placed her empty cup on the table and rose to leave. "I just thought you'd like to know where I stand before we depart."

"That was thoughtful. Thank you. I'm reassured. Do

you feel you've been able to make an informed decision about the journey to Devet? Was the stress too much?"

Cash chuckled. "Relax, Lanaq, I don't wilt under a little stress. I've bought the pitch. I'm not backing out at the last minute."

"Good to know." He joined her in standing. They exchanged bows and the Vashallen took her leave.

Following Cash's departure, Lanaq took the time to update her file with a report of their interaction, adding his own impressions to the factual account of their conversation. He stopped short of adding too many glowing adjectives. He felt certain Cashondra would make a fine Matriarch for whichever house she chose. With a lighter heart and a bemused smile in place, Lanaq sought his bunk once more.

# Chapter Eight

# Starship Revival

"Lanaq. Lanaq, wake up."

"Yes, Shay." His voice was groggy with sleep.

"As soon as we entered transporter range, your mother boarded. She's on her way up."

Lanaq tried to shake the confusion from his head, running a hand across his sleep slack face. It took him a brief moment to gather his thoughts enough to respond. "Tell her to meet me in my study, please."

He took the few minutes necessary to neaten his appearance before making his way down the corridor. The door to his study whooshed open. His mother stood stock-still by the fireplace, a glad smile trembling on her lips. Lanaq strode forward, opening his arms to engulf her in a hug. Mother and son stood in a mutual embrace for many moments, as if they could make up for all the time apart with touch.

Lanaq relinquished his embrace, stepping back to look at the woman he hadn't seen in several millenia. She looked much the same as she ever did; her ebony hair gathered in a loose chignon, her honey-colored skin unwrinkled, though he detected a tightness around her temples that spoke of sleepless nights and stress. Her face and figure appeared ageless; the weight of her years carried in her gaze. It was her eyes, the exact shade of espresso as those he met in the mirror each morning, shining up at him with affection, that nearly brought him to his knees.

"Come my son, offer your mother a seat and something to drink." Patrain's normally husky voice was made thicker by emotion. She too was affected by their reunion.

"A cup of banga or fosh?"

"Fosh, please. We'll both need the energy for the day ahead."

Patrain arranged her voluminous skirt as she made herself comfortable in one of the matching wingbacks. Settling herself, she crossed her legs, a deep slit in her skirt revealed slim pants in matching fabric. The dress was unusually unadorned for Patrain, the sumptuousness of the vibrant fabric needing no help. Lanaq could picture his mother in his mind's eye striding down the halls of the Quorum, skirt tails whipping behind her as if she were creating her own wind. Diminutive of stature, his mother might be, but her presence was large. Her energy filled his study in a familiar, comforting way.

"I like what you've done with this room. Are the paintings by Earth artists?"

"Indeed. Each was considered a master. Which one is your favorite?"

Patrain examined the paintings that graced the study while Lanaq finished brewing their cups of fosh. He added plenty of sweetener to his mother's cup, smiling as he presented her with the steaming mug.

"I am drawn to the naturescape you have hanging above the fireplace. It's so delicate and lifelike."

"It's also the only one that is real. I bought it from the artist as a gift for you."

"Really? Thank you, Son. I'll treasure it. Tell me about the artist."

"His name was Albrecht Durer. The first time I saw him I was stunned; he looked so much like Darval it was uncanny. A DNA sample confirmed what I suspected."

"He was from the Adderigus line?"

"He was."

"And so you brought me his painting."

"And so I brought you one of his paintings."

A single tear escaped his mother's eye, running down her cheek. She flicked it away with a slim digit.

"You are a good son, Lanaq. You prove over and over again why you were the only choice for this mission."

"You might not think so kindly of me when you hear what I have to report."

His mother's eyes widened, then narrowed. "Well, don't keep me guessing. What has gone awry?"

"Not awry exactly. I share frisson with the first Vashallen, Beatrix."

"Congratulations! That is wonderful news. I look forward to telling your father; he will be very excited for you."

"I thought you'd be more upset."

"Politically speaking it will be a nuisance, but one I anticipated. When the Quorum could not be swayed to accept a synthetic pilot for the mission, I knew this outcome was a possibility." Patrain made light of a situation which was not of her son's making; the onus of which he shouldn't have to carry. "I am, however, grateful you are wise enough to understand the sensitivity of this information. Now, tell me about the Vashallen. How are they?"

"As well as can be expected; better, actually. They are strong and resilient. I've been constantly amazed by them."

"I'd like to hear all about Beatrix specifically, but we haven't the time right now. The Quorum is aware of the Revival's return, and you are expected in chambers to provide a report on the outcome of the mission."

"Don't you mean a grilling? I'm aware the small number of Vashallen aboard the Revival will cause consternation among the members. Did you come to offer advice?"

"I came to see my son," Patrain feigned hurt, a hand clutching her wounded breast. "But since you ask, my advice is, tell them the truth. Don't spare them on my account."

"You anticipated this outcome as well?"

"Let's just say I saw it as a distinct possibility."

"How widely known is the total?"

"Only the thirteen know. They have held the information tightly, hoping your results would improve."

Lanaq sighed a heavy sigh, his frustration evident. "They tied my hands at every turn."

"I know, Son, and they know it too. They are loath to

admit their mistakes. I am sorry you will bear the brunt of their disappointment."

"You needn't worry. I have big shoulders. I'll manage."

They rose simultaneously, wrapping their arms around one another again.

"It's good to have you home. We'll see you at the Residence after your thorough roasting. Your fathers and brothers are all waiting to welcome you home."

His mother gave him her best reassuring smile and a last squeeze before stepping out of his embrace, making her way to the door. She paused before exiting, pointing to the watercolor hanging above the mantel. "I think that will look splendid in my office."

After his mother's departure, Lanaq hurriedly packed his personal items. Removing the watercolor from pride of place, he wrapped it carefully for its journey to his mother's office. He then checked in with Shay regarding the Vashallen. All were still sound asleep in their beds.

Over the course of the last few weeks, Shay had slowly altered the ship's day-night cycle to match that of Devet. The current time was too late to be called night, yet still somewhere short of morning. The Vashallen shouldn't wake for several more hours. With a last look around the rooms he had called home for several millennia, Lanaq took his leave of the ship, heading planetside to face the Quorum.

His mother's personal assistant met him as he exited the transport cradle. The synth had instructions to take Lanaq directly to the Quorum chambers. He followed the synth without objection, pausing outside the double doors to hand over the wrapped parcel tucked beneath his arm. "Would you see this gets hung in my mother's office, Anile? My gift to her from Earth. It's fragile, please use care."

The synth accepted the package mutely, their free hand indicating Lanaq should enter the Quorum chambers without delay. Lanaq watched Anile scurry away, painting cradled carefully. They never said much, but their efficiency was unequaled. He had no doubt the watercolor would end up in the perfect spot for optimal viewing.

He could put off the unpleasant task awaiting him beyond the stone portal no longer. Lanaq straightened his tunic, took a calming breath, and pushed open the heavy doors of the Quorum chambers.

Surprise was Lanaq's initial reaction to the number of people milling about the chamber. Due to the extremely early hour, he had expected no more than the thirteen Quorum members to be present. He realized how short-sighted his assumption had been. Every House had a stake in the results of Project Ferax, so of course their representatives were here for his firsthand report, no matter the hour.

Lanaq stood in what was inelegantly called the pit, the tiers of the chamber rising around him. The thirteen Quorum members were already in their places. He had kept them waiting. He dropped into a deep bow, holding the position long enough to apologize for his tardiness. No need to antagonize the members before he even opened his mouth.

A chair materialized, Lanaq seating himself while his mother addressed the assembly. "Today we welcome home

Lanaq Adderigus, pilot of the Starship Revival. All Devet rejoices in his return." The sound of feet stamping against the time-worn stone of the chamber signaled the listeners' approval of the speaker's words: a single stamp that faded away quickly. "We await your report, Pilot Adderigus. What can you tell us of your mission?"

Lanaq knew he needed to project confidence. Any sign of hesitation or weakness would be as blood in the water. He was determined not to be put on the defensive. "Thank you for the warm welcome, Elder Patrain. It is good to be home. On a personal note, it's wonderful to see you and Father looking so well." Lanaq offered a deep bow to his father, who sat several chairs to his mother's right. Lassitor had a satisfied look about him, his chest puffed up with pride. He returned Lanaq's bow with his own inclination of head and shoulders.

Lanaq pressed on with confidence, saying, "I'm heartened to see so many members of the Mavinarium in attendance at such an early hour. It gives me a great deal of pleasure to report to you all that Project Ferax has been a success. It has produced Vashallen."

A cheer rose from the assembled members, breaking protocol. Anyone watching closely might have noted none of the thirteen added their voices to the joyful noise. Lanaq continued, "A full nine percent of the Earth's population has completed recombination. That equates to nearly a quarter billion living and breathing Vashallen. Aboard the Revival are fifty-two Vashallen who have come here..."

"Fifty-two?" The representative from House Bellinger

was on his feet. "Two hundred and fifty million women, and you bring home a measly fifty-two?"

"Sit down, Geanole. You are out of order." Patrain did not raise her voice. She did not have to; her censure was enough to wither the Mavinar's outburst. He retook his seat, indignity clearly painted across his face. Patrain pursed her lips before she continued, "While the Bellinger member is out of order, Pilot Adderigus, he does ask a pertinent question. Could you explain to this body why so few Vashallen have been returned to Devet?"

"Happily, Madam Elder. First, I think this honored body should consider the quality of these Vashallen before deciding fifty-two is an insufficient number. I was tasked by the Quorum with bringing home Vashallen who were willing to join and grow our citizenry. I have brought home fifty-two courageous women who are cognizant of our situation, who are moreover ready to be the solution.

"Additionally, if the Quorum finds that the results of my mission are less than acceptable, they should begin by examining the procedures put in place by their predecessors. I adhered rigorously to all guidelines for the identification and retrieval of Vashallen."

"Are you saying the Quorum is to blame for so few Vashallen?" The new voice was that of Moina Quemcara, Matriarch of House Quemcara and longtime Adderigus ally.

"No, Madam Quemcara. There is no blame to assign, for there is nothing to lament in this situation. Fifty-two smart, determined women have agreed to join us. They and their daughters will bring new life to Houses long in decline. How can anyone be other than happy about that news?"

The Quemcara Matriarch nodded her approval of his answer. Lanaq suspected his mother had spoken to many of the thirteen prior to this public forum; the next question confirmed his suspicion.

"In your opinion, what adjustments should this body consider to improve results on future missions?" The frank, considered query came from Tuhan, member from House Ukanii, generally considered a neutral House.

"I believe the problem lies in having both restrictive rules and limited resources. The Quorum might consider relaxing one or the other."

"I'm not sure I follow, Pilot Adderigus."

"Allow me to illustrate with an example. The majority of the final few Vashallen came from a single night. A natural disaster on Earth killed many people. That night I retrieved three Vashallen, but Shay was tracking many more. I was limited by resources, namely that I am only one man. Had I been authorized to utilize the synthetics for emergency retrieval I might have been able to save some thirty or forty Vashallen."

"You believe we need to relax the rules?"

"Not necessarily. I understand why the rules are in place, sir. They protect Earth, Devet, and the Vashallen. The guidelines have proven their worth, insofar as they resulted in the retrieval of fifty-two exceptional women, all while Earth remains ignorant of our existence. If the result is unacceptable to this august body, I suggest an adjustment of expectations is in order."

"I see." Tuhan resumed his seat without further comment, leaving Lanaq unsure whether the exchange benefited his mother's position or the member's own. Certainly, Tuhan gave nothing away in tone or expression.

"Regardless of the outcome of this mission," he continued, projecting confidence, "I believe the Quorum will need to examine their guidelines before any future missions, Madam Elder."

"Why is that, Pilot?"

"Earth's advancing technology is making undetected retrieval increasingly difficult. Under the current guidelines, future pilots may return with even fewer numbers."

"On what do you base your supposition?"

"I have data that supports my conclusion. I'm happy to share the statistical models."

"Is there anything further you'd like to add that will help the Quorum in its discussions on this topic?"

"No, Madam Elder. My mission reports and ship's AI should provide everything you need. As always, I am at this body's pleasure."

"If there are no further questions from my fellow members," Patrain glanced to her left, then her right, "the pilot is excused, and this meeting of the Quorum is adjourned."

Lanaq rose and snapped a deep bow as the thirteen vacated the dais. He too made a hasty retreat from the chamber, the sound of rising voices at his back.

Being first out of the chamber gave him the opportunity

to reach the transport terminal before anyone could accost him. If he got stopped, it would be hours before he could get away politely. Thankfully, no one was lingering in the ante-chamber. Lanaq crossed the deserted space with haste and was soon standing in the foyer of the Adderigus Residence. "Home," he thought, letting out a breath he hadn't known he'd been holding for the last three millennia.

The Residence was quiet. He peered toward the library; no light or sound emanated from that direction. The hour was early, there was no reason to expect that anyone who didn't have to, would be awake. His slight disappointment was curtailed by the sound of the transport and his father's footfalls across the cut stone floor. Lanaq turned, expectation lighting his expression.

Lassitor Adderigus was a man of average height. Cut from the same cloth as his Vassen, it was his presence that made him feel larger than his size. Broad of shoulder but lean of body, he moved with languid grace. Well, normally, he was graceful, today he launched himself across the distance of the foyer to gather his son in a bear hug.

Lanaq returned his father's fierce embrace, enjoying the personal contact after his time alone.

"Let me look at you," Lassitor said, taking a step back. "You've grown your hair," he proffered after a lengthy appraisal.

"I still don't keep it as long as yours, but yes, some." Lanaq chuckled, grateful for the light banter rather than an emotional display. His father understood him; the pride shining in his eyes was all that Lanaq needed.

Lanaq and Lassitor were much alike. The two shared the same build, though Lanaq was taller, the same aquiline nose and almond eyes, and the same fall of straight hair inherent to Lassitor's family lineage. Beyond the physical, they were of like minds on most topics, shared a similar sense of humor, and shouldered their duty to House and family with pride. Lanaq might share Patrain's coloring, but he was his father's son.

"Your mother told me of your predicament," Lassitor turned them toward the stairs as he spoke.

"She said she had it under control." Lanaq's voice was a whisper, yet it carried urgency.

"She does. She does," Lassitor repeated for emphasis, attempting to allay Lanaq's concern. He waited for his words to penetrate, the arm he had draped across his son's shoulders gently squeezing his reassurance.

Lanaq's muscles were like wound springs, bunched and tight. "The last thing I intended was for my return to add drama," he hissed between clenched teeth. "I know the last thing Mother needs right now is another reason for the Mavinarium to question her."

"Don't trouble yourself. Patrain and I are prepared. After all," he shared a conspiratorial grin, "we've had a couple of years to think about and plan solutions for any eventuality."

Lanaq studied his father's face, searching for certainty in his unchanged features. He trusted what Lassitor said was true. This cause meant as much to he and Patrain as it did to him, more even, as they were the architects of Project

Ferax. He capitulated, both his body and his mind freeing themselves of the strain he'd operated under for the last few thousand years.

Lassitor's troubled expression lifted when he felt the tension drain from the son's body. "I brought up your predicament, solely because I wanted to enquire how you were handling the separation."

"I'm a grown man, Father. I control my emotions; they don't control me."

"As you have since you were a young boy. You've always been self-possessed, in control. I wasn't implying otherwise. I don't mean to offend, Lanaq, so stop looking for offense. I'm trying to sympathize with the unorthodox beginning of your courtship with Beatrix," Lassitor finished with a hint of frustration.

"Forgive me, Father, three millennia without company has rendered my social graces nearly nonexistent." Lanaq lowered his voice, "I would like to discuss my feelings on the matter, perhaps at a more appropriate time?" Lanaq nodded toward the head of the stairs where his three brothers, Rexin, Maliq, and Darval, had just appeared.

"Glad to have you home, Son," Lassitor took the hint, raising his voice to include the three men who were crossing the foyer. "I'll leave you to the tender mercy of your brothers." With a final squeeze of Lanaq's shoulder, Lassitor made for the family quarters, leaving Lanaq alone with three eager faces.

Rexin, the most gregarious of the bunch, wasted no time. "Let's get some breakfast." He linked arms with Lanaq, turning him in the direction of the dining room. "While we eat you can regale us with tales of the Vashallen; ones not included in the public reports."

"If you insist," Lanaq capitulated gracefully, to do otherwise would be churlish. He allowed himself to be led away.

# Chapter Nine

# Starship Revival

eatrix's door chimed. Tapping her strap, she called out, "Come in."

The door slid open, and an unfamiliar face appeared in her mirror. Beatrix suppressed a gasp and spun around on her stool. "Hello?" she said to the newcomer, voice uncertain.

"Good morning, Madam Beatrix. My name is Indik. I have been assigned as your personal attendant. May I come in?"

"Yes, of course, come in." Standing, she adjusted her robe, securing the belt as she approached the living area of her quarters. She offered Indik a seat, taking a moment to study the attendant.

Indik was only slightly taller than Beatrix herself, with chestnut hair, arching eyebrows, and perfect cheekbones beneath flawless skin. Bright umber eyes shone out from an androgynous face. "Where is Joan?" Beatrix asked.

"Now that you have reached Devet you will need a

dedicated attendant. Joan and the others will stay with the ship."

"What does being my personal attendant entail?"

"My function is to provide any assistance you need to integrate into Devetian society, Madam Beatrix."

"You may have your work cut out for you, Indik. Can we drop the Madam? It's just Beatrix."

Indik smiled for the first time. "Certainly, in private I may call you Beatrix. In public, it would be best to maintain protocols."

"Understood. I'm told the Vashallen are attending an arrival ceremony today."

"That is precisely why I have arrived, Madam. I'm here to help you prepare. As with most things Devetian, it will be a formal event."

"And the Vashallen will be on public display."

"Frankly Madam, yes, you will." Moving with purpose, the attendant crossed the room to open the cupboard containing her finery. "This should suit you well." Indik fingered the material of the gown. "It does seem appropriate for you to wear House Adderigus colors."

"Pardon, what do you mean? And remember, it's just Beatrix."

"House Adderigus is largely responsible for the solution to the problem plaguing Devetians. As the first Vashallen chosen, it is appropriate that you should wear their House colors."

"All right, that makes sense. I thought you were referring to me sharing frisson with Lanaq. Oh no!," Beatrix slapped a hand over her mouth. "I promised not to say anything and look at me blabbing at the first opportunity."

Indik allowed the heavy fabric to slip from his fingers. Beatrix's news was indeed unexpected and inconvenient for House Adderigus should certain other Houses catch wind. "Most felicitous. House Adderigus already has a possible mate for one of its sons. Might I suggest, Madam, that this information is best kept to oneself for the time being?"

"Why? I don't understand the problem. Explain the situation to me as if I were a child."

"You haven't done anything wrong, Beatrix. House Adderigus is the architect of Project Ferax. Madam Patrain and her Ventir Lassitor have served many terms on the Quorum, ensuring the project reaches fruition in the manner envisioned. Opposing factions feel House Adderigus has exerted too much influence over the direction of the project. They will see frisson between yourself and Lanaq as proof House Adderigus has had an unfair advantage in this matter."

"An unfair advantage?" Beatrix was silent for many moments as she pondered this new information. "Frisson is important?"

"For Devetians? Very much so." Indik clapped his hands together twice. "We will have lots of time for questions, right now we need to make a start. You have a party to attend. Into the cleanser with you," he ordered, shooing her toward the bathroom.

Beatrix responded to the authority of the voice, hopping to her feet. She started toward the bathing room, unbelting her robe automatically. Her hands and feet came to a halt at the same moment, freezing her place.

Pausing in the organization of accruements, Indik shot her a questioning glance.

Beatrix peered at her hands clutching together the edges of her robe, before shifting her gaze to Indik. "Should I be undressing in front of you? I'm sorry to ask, embarrassed in fact."

"Didn't Joan explain about synths, Madam?"

Beatrix searched her memory, to no avail. If Joan had told them about synth birds and bees, she hadn't been listening. She employed Npheba's habit, she shrugged.

"And your implanted knowledge isn't helping," the attendant surmised. "That isn't surprising in your case. You've had a great deal of knowledge stuffed into your memory. Occasionally, like a misplaced file, some information isn't readily available. Give it time, your brain will assimilate more each day.

"As to your concern," Indik nodded at the flimsy material still clasped about her nakedness, "your comfort is all that matters. If it helps, synths are asexual, reproductively speaking."

"Meaning what exactly?"

"Synths are created, not born. We don't require sex traits for the purpose of attracting a mate; therefore, synth shells aren't normally sexed."

"Joan did explain that she was an android. I didn't think beyond her explanation at the time"

"The attendants aboard the Revival were made to

appear female for your comfort. Devetian bound synths, with slight variations, will look very much like me."

"Not male then?" she asked, her modesty feeling less in jeopardy.

"Our creators designed our shells with utility in mind, but programmed their paradigms in our coding."

"You're hurting my brain, Indik. Could you say it plainly?"

"Upon start up, each synth is randomly assigned a gender. To coincide with the language, to reflect our creators, either he, she, or they."

"Rather arbitrary."

"Perhaps, but it is the Devetian way. Joan really didn't explain?"

Indik was distracted for a fraction of a second, giving Beatrix an opening to ask a question rather than answer the one which would expose her less studious side, "So which were you assigned? How am I supposed to know?"

Indik actually frowned. The small movement, so normal on an organic face, struck trepidation in Beatrix. *Had she offended?*

Indik's expression was once again smooth when he spoke, confirming Bea's fear, "Synths interface directly, exchanging digital signatures, we have no need for such inquiries among ourselves. Organics know by the piping on our uniforms, yellow indicates female, brown, male, and the two colors twisted together indicates neither. If nothing else Joan should have explained that in preparation for our arrival on Devet."

Bea shrugged once again. She was beginning to appreciate Npheba's strategy. "You've explained now," she dismissed his concern. She looked down at her robe once again, indecision apparent in her hesitation. The brown piping on Indik's one piece uniform gave her pause. Maybe, one day, she would let go of the lessons ingrained by her former life, but today was not the day. She kept her robe secured until the door to the necessary room closed behind her.

When she emerged, Indik took complete charge, and for the next couple of hours Beatrix submitted to his ministrations. Her hair became an elaborate configuration, beads and gems winking from among her strawberry intricately piled curls. Her makeup was equally elaborate. A mist from the shower had coated her from head to toe in a fine opalescent sheen. To her pearlescent skin, Indik added rosy hints on her cheeks and lips. Glittery green shadow was swept across her lids, the edges lined in silver swirls and whorls, which trailed upward to her temples and down the outer edges of her cheeks. Indik pressed a small device to her upper and lower eyelids, and her lashes became darker, fuller, and longer.

"Nanite lashes," he explained when she shot a questioning look in the mirror.

Beatrix had spent a lifetime caring for her mistress in this exact manner. It felt wonderful, but oh-so-very strange, to be on the receiving end of such treatment.

Turning her face this way and that way, Indik pronounced her makeup finished. Wasting no time, the synth drew the gossamer gown from the wardrobe. The dress glided over her hips, the lining molding itself to her frame, providing lift and support where needed. A bejeweled collar fastened at her neck with the wave of a wand by Indik.

After sliding her feet into the provided sandals, securing a sparkling tiara to her head, Indik gave her a final once-over before pronouncing her prepared. "We have a little time before your scheduled departure, so let's talk about what you can expect when you reach Hekaria. Upon arrival, you will have some time with the thirty-two Matriarchs. Following that, you are scheduled to meet with the thirteen Quorum members. These first two meetings will be small."

"The Quorum are your leaders, right? Lanaq told us about them, and the Madarium."

"Mavinarium, Madam."

"Right. Mav...i...nar...ium. Got it. That doesn't sound so overwhelming." Beatrix let out a shaky breath. "I didn't think I'd be so nervous."

"All new experiences are scary. If your nerves feel too frayed, I can get you a cup of banga." Indik raised his brows and made a sip-sipping motion with his thumb and forefinger.

Beatrix thought of the relaxed, blissful feeling banga produced; she then imagined herself slumped in a chair, snoring lightly, and chuckled. "Thank you, no. That probably isn't a good idea either." But Indik's joke had banished the tension. "So, first the Matriarchs, then the Quorum. What next?"

"Your first true public appearance. You'll make your way from the Quorum chambers into Hekaria Square, where you will attend the arrival celebration. Each Vashallen's entrance into the square will be broadcast, but after that you need only contend with the scrutiny of those in attendance."

"Broadcast?"

"No one wanted to overwhelm you on your first day. The single males have been barred from attending. I imagine they will all be glued to their screens, eager to get a look at the new arrivals."

"You're making me feel a little like a broodmare. Will they check my teeth to see if they're good?"

"No broodmare ever had much say in the stallion that covered her. Remember, when the presentation festival gets underway, the single males might feel it is you who are checking their teeth."

"Presentation festival?"

A chime came from Indik's strap. "Time to go. I'll walk you to the transport room." He offered his hand to help her rise from the sofa. "I can't accompany you to the private meetings, but once you reach the public space I'll only be a tap away." He gave her a reassuring smile as he secured a dainty bejeweled version of her strap around her wrist.

They took the lift to another part of the ship. The corridors all looked the same to Beatrix, but Indik confidently navigated them to the transport room. In the center of the otherwise empty room was a metal sphere. The sphere hovered a hair's breadth above a cradle.

Indik opened a door and indicated that Beatrix should step inside. Beatrix peered in; there was nothing to see. She stepped in hesitantly.

Indik stepped back with a smile and a wave, and the opening slid shut. A few seconds passed, and then the door unsealed with a pop. Beatrix was surprised when an unfamiliar synth greeted her with a smile, saying, "Welcome to Devet, Madam Beatrix."

The Vashallen milled about an antechamber, waiting for the rest of their number to arrive. Beatrix found her group and spent a few minutes admiring everyone's gowns. They resembled a flock of brightly feathered birds.

The heavy double doors of the antechamber began to swing open, the massive stone slabs pivoting with ease. Beyond the doorway a large circular chamber was revealed. The Vashallen made their way inside, emerging from the tunnel-like doorway into the pit.

Two-thirds of the room rose sharply in tiers; on each tier sat evenly spaced trios of stone chairs. High-backed and intricately carved, most of the seats were empty, though a small number were occupied by women. *Thirty-two in all,* Beatrix thought, *exactly the number of remaining Matriarchs.* The stark contrast between the size of the room and the Matriarchs' pitiably small number brought home, as nothing else had, the dire circumstances the Devetians faced.

The final third of the room was dominated by a curved dais upon which stood thirteen thrones, the seats of the Quorum. In sharp contrast to the highly decorated trios that inhabited the tiers, the thirteen chairs for the Quorum were plain, lacking even a cushion to soften the seat. Tucked under the dais was another set of double doors.

The walls of the massive chamber were lined with

House banners, providing bright shocks of color. Beatrix was able to identify the House Adderigus banner unfurled directly behind the centermost Quorum seat.

"Please come in, ladies."

Beatrix had her back to the speaker, but she was sure the voice belonged to Patrain Adderigus, leader of the Devetian people. It held authority, and it spurred the women to action. She followed Gina. Their group claimed five places on the first tier.

When everyone had found a seat, Patrain spoke. "Ladies, blessed Vashallen, welcome to Devet. Thank you for your decision to begin a new life here. Your arrival brings hope of a future to our people."

Patrain's voice, though firm and steady, was also rich and pleasing, the voice of a mother greeting her daughters. Gone was the authoritative edge, replaced with genuine warmth. "I look forward to knowing each of you," she concluded, retaking her seat.

A tall, lithe woman took Patrain's place. "Good afternoon. I am Moina Quemcara. I'd like to reassure each of you that we Matriarchs want your happiness, not just your wombs." There were a few titters around the room, even some outright guffaws. Tension vanished, like a bubble popping. "We understand that immersing yourselves in a new culture is a daunting prospect. I encourage you to rely on the advice of your host Matriarch. They will provide you with a broad outline of the presentation festival and are happy to answer any specific questions you may have.

"Regarding today's activities, we have allowed time

before your presentation to the Quorum to meet and speak with your host Matriarch. They know who you are and will seek you out.

"Lastly, on behalf of myself and House Quemcara, welcome to Devet."

Moina retook her seat, signaling an end to the official part of the meeting. For the next half hour, the Vashallen and Matriarchs mingled. The first five met their hostess, Lorral Stengot, an elegant woman with raven dark hair and amethyst eyes. Her demeanor was warm and friendly.

Beatrix was standing on the periphery of her group, listening to Madam Stengot describe the beauty of the Stengot caszartera. She felt a tap on her shoulder and turned to find Elder Patrain at her elbow.

"Might we speak for a moment?" Patrain glided away, assuming Beatrix's compliance. Beatrix hurried to fall in step with the Matriarch, but stayed silent, unsure of her purpose.

Once they were far enough from the others, Patrain turned and fixed her with an intent stare. "My son has told me that you and he share frisson."

Though it was a statement rather than a question, Beatrix felt compelled to offer a reply. She did so quietly. "We do," she nearly whispered.

Patrain nodded, as if she approved of Beatrix's caution. "In this private moment, as Lanaq's mother, I can tell you I am overjoyed that one of my sons has found a possible mate. But, as Devet's Quorum Elder, I must inform you this poses a political difficulty which could threaten the future of Project Ferax."

Beatrix, blameless in this matter, squared her shoulders. "No one has yet explained frisson to me, except to say its existence between Lanaq and myself could create political difficulty. I assure you; it is not my intention to broadcast the knowledge."

"Your discretion is appreciated. The situation is regrettable." Beatrix blanched at Patrain's words. Seeing her reaction, Patrain continued, "It isn't anything to do with you, Beatrix. This was bound to happen and would be regrettable regardless of who was involved."

"Then why send Lanaq and create this very situation?"

"Because, child, even the Quorum is fallible. They wouldn't approve a synth, and Lanaq was the only available pilot I trusted to see the mission through with the integrity it required."

"I see." Obviously, political currents were stirring under the calm surface of Devetian society. Beatrix didn't yet understand the nuances.

"In order to prevent further speculation, I have decided that you must find frisson with at least one other before you meet with Lanaq again. More than one would be ideal."

"Excuse me? I don't understand."

A chime sounded from the strap on Patrain's wrist. "Our time is almost at an end," she announced. "I must take my leave, but it was a pleasure to meet you, Beatrix. You are exactly as Lanaq described you. I wish you good fortune during the festival."

Patrain's departing bow was more an incline of her head, which Beatrix attempted to return with an inept gesture of her own. A curtsy she could have managed with grace, but the Devetian penchant for bowing was beyond her comprehension. She needed a crash course on the subtleties of the custom, post-haste.

The Matriarchs departed. Before long, a grinding sound drew the Vashallen's attention to the dais. Large stone plates slid away at either end of the platform to reveal stairs in the floor. Warm yellow light filtered upward as the thirteen members of the Quorum filed in to take their seats.

Patrain, as the Quorum Elder, seated herself in the center directly under the Adderigus banner. To her left, six Matriarchs, each holding herself with a regal rigidity that had been absent during the earlier meeting, seated themselves under their House banners. Beatrix identified two of the six women as the leaders of Houses Quemcara and Stengot.

To Patrain's right the six members of the Mavinarium elected to serve on the Quorum, also proceeded to their seats. Beatrix recognized Lassitor, Lanaq's father, from a photo he'd shown her aboard the Revival. In person, the resemblance between father and son was unmistakable. They shared similar frames and dark hair, not to mention they both held their heads with the exact same quizzical tilt when questioning something.

With the Quorum members seated, Patrain stood once more to address the room. "The Quorum welcomes the Vashallen to Devet. We thank you for your willingness to join our society. It is, however, this body's responsibility to ensure your presence here is your own choice. Please stand and testify when your name is called."

All conversation in the room ceased. The solemnity with which the Devetians treated the moment spoke volumes about Devetian society.

"Beatrix, first Vashallen, do you affirm that your arrival on Devet is of your own free will?" Patrain's eye was fixed upon her. In fact, every person in the council chambers was staring at her.

Her lips and throat felt dry as she spoke, but her words came out strong and confident. "I am Beatrix, first Vashallen. I choose my place on Devet of my own free will."

An expression of pride passed fleetingly across Patrain's face, and Beatrix was sure she detected a sigh of relief. "So noted. Regina, second Vashallen, do you affirm your arrival on Devet is of your own free will?"

Patrain continued until all fifty-two Vashallen declared their free choice. Once the formalities were complete, Patrain issued a lengthier welcome and thank you on behalf of the Devetian government. Then, the meeting concluded as abruptly as it began. The Quorum members filed back down the stone steps, disappearing into the floor.

Once the stone slabs slid closed the Vashallen were left again on their own, but only for a moment. En masse, their attendants arrived from the antechamber; finding Beatrix, Indik gave her the once-over. Slipping a small wand like device from his pocket, Indik waved it over the wrinkles that had formed in her skirt while she sat. Wrinkles gone,

Indik examined her hair and face, touching up the color on her lips.

"Everything going okay so far?"

Beatrix wasn't sure how to answer the question, as she wasn't really sure if everything had gone 'okay' so far. "I think so. The Matriarchs seemed nice, but the Quorum was a little intimidating."

"The Quorum aren't used to having their proceedings broadcast. They did seem extra stiff as a result. You were charming." Indik gave her hand a squeeze of reassurance.

"We aren't being broadcast now, are we?"

"No. The formal greeting by the council, and your entrance into the square, are all that will be shown today."

"Any advice for how to behave at the party? For instance, what's the correct way to bow?"

"You've had no instruction on bowing?"

Beatrix shook her head in the negative.

"Forgive my oversight in this matter. I will give you the basics now, and we can go over finer points later."

Beatrix only nodded her agreement, reluctant to waste their limited time.

"Devetian society is hierarchical, like most groups in nature. At the top of our hierarchy is the Quorum Elder, followed by the other Quorum members. Next are the Matriarchs, the Heirs, then the Mavinar, followed by the Ventinar, the Ventir, and lastly the single males."

Indik paused to ensure that Beatrix was following the explanation thus far.

"The England of my day also lived by a caste system,"

she confirmed her understanding. "Where do the synths fall in the hierarchy?"

"We have no position in the hierarchy. We were created to be of service."

"You are aware I was a servant in my former life, Indik. I understand what it is to be invisible even when you're present."

Indik squeezed Beatrix's hand, acknowledging her sentiment even as he continued with his explanation. "Understanding one's place in the hierarchy is essential to understanding how to bow. One uses more of one's body in the bow and holds the bow longer if addressing someone of higher rank. How much and how long are determined by the distance in rank; this also inversely applies to those beneath you."

"I understand. Madam Patrain merely inclines her head because she sits atop the hierarchy."

"Correct."

"So where do Vashallen place within the hierarchy?"

"For the next year, I would place you within the Heirs category."

"The Quorum members and the Matriarchs rank above us?"

"Correct."

"So, the appropriate amount to bow to them would be...?" Beatrix trailed off, implying that Indik should fill in the answer.

"Difficult to approximate, because intent and perception are factors. A good rule of thumb is to bow from the shoulders and pause for the briefest of seconds." A single beep emitted from Indik's strap. He glanced down, then gave her hand another quick squeeze.

"Don't worry, no one will be judging you on your bows today. We will have plenty of time to discuss the intricacies of Devetian manners once we reach the Stengot caszartera. Now, time to make that entrance I told you about."

Indik turned her by the shoulders. The heavy stone doors under the Quorum dais swung open, revealing a column-lined hallway ending at a sunlit portal: literally, a light at the end of the tunnel.

Indik took charge, stepping to the front of the room just inside the stone doors. "All right ladies. One at a time — in chronological order, if you please. Beatrix, you're first."

Beatrix made her way along the row and down the stairs. Soft words and gentle touches of encouragement were offered as she made her way to the front. When she stood at Indik's side, she offered him a weak smile. "Any last-minute words of advice?"

"You have nothing to be nervous about this evening. Remember, you are a much-needed breath of fresh air. They will all be charmed. On a practical note, take the stairs slowly, and don't look down at your feet." With that, Indik laid his hand on the small of her back, urging her forward down the hallway.

Beatrix took a deep breath, squared her shoulders, and headed for the sunlight at the end of the tunnel.

## Chapter Ten

# Hekaria City

Beatrix emerged into the late afternoon sun. Her appearance at the top of a monumental staircase was met with cheers and applause. Heartened by the warm welcome, Beatrix beamed. She executed what she felt was a passable bow, holding it for an extra second to show her gratitude. The cheers grew louder.

Draped in deep purple carpet with a gold geometric pattern, the stairs before her weren't steep, just numerous. Beatrix was mindful of Indik's advice. Fixing her eyes on a spot near the bottom, she began her slow descent.

At home on his screen, Lanaq watched Beatrix's progress down the Quorum house stairs with pride. The polished voice of the announcer introduced Beatrix to the audience while the camera followed her descent. She reached the bottom of the stairs, and Lanaq saw his father step forward to offer a bow. Beatrix returned the greeting and accepted Lassitor's proffered arm. They melted into the crowd, and the broadcast switched focus to Gina's arrival in the square.

Lanaq sighed, knowing this would be his last glimpse of Beatrix for some time.

Beatrix looked out on Hekaria Square as she made her descent. It consisted of five pavilions; one large rectangular pavilion flanked at its ordinal points by four smaller pavilions. These were supported by numerous columns, each topped with brightly colored pennants that unfurled lazily in a sultry breeze.

The columns and canopy appeared to be natural formations enhanced by Devetian sensibilities. Beatrix was reminded of the gazebo Shay had created for their last luncheon aboard the Revival. Twisting vines grew around and up the carved stone columns, plaiting overhead in intricate patterns. Soft lighting hung from overhead branches, massive blooms adding an intoxicating fragrance.

As she reached the last step, Beatrix was grateful to see a familiar face. Lassitor stepped forward to greet her, offering his escort; she thankfully took his arm and allowed him to lead her into the crowd, knees wobbling.

"Welcome to Devet, Beatrix. I'm Lassitor, La…"

"Lanaq's father," she finished for him. She was surprised she could speak. Her heart was hammering so hard in her chest she could hear the blood pumping to her brain. "Those stairs are not for the faint of heart."

"Someone faint of heart would not have made the journey to Devet. You humble us all with your courage."

"Ah, flattery, you are as the sun to the flower." Beatrix's joke allowed the two to relax into one another's company. "Seeing you in person, the resemblance between father and son is remarkable. I would have suspected a familial connection even if Lanaq hadn't shown us a picture." She smiled up at Lassitor, a merry twinkle in her eye.

"And you are as charming as Lanaq said you would be. How about something to drink and eat? In that order, I think."

"That would be lovely. It seems like a long time since breakfast."

The attention of most attendees was still focused on the introductions. Beatrix and Lassitor made their way unmolested to the pavilion, where refreshments were being served.

"What can I get for you? Something hot, cold, altering, non-altering?"

"Something cool, I think." Beatrix avoided the question of altering, hoping Lassitor would make the right choice for her.

"Here, try this." Lassitor handed her a goblet filled with a pink liquid. "I think you'll like it. It's made from del-dell fruit. Refreshing, and it will take the edge off your nerves without the lethargy of banga."

Beatrix took her first sip. The juice was tart on her tongue, but left a pleasant aftertaste unlike anything she'd experienced before. By the time Lassitor steered them toward the pavilion of savory delights, Beatrix felt less nervous. The del-dell juice was having an effect. She began to enjoy the experience. "Will you tell me about House Adderigus?"

"With pleasure. Much Adderigus land is mountainous

and rocky; most of the caszartera is built into the heart of a mountain, so we tend to feel very close to nature."

"Lanaq showed us pictures of his home and family during our journey. The Adderigus caszartera was indeed impressive. It appears to cling to the mountainside by sheer force of will."

"The first time I saw the caszartera, after my joining with Patrain, I thought the same thing. Adderigans are a lot like the caszartera, strong and tenacious." Lassitor smiled over her shoulder as he spoke, causing Beatrix to turn. "Beatrix, allow me to introduce Hugen and Aftin, my fellow Ventir."

"Welcome, Vashallen Beatrix," the two men said in unison, bowing.

Beatrix quickly gave up trying to decide on the correct reciprocal bow. "A pleasure to meet you both," she said with a wide smile, hoping to make up for her lack of expertise. "Fellow Ventir? Does that mean House Adderigus is your home also?"

"Yes. House Adderigus has been home since our joining," Hugen answered for both men. "It really is majestic. I hope you'll visit someday."

"Thank you for the invitation. I'd like that."

They spent several minutes in conversation with the two men, who made Beatrix feel welcome with warm words and smiles. Soon enough Lassitor made their excuses, leading Beatrix off to meet and greet another group. Everyone wanted a moment with the Vashallen, so Lassitor kept them moving throughout the evening, never stopping more than a few minutes in any one place. Beatrix kept smiling and making polite small talk, coming to appreciate Lassitor's ability to sense when she needed a brief respite. He would make their excuses and lead her away, always the perfect social escort.

Not that it was difficult to be pleasant. Everyone was cordial, going to great lengths to make the newest Devetian citizens feel at home, but Beatrix was feeling the strain of a long day. Her feet ached in the unfamiliar shoes, and she longed to pull her hair free of its complicated confines.

Lassitor circled them back to the refreshment tables to get a pick-me-up, almost as if he could read her mind. Patrain joined them as they reached the pavilion. Her hand found Lassitor's as if by homing beacon, and they shared a glance. In that look, Beatrix could tell, the Vassen and her Ventir exchanged an entire conversation. She felt a tiny bit jealous watching the exchange.

Lassitor made polite excuses, stepping away to grab more drinks, leaving Patrain and Beatrix alone.

"Have you enjoyed the welcome party?"

"So many names and faces. I'll never remember them all. I hope I don't embarrass myself at some future event." A grimace flashed across Beatrix's features as she imagined a diplomatic crisis between Houses, all because she forgot so and so's name or title. "I met Hugen and Aftin from House Adderigus. They were very welcoming."

"They told me of your meeting. They were impressed by your graciousness."

"I don't think I was particularly witty or vivacious when we met."

Lassitor returned, handing them a tall glass filled with a bubbling green concoction. Bea's first sip tasted like springtime in a glass.

"Though Lanaq is my youngest son," Patrain attempted to explain, "he outranks his brothers because Lassitor is my Ventinar. You showed Hugen and Aftin courtesy nevertheless." Patrain spoke between sips from her glass. "Very socially adroit."

"Where and when I'm from, we call that good manners."

Patrain laughed a hearty laugh that drew looks from people nearby. Leaning in and lowering her voice to avoid being overheard, she added, "I begin to see why you and Lanaq are suited. Intelligence. Frankness. He will be pleased to hear you got along well with his fathers."

Beatrix was taken aback by the leader's compliment; the woman was daunting to say the least. Heart fluttering, palms sweating, Beatrix missed the implication in Patrain's words, as she stuttered a 'Thank you' that was more question than statement.

Patrain, unfazed by the young Vashallen's disconcerted stare, turned her attention to Lassitor. "I'm going to wrap up the festivities. Would you please ensure Beatrix reaches the transport cradle? Lorral is waiting." Pausing only long enough for Lassitor's acknowledgment, she turned and set off through the crowd, which parted like an ocean cleaved by the prow of a great ship.

"She said 'fathers,' plural," Bea's flustered brain finally caught up.

"Yes." Lassitor began to lead Beatrix through the crowd.

"I'm not sure I understand."

They approached the Quorum building, but rather than climb the stairs, where Patrain was currently holding everyone's attention with a closing speech, they veered off down a side path.

"Hugen, Aftin, and myself are Patrain's Ventir. We are a Venvastum, a family unit." The path led to a nondescript door at the side of the building. Lassitor thumbed his strap, and the portal opened. He motioned Beatrix inside. "Did Lanaq not explain our ways to you aboard the Revival?"

"He might have. I wasn't always present when he spoke." They navigated the corridors toward the transport room.

"And still you came? I'm amazed, impressed. You are a brave woman, Beatrix."

"Or maybe a foolish one," she mumbled under her breath. Sky-blue irises, luminous twin candles in the gathering gloom, filled her owlish expression. Her footsteps faltered, coming to an abrupt halt as the enormity of her decision finally hit home.

Lassitor too came to a halt. Her lack of forward momentum caused him to turn. A questioning eyebrow rose. He would have spoken but Beatrix reassured, "I'm fine. Just sore feet." She rotated her ankle, displaying the offending shoes. His doubtful stare probed, but he didn't question her veracity. He offered her his arm and they continued toward their destination.

Further conversation was curtailed by their arrival at the transport cradle. Waiting there were Madam Stengot and the other members of the first five. "Thank you for showing Beatrix the way, Lassitor. I will take the Vashallen to Stengot straight away. I'm sure they are tired after such an eventful day."

"Look after them well, Lorral." Turning to Beatrix, Lassitor offered a deep extended bow. "It has been a pleasure to meet you, Beatrix." With a quick bow to the rest of the room, he then turned on his heel, disappearing into the dark corridor.

Lorral Stengot gathered herself. Lines of tiredness showed under her eyes, but her voice was still lively as she said, "Come, ladies. Let's go home and get comfortable."

One after another they climbed into the transport. Lorral was the last to enter, tapping her strap to shut the door as she settled inside. Beatrix barely had time to blink before the door popped open again; Lorral ushered them out.

Emerging from the Stengot transport room into a cavernous foyer, Beatrix was comforted to see Indik's familiar face. He and five other synthetics stood waiting. Beatrix recognized those who had attended her groupmates earlier; she could only assume the sixth was Madam Stengot's personal attendant.

"Welcome to Stengot, Ladies," Lorral waved an effusive arm, encompassing the grand foyer. The family caszar is at your disposal. This level houses all the public rooms, library, dining, ballroom, sunroom and such. Guest rooms are located upstairs," Lorral waved at the sweeping staircase which split in two at the first landing. "Family rooms are on the lower floor. You will have plenty of time to explore the caszar and the greater caszartera in the coming months. Right now, I'd lay odds you would all like to change out of your formal attire." Five nods elicited a knowing smile from the older woman. "Off you go then," she waved the women toward the waiting synths.

Indik whisked Beatrix upstairs to her room, where he began defrocking her. In no time she was clean-faced and clothed in soft pajamas, a cup of warm and frothy fosh in her hands.

Indik guided her to sit upon a stool before a mirror. He began to unwind her elaborate hairdo. "Did you have a good time?"

Beatrix contemplated everything she had learned in a single day. *And this is just the beginning.* "It wasn't bad," she answered. "Maybe a little overwhelming. So much to absorb. I feel numb."

Indik had removed all the frippery and tangles from her hair, was now rhythmically stroking a soft brush through its strands. "Tell me one thing you particularly enjoyed from the day."

Beatrix relaxed into Indik's capable hands. "I enjoyed meeting Lanaq's father. He was very welcoming."

"Which one?"

"I met all three, actually. That was a bit of a shock. Patrain having three spouses, that is."

"Yes, her final selection was a little sparse. A bit of a controversy in its day."

Beatrix was silent, processing the revelation. Indik filled the silence. "Tell me one thing you didn't enjoy today?"

Beatrix thought for a moment, her nose wrinkling with distaste. "I didn't like lugs knot far. It was squidgy, rubbery, and gritty all at the same time."

Indik couldn't help the laugh that bubbled up. "You mean Lugst-nough-argh. It is an acquired taste."

"Whatever it's called, one would need to acquire the taste for congealed snot to enjoy the dish."

Indik continued to stroke the brush through her hair for several more minutes while Beatrix sipped from her mug. Then, putting down the brush, he disappeared into the gigantic wardrobe which occupied one entire wall of her room, emerging after a few moments with a robe and slippers in hand. "Madam Lorral has arranged a cold collation in the library. She requests the pleasure of your company, but understands if you're tired and would prefer to retire."

Revived by her mug of fosh, Beatrix wouldn't dream of disappointing her hostess. She slipped into the robe and slippers and followed Indik downstairs to the room designated, the library.

The space was alive with art from many mediums. Watercolor and oil paintings lived on the walls, while sculptures of stone and metal inhabited much of the floor and table space. Books rose above their heads, volume on volume, colorful spines framed in fancifully carved book-shelves; there were even delicate glass pieces floating in the air, reflecting glints of lamplight.

Madam Stengot and Sophia were in quiet conversation across the room when Beatrix entered, her presence going unnoticed until she spoke. "Hello?"

The two women turned at once. Lorral hurried forward. "Beatrix, come in. Let me get you a glass of tafron. I'm told it's very similar to Earth's wine."

The others arrived while Lorral was pouring a glass of the dark purple liquid for Beatrix. She continued pouring until everyone was provided for, then settled herself in the corner of a large sofa, kicking off her slippers and tucking up her feet in a relaxed familial way.

"Welcome ladies, your first night at House Stengot," their hostess sighed in a completely satisfied way. "Make yourselves at home. I want House Stengot to feel like your home. Explore the caszar to your heart's content, however for the duration of the festival, the lower level, the family quarters, is off limits. Please respect those boundaries." Lorral quickly switched to a more pleasant topic, "You all survived your first day Devetian pomp and circumstance. How do you feel?"

"Ready to know what happens next," Gina said, frown reflected in her tone.

Lorral merely chuckled. "Your enthusiasm and forth-rightness are refreshing, Gina. I was expecting more hesi-tance to jump into Devetian society."

"I would just like to know what is expected of me. Of us."

"That's understandable. As is the excitement of our unattached males. They have all waited a very long time to meet each of you. I've arranged for formal introductions to begin tomorrow."

"So soon?" Rather than sharing Gina's pessimism, Phe's question was practical.

"If you prefer a few days to settle in, I understand. I can alter the arrangements."

"No. It's not...I just wasn't expecting formal introductions."

"While our population numbers are dreadfully low, there are still close to nine hundred single males. It is only fair they each have the opportunity to meet every one of the Vashallen. It will take an entire year to accomplish such a feat. Formal introductions, it was decided, were essential to preserve fairness."

"Who decided?"

"Why the Quorum, of course."

"Your Quorum concerns itself with such trivial matters?"

"My dear Npheba, our population is approaching extinction. I assure you even the most trivial of details concerning the preservation of our species is of paramount importance to the Quorum." Seeing the frown marring Phe's brow, Lorral added, "We have done our utmost to hold all our responsibilities equally in this matter. Our responsibility to save our citizens, to preserve choice for the Vashallen, to protect Earth, to protect the universe in fact. It hasn't been easy, and to be frank no one is perfect, even if they have the best of intentions."

Npheba shrugged in the quiet way she had of saying many things. In this case, she indicated her willingness to accept Lorral's answer.

Lorral inclined her head in Phe's direction before continuing. "The single males have been divided up into roughly even-numbered groups, and a new group will be presented here each month for the next year. You'll have five weeks to get to know each group and establish frisson with candidates."

*There's that word again,* Bea's train of thought veered off topic. *Why will no one explain the phenomenon?*

"Five weeks? Is that the length of a Devetian month?"

Trudy's question elicited a shake of Sophia's head. "Didn't you read any of the information provided during our stay on the Revival?" Her frustration made Beatrix feel guilty, as she hadn't read the information either. Sophia educated them: "Devet's year has four hundred fifty days divided into ten months. A month consists of forty-five days, five weeks, each nine days in length. A Devetian day is twenty-six hours long. Similar to Earth's leap year, every seven Devetian years an adjustment is made to the calendar. The adjustment is referred to as the Hours of Rashvadallid, the only religious holiday celebrated on Devet. On average, the holiday ranges in length from 1.7 to 2.2 days in length."

"Goodness gracious Sophia, did you memorize that word for word?"

Sophia looked uncomfortable, or maybe embarrassed would be a better word to describe the emotions that flitted across her face. Trudy's blunt question sounded more like an accusation than an inquiry. Lorral stepped in to ease the tense moment.

"I suspect Sophia has an eidetic memory. What a wonderful gift. Great recall can be invaluable." Turning her focus to Sophia alone, Lorral continued, "I also like to be highly prepared when I enter a new situation. It gives me a sense of control where I can find no other."

Lorral's kindness had Sophia looking a little less defeated, standing a little straighter. Her comment to Sophia was also a gentle rebuke to Trudy.

As was usually the case in these situations, Trudy looked contrite. She had taken Lorral's meaning. "You all know my mouth runs away with me. I don't mean to be, well, mean."

"It's okay, Trudy," supplied Gina. "We all understand your nerves make your lips loose, and Sophia becomes a talking tome. We accept you both as you are."

"I think you are a remarkably cohesive group, considering how little time you've known one another." Lorral's effervescence didn't quite lift every face in the room; Bea's was still lined with consternation.

## Chapter Eleven

# Stengot Caszar

Early morning sunshine woke Trudy as Verka drew open the window shutters. "Good morning, Madam Trudy," she chirped when Trudy lifted her groggy head from the pillow. "Shall I bring you a cup of fosh?"

"Morning Verka. Yes, please." Trudy pushed into a sitting position. "Oh, my head. Too much tafron last night." Trudy pulled on her robe and made her way to the small table in front of the window.

Verka approached with a cup of fosh in one hand and a small glass of green liquid in the other. "Take this for your headache," she said, offering the green glass.

Trudy took the proffered drink, sniffing before she brought the liquid to her lips. It smelled of sunshine and springtime. She took a hesitant sip. The slightly viscous liquid was delicious; she downed the remaining contents of the glass. Verka placed the fosh in Trudy's free hand, retrieving the now-empty juice glass from her other.

In just a few minutes Trudy began to feel better, and

told Verka so, inquiring about the remedy. "What is that called, Verka? It reminded me of something I drank at the party last night."

"This was undiluted ginula juice," Verka replied, swirling the remnants around the glass. It has uplifting properties for the mind and body; nature's perfect cure for too much tafron. What you tasted last night was diluted, a nice lift on a tiring day."

"Medicine sweet enough to entice the most reluctant patient," she granted, then asked, "Is the fruit grown here at House Stengot?"

"The juice is from a berry grown on one of Devet's claimed farming worlds. Drones tend the wild berry bushes, encouraging propagation. Then harvest the fruit, leaving a predetermined percentage to support the indigenous wildlife and their ecosystem. The berries are then processed at a facility on a nearby moon."

"Thank you, a most edifying explanation."

"One of my primary purposes is to be a useful resource during your stay at House Stengot. Please feel free to ask me anything, Madam Trudy." Verka's digits flew across the control panel of the food dispenser while she spoke.

Trudy liked her new synth attendant, grateful for both her thoughtful care and her relaxed chatty manner. She felt comfortable commenting. "On board the Revival, everything was very advanced. Many things on Devet seem simpler."

"Devetian principles require that Balance be maintained. This principle extends to the treatment of the environment. In order to maintain such a balance, simple solutions are often the best practice." Verka placed a breakfast tray on the table before Trudy.

"So manual window coverings, but magical instantaneous food?"

Verka tilted her head quizzically. "Devetians are anachronistic. Fair point, Madam Trudy."

"Can I ask another question?" Trudy's fidgeting gave away her qualms.

"I think you just did," Verka replied with a chuckle. "Go on. Difficult conversations are usually the ones best tackled first." Verka brought Trudy's breakfast, waiting next to the table for the young woman to voice her concern.

Trudy wanted to know if the population of Devet was going to treat her like a leper. Outside of her own cadre, not many of the other Vashallen would have much to do with her. They were civil, but certainly not friendly. Her nerve failed her. She asked instead, "What can you tell me about House Stengot?"

Verka didn't bother to probe, merely answered the query put before her. "The House Stengot caszar is one of the oldest and largest surviving domiciles, boasting a full twelve venvastum suites. The site was chosen and established by Eldincara, the first Stengot Matriarch of Devet.

"Holy cow! Twelve? She was a busy woman."

Verka gave Trudy an odd look, one that questioned the Vashallen's intellect. "History did not record the exact number of Ventir tied to Eldincara. At the time it was common practice for the Heir and her venvastum to share the caszar with the ruling Matriarch."

"Ohhhhh." Trudy drew out the word, her understanding dawning slowly. "Has the custom changed?"

"Many Houses have a secondary separate caszar for the Heir's use, but accommodations vary by House."

"Does House Stengot have separate accommodation for the Heir?"

"No, it does not."

"What else can you tell me of interest?"

"The outer walls of the caszartera also date back to the first age, though many of the caszartera's buildings are newer."

"Caszar? Caszartera? What's the difference?" Trudy looked bewildered.

"Caszar is the dwelling occupied by the Matriarch and her venvastum. The caszartera is the larger compound which provides accommodation and workspace for the remaining House members.

"What is House Stengot's specialty? I know each of the Houses focuses on one area of expertise."

"Stengotonians are trained as diplomats and negotiators. Madam Lorral is Devet's most illustrious ambassador. She is responsible for many of the positive relationships we enjoy with our galactic neighbors. Devetian ships always have Stengot personnel assigned to the crew."

"The Revival didn't."

"The Revival is special because of her synth pilot. Shay is fully versed in Stengot training."

"Thank you, Verka," Trudy said between bites.

Verka left Trudy to finish her breakfast, promising to

return to help her dress for the day. Trudy picked at the offerings on her tray, pouring herself a second cup of fosh. She couldn't stop thinking about Verka's advice to tackle difficult conversations. Making a decision, she rose from her seat and made her way down the hall. She took a calming breath and rapped lightly at Phe's door.

"Who is it?"

"Npheba, it's Trudy. May I speak to you?"

The door opened to reveal a similarly clad Phe. She swept her arm backward. "Please, come in. May I offer you some fosh?"

"I'd better not. I've had two cups already, and I'm nervous enough as it is. Oh goodness, I said that out loud, didn't I? See, I shouldn't have more fosh. Definitely not."

"Trudy, calm down. What has you so flustered?"

"I feel the need to keep apologizing. To you, to Cash, to pretty much everyone." Realizing she hadn't yet actually said the words, she hastened to add, "I am sorry for all your losses and suffering."

Npheba looked at her intently for a moment before responding, "You have treated me with respect. As far as I am concerned, you and I are good. I want no more of these self-recriminations, Trudy. Reassuring you grows tiresome."

"How do I make things right with Cashondra?"

"I don't know. Maybe you can't. All you can do is speak to her the same way you are speaking to me. The rest is up to Cash. It's not her responsibility to exonerate you, or to assuage your guilt."

Silence fell between the two women. Trudy took Phe's

hint, changing the topic to ask, "Will you tell me about your son? What was his name?"

A smile lit Phe's face. "His name was Ezikimbe. He was full of sunshine, my little Kimbe. He would have become a man full of life. He would have forged a strong path. These days I can smile when I think of him. He was my joy. Did you have children?" she asked Trudy in turn, before the topic became maudlin.

"I had two stepchildren from my marriage, but no, none of my own."

"Did you want children?"

"They were never a possibility for me. I lost the use of my legs in a riding accident when I was fifteen."

"Ah, I remember you said you couldn't walk before. Yet someone married you. Surely the loss of your legs didn't mean the loss of your womb."

"My husband, he never...well, we never. ... We didn't have that sort of marriage. It was understood when Father made the arrangements that Mr. Greene and his children would become heirs to the farm. My womb, working or no, was not required."

"How sad for you."

"All the more reason to grab hold of the opportunities presented in this new life with both hands. Don't you agree?" Trudy too wanted to prevent the conversation from taking a melancholy turn.

"My mother had a saying: 'Always seek to fill your cup and you won't have time to stop and worry if it is half full or half empty.'"

"She sounds wise."

"She was full of wise sayings at least," Phe joked. When their mirth ended Phe changed the subject. "Are you nervous or excited about today's introductions?"

"Both. Every event here feels momentous. I'm afraid to put a foot wrong in case they decide they made a mistake choosing me. They might send me packing back to Earth."

"Fat chance! These Devetians spent too much time and effort acquiring Vashallen. Gina's right. She might be overly suspicious, but she's right when she says they aren't telling us everything."

"You too believe they're holding something back? Something important?"

"Probably. Maybe. I don't know. I just hope if they are hiding something, it is something with which we can live."

# Chapter Twelve

# Stengot Caszar

"Let's move those chairs a little further into the shade. I don't want the Vashallen to get heat stroke. These introductions could be lengthy." Lorral directed the flurry of activity with a confidence derived from years of experience, tapping out orders on her strap while calling verbal orders as well. A line of synths followed in her wake, peeling off one by one to carry out her instructions.

The Stengot grounds were alive with preparations, synths scurrying to and fro as the final touches were added. A low dais had been raised at one end of the manicured expanse, while refreshment tables and seating areas were strategically placed under awnings or shaded areas. Musicians were setting up on the terrace, their practice notes floating across the garden. The first five tried to take in all the hubbub as they joined Lorral on the lawn.

Lorral graced the Vashallen with a wide smile as they arrived at her side. "Good morning to you ladies. I hope everyone had a restful night. I have eighty-five enthusiastic

Ventir candidates waiting to make your acquaintance this afternoon."

On her third full day as a resident of Devet, Beatrix found herself in the Stengot gardens with her fellow Vashallen. Madam Lorral had rearranged the schedule, giving the Vashallen two days to settle in and explore the caszar before the first round of introductions. The formal ceremony would begin shortly; Beatrix was beginning to think the Devetians loved any excuse for a ritual celebration.

A synth approached the group of women with a tray. Lorral's already-animated face drew into an even bigger smile. "Perfect timing, Yanaq," she said, addressing the synth attendant. "These," she indicated the tray of golden circlets, "are your new straps. They are equipped with the ability to test frisson events."

At mention of the word, Beatrix's ears perked up. Ever since she'd felt the sensation with Lanaq she'd waited for someone to explain. She hoped to learn something when Patrain confronted her at the Quorum, no such luck. She'd been too anxious that she would expose her connection to Lanaq if she asked anyone else. She waited now with bated breath for someone to ask. Gina obliged her, and Lorral explained.

"Frisson is a psychophysiological response to a positive stimulus. Put simply, frisson is how the women of Devet identify possible mates. The chemical release of pheromones and hormones in the body creates a rush of sensation, like pins and needles, or the hairs on the back of your neck standing on end. In very strong instances of frisson the pupils will dilate, or the skin may flush. Trust me, when it happens, you'll know."

"What causes frisson to happen?" Beatrix asked, finally free to join the conversation.

"The positive stimulus is unique to each couple, but may be visual, auditory, scent-based, any combination of the senses really. Frisson alerts us to possible mates by signaling a mental and physical compatibility. In the aftermath of a frisson event, we measure the types and levels of pheromones produced; this indicates the strength of the compatibility. Earthlings share a lesser-but-similar experience, often referred to as love at first sight. What's important is, no Devetian would consider a partner with whom they did not share a confirmed mental and physical compatibility. Frisson provides that, but shouldn't be the only tool you employ in your decision-making process."

"You said 'possible mates.' Is it possible to share frisson with more than one person?" Gina inquired, incredulity coloring her question.

Lorral's answer was nonchalant. "It is probable that each of you will share frisson with as many as half a dozen males. It does not follow that you will be equally compatible with all six. The courtship phase will help to..." Lorral wavered in her choice of words, before finishing, "winnow the field, so to speak."

The five Vashallen were silent, sharing a series of looks with one another. Beatrix thought about Patrain's three Ventir. The Vashallen may have agreed to more than they were expecting.

"When you experience frisson, just press this button," Lorral continued, pointing to a slightly raised area at the top of the strap. "The event will be registered, and the strength of the connection measured. Always wear your strap, frisson can happen anytime, anywhere, and usually when you least expect it," Lorral rolled her eyes, indicating her annoyance at the inconvenience of being female.

The women each took one of the new straps from the tray, hesitantly placing the devices on their arms. "Could you tell us more about what frisson feels like?" Trudy asked.

"There is some variation, depending on the strength of the connection, but in general frisson engenders similar sensations for most people, just as I described."

Raising her arm, Lorral waved a greeting to four men who were crossing the lawn toward their gathering, effectively putting an end to their discussion of frisson. "Come, meet my Ventir before we begin the formal introductions."

Lorral introduced her Ventir in order of rank. Her Ventinar, Kaigor, was a Viking of a man, all chest, arms, and towering height. Rendre was several inches shorter in stature, his frame covered in sinewy muscle and not an ounce of spare fat. He had the body of a dancer and a face that any painter would love. Nikaal was gregarious, his mischievous attitude lifting the spirits of all in his presence. The last of Lorral's Ventir, Fieren, was also the quietest. He offered the Vashallen a respectful bow when introduced, but refrained from speaking.

"Are we ready to begin, Kai?"

"We are my love. The transport schedule is confirmed. The first candidate will arrive momentarily."

"Ladies let's take our places. The sooner we get the formalities out of the way, the sooner you can relax and mingle."

Lorral led the way to the dais. She and her Ventir took the top tier, Lorral in the center flanked by her mates. The five Vashallen sat in the bottom row, nervously smoothing imagined wrinkles from their attire.

Without further preamble Lorral gave a signal, and the veranda's double doors parted. A single figure emerged, making his way down the steps and across the lawn. Reaching the edge of the shade, he placed his hands on his thighs and made a deep bow.

"Greetings, Madams Vashallen. I am Trimain, second son of House Wittingmer. It is a great honor to be presented for your consideration today."

Trimain made another bow and stepped aside. A second figure was already walking across the lawn to greet them.

Beatrix was stunned by Trimain's words. Now she understood what Lanaq and Indik had tried to convey. The shoe was definitely on the other foot for Devetian men when it came to courtship. She briefly wondered if her Vashallen sisters were as thrown by the reversal of mores as she was. In deep contemplation, she missed a few introductions.

Beatrix was brought out of her reverie when she felt Gina tense beside her. She glanced in her periphery to see Gina's eyes had grown wide. She gave her friend's hand a slight squeeze, and felt her friend release a breath. Beatrix had a suspicion that Gina was experiencing frisson. She turned her attention to the man who was discombobulating her sister.

He was about six feet, dark hair tumbling to his shoulders in soft waves. Blue eyes were set in a chiseled face, marked with a cleft chin and sharp cheekbones. He was beautiful in the way of marble statues. "Maxeem of House Mivane," he introduced himself.

"If you are experiencing something, you should push the button on your strap." Beatrix's whisper shook Gina out of her trance. She squeezed Bea's hand in return. Gathering her wits, Gina smiled hesitantly at the man standing before her. Her skin was sensitized, and she felt tipsy, though she'd imbibed no spirits. She pushed the button on her golden strap as instructed, looking up in time to see Maxeem do the same.

Seconds later, Gina's wrist beeped. The screen flashed, *FRISSON EVENT LOGGED: 7.8 FULL RESULTS PENDING.* Behind her there was an explosion of excitement.

"Marvelous! Absolutely marvelous! Our first frisson event, and during introductions no less." Lorral was out of her chair. In a few quick steps she had vacated the dais, standing in front of Gina with her hand extended, encouraging the man to come closer. "Maxeem, you and Regina may make history as the first pairing to occur as a result of Project Ferax. Congratulations."

Both Maxeem and Gina looked mortified to be the center of attention. Their mutual embarrassment made sense to Beatrix. Frisson was supposed to indicate they were suited to one another; Gina didn't mind being the center of attention if she was on the path of a righteous cause, but hated what she called "sappy sentimental showings." Bea was pretty sure this situation fell into the sappy category.

By focusing the attention on Gina, Lorral was definitely not earning goodwill; Beatrix prepared herself for a Gina-sized outburst. You could have knocked her over with a feather when Gina rose gracefully, spouting the proper Devetian greeting for just this occasion: "Greetings, Maxeem of Mivane. On behalf of my host House, Stengot, I welcome you and extend an invitation to partake of our hospitality." Gina placed her hand in Maxeem's and, in a quieter voice, added, "Later, I hope we may speak while suffering less scrutiny."

It was hard to judge Maxeem's reaction, as his face remained impassive. He snapped a sharp bow over Gina's proffered hand. "I look forward to it," he said, then stepped aside. Lorral and Gina returned to their seats, Lorral still crowing over House Stengot's good fortune, and the formal introductions resumed.

Eighty-one candidates later, the formalities were finally over and everyone could relax. Trudy, seated on a bench under a shady awning, held court to no less than five gentlemen at a time. Her tittering laughter could be heard wafting on the afternoon breeze. Meanwhile, Gina retreated to the veranda with Maxeem, remaining there in deep discussion for the rest of the afternoon. Phe, Sophia, and Beatrix spent the afternoon being squired around on the arms of

Lorral's Ventir, none of them possessing Trudy's natural flair for small talk.

For Beatrix it was a whirlwind of names and faces, but no frisson events. It was a relief when, as late afternoon approached, Lorral called an end to the garden party. Devetian custom dictated taking a few hours for relaxation before the evening meal. The Vashallen gladly retreated from the garden, congregating in Bea's room.

Phe and Trudy draped themselves across Bea's bed, stripping off their shoes as they climbed atop the plush bedding. Gina collapsed into one of the tufted chairs flanking the window.

"Well?" questioned Sophia.

"Well, what, Soph?" Trudy's slurred abbreviation of Sophia's name left no doubt she had indulged in too much tafron and too little sustenance during the party.

"I wasn't addressing you, Trudy. I want to hear from Gina about Maxeem." Sophia's sharp rejoinder took Trudy by surprise.

"What exactly are you implying?"

"I'm not implying anything; I'm saying it flat out. You are intoxicated."

"Who are you to judge?"

"I'm not judging. I'm annoyed. I don't care that you are intoxicated, only that you control yourself long enough for someone else to be the center of attention."

Trudy was clearly taken aback. Her mouth snapped shut. Crestfallen, she seemed to shrink in on herself. Seeing Trudy's reaction to her criticism, Sophia threw herself into the empty tufted chair, frustration written across her features.

Beatrix sagged. She folded herself onto the long, padded bench at the end of her bed. Removing her strappy sandals, she released a heavy sigh. "It's been an eventful few days. I think the pressure and stress has us all understandably on edge. Let's not cut one another to shreds with those edges."

Phe, who had been rather quiet during the afternoon, broke the foul mood in her singular way. "I believe these Devetians have duped us. Every last man they presented today was strong, tall, able-bodied. It's most obvious: they have imported Igbo men."

On cue the women laughed, and the tense moment between Sophia and Trudy passed. Humor still lifting her tone, Gina spoke in an uncharacteristically shy voice. "Max is very handsome, certainly, but there is more to like than his looks."

Phe smiled. "Tell us about him."

"We talked all day, and it was easy. We were so comfortable in one another's company. He's well-spoken and kind. We share a similar sense of humor. The most important thing I learned about him today is that he's a Max-and-Gina kind of man, versus a Maxeem-and-Regina kind of man."

"He sounds like a dream."

Gina looked directly at Sophia. "I understand your skepticism. When Lorral was talking about frisson I thought the idea must be a figment of Devetian imagination, with no substance in reality. Of course, I learned differently today."

"So you felt it?" four voices asked in unison. Or at least, each expressed a similar sentiment, the words overlapping.

Gina tilted her head, nodding sagely. "It was exactly as Madam Lorral described. What she didn't tell you is how you feel afterward. You are left with a knowing, a certainty."

"A certainty of what?"

"That you belong to one another. I find it hard to believe I'll be able to feel the same for more than one person, but now that I understand, I'm taking this festival more seriously. Trudy, I think that's why Sophia gets frustrated with you. Sometimes you seem flippant about this process."

"Exactly!" Sophia couldn't hold in her triumph.

Trudy pushed herself to her feet, sort of sliding backwards across the bed till her feet met the floor. She swayed slightly before drawing herself to her full five-foot-three-inch height. A scowl and a pout ruled her expression.

"I take the result very seriously. I won't apologize for taking a different approach to the meet and greet portion of the process." Trudy's serious demeanor was belied by the hiccup which punctuated her statement.

"You don't have to apologize," Sophia said, jumping to her feet to steady her tipsy friend. "I'm sorry. You're right. I am judging you." She contemplated for a moment before continuing, "Not for the reasons you might think, either. I envy how easy it is for you to socialize with the men. I find the social aspect stressful. It's not fair of me to take my frustrations out on you." The two women hugged; fences mended. "I think we should rest a little before dinner. What do you say, Trudy?"

Trudy agreed, and the two took their leave. They were followed not long after by Gina and Phe.

Left to her own devices, Beatrix stretched out on her sumptuous bed, only meaning to rest her eyes for a moment. Indik woke her up a while later; sleep still clouded her mind as he herded her into the bathing cubicle. Upon exiting, he wrapped her snugly in a robe and handed her a cup of citrusy ginula juice. Seated in front of her mirror, she sipped while Indik arranged her hair.

"I'm in awe of your efficiency, Indik. You are taking such good care of me, and I know I'd be lost without you. Thank you."

Indik's hands paused in their task, and he met Beatrix's gaze in the mirror. Time seemed to freeze while he came to some internal decision. "You are most welcome, M...Beatrix. It's my pleasure to be of service." His hands resumed combing and curling Beatrix's hair into a complicated chignon. "It's always nice to hear one's efforts are appreciated."

"Have I offended you in some way, Indik?"

"You mistake me, Madam. I am genuinely pleased by your appreciation. It's not often a synth hears praise for their work."

"I know what it is to be a servant. The Devetians take synths for granted."

"No more than one takes for granted any tool built for a purpose."

"You see yourself as a tool?"

"Built to serve."

"That's terrible. I don't see you that way, Indik."

"Please don't upset yourself on my behalf, Beatrix. It isn't necessary. My programming keeps me satisfied."

"You say that, but you are far more than just programming, Indik. At least to me."

"Thank you, Beatrix. It's nice of you to say so."

# Chapter Thirteen

# Hekaria City

At the end of her first full week on Devet, Beatrix was awakened by bright sunshine gleaming through the filmy gauze of her curtains. She stretched, rolling over lazily. There was an urgent rap on her door. She lifted her head from the pillow in time to see Trudy come barging in without waiting for Bea's reply.

"You'll never guess what happened last night." She didn't pause for Beatrix to try guessing. "I was invited to go swimming at House Ukanii by Nokhoa. He was one of my dinner companions. I liked him, but didn't feel anything special at the time. Anyway, he asked if I'd like to see the ocean by moonlight..."

Beatrix smiled at Indik as he entered to prepare her morning meal. She was relatively sure she knew where Trudy's tale was headed, but she remained quiet, letting Trudy tell it in her own time, in her own chatty way. Not that Bea could have gotten a word in, had she wanted: Trudy's enthusiasm was in full force.

"...when the wave nearly knocked me off my feet,

Khoa reached out to steady me and — wow! It was just as described, pins and needles all over. I had goosebumps too. Though in retrospect the goosebumps could have been because the water was cold. That doesn't negate the fact that I felt the frisson."

Before Trudy could take a breath and launch into further details, Beatrix inserted, "What did your frisson measure?"

"7.5. Is that good? Or bad?" Trudy's brows drew together as she looked back and forth between Beatrix and Indik.

"I'm not sure what those numbers mean. Indik, can you enlighten us?"

"Certainly, Madam Beatrix. The scale ranges from zero to twelve. The statistical average of measured frisson events among Devetian pairings ranges between five and eight. Anything approaching a nine or above is considered an extraordinarily strong connection. Madam Trudy's 7.5 event is on the high end of average."

"That should give you some perspective, Trudy."

"Yes, but what does it mean?" Trudy stressed her final word, looking expectantly at Indik.

"The number represents the possibility of a strong relationship between two people. The higher the number, the stronger the possibility. Of course, the measurement also determines a Ventir's rank within his Venvastum."

Trudy's mouth pursed into an 'O' as she considered the ramifications of Indik's explanation. Shortly thereafter, three more Vashallen appeared in Bea's doorway, to be regaled with Trudy's news.

The entire breakfast hour was spent listening to Trudy recount her frisson event with Nokhoa. By the time the other four Vashallen vacated the table to attire themselves for an impending outing, Beatrix was ready for a little peace and quiet. The calm, even tones of Indik's voice were always settling for her. "Tell me about the Hall of Houses, Indik," she asked, putting herself in his capable hands.

"What would you care to know, Beatrix?"

"What is the purpose of the Hall?"

"The Hall displays a House's history, as well as the House colors and insignia. There you will find examples of significant contributions made by the House in their respective field. In addition, the Hall serves to memorialize dormant Houses."

"Dormant Houses?"

"Those Houses that no longer have any living members. Hekaria City was renamed in memory of the first House to go extinct."

"How many Houses are there?"

"There are two hundred and fifty Devetian Houses; thirty-two currently have living Matriarchs. A further thirty-nine have living members but lack a Matriarch. And of course there is House Eschenwell."

"House Eschenwell?"

"Eschenwell's leader is Patriarch Jeridian."

"I thought all Devetian leaders were women."

"There have always been two Houses which represent

our homosexual population: House Eschenwell for the males and House Ibinaya for the females. Ibinaya, unfortunately, has gone dormant."

"So many dormant Houses." Bea's soft voice made the comment a lamentation.

"Indeed, the losses have been many. On a brighter note, the vacancies leave many choices for the Vashallen."

"What happens if we want to choose a House that already has a Matriarch?"

Indik was silent and still for several seconds. "Pardon the delay," he said at last, "I needed to consult the Quorum minutes on the subject. Vashallen may apply for Heir status. Ruling Matriarchs retain the right to accept or reject applications."

"Thank you, Indik. I feel better prepared for today's excursion."

Stepping out of the transporter later, Beatrix was surprised by the Hall of Houses building. It was more open-air than it was enclosed; like most Devetian buildings it made as much use of the natural landscape as possible, the man-made portions blending unobtrusively.

The building was massive, but laid out in as logical a pattern as the natural landscape allowed. Brightly colored banners and intricately carved friezes told House stories. Thoughtful displays evoked House specialties. House Dovic's display captured the group's attention immediately, their forte being all things animal. A House Dovic synth was on hand to introduce the Vashallen to a litter of sylix kits. Beatrix had seen Lorral with her pet sylix, Zooks, wrapped around her neck like a scarf. The kits were a delight, soft and affectionate. Phe was obviously enchanted. She immediately began asking all sorts of questions about the wriggling little bundles. Beatrix handed off her sylix and wandered away to explore other Houses.

She was drawn to the House Quemcara display. A bolt of lustrous fabric rested on a table under the House banner. Beatrix couldn't help herself, fingers itching to touch the fabric. She wasn't disappointed. It felt like warm water against her palms, sliding across her fingers with silky slickness. However, what captivated her most about the Quemcara display were the story panels. They told a tale of conservation, of producing fabrics and dyes using leftovers from other processes.

"Did you know Hekaria City was once called Yaginmar?" Sophia had come up silently behind Beatrix, but her soft voice didn't startle. "It was renamed in honor of the first House to go extinct."

"I didn't know the original name. Are you finding the Hall informative?"

"It's pretty, and the visuals for each House are appealing, but I've already done my own research."

"Your diligence puts us all to shame, Sophia. Have you already decided on a House you'd like to lead?"

"I plan to revive House Hekaria. Hekarians were historians and archaeologists, librarians and anthropologists. They sought and preserved knowledge. Seems like a good fit for me. How about you, any thoughts?"

"I'm not as organized as you. I've given the matter some thought, but I haven't done any research."

"Do you really need to do more? House Quemcara is the perfect fit for you."

Beatrix turned to face Sophia. "Maybe. Choosing a House that already has a Matriarch…" Beatrix let the thought trail off, not sure how to finish the statement. "Could be problematic," she eventually concluded.

Sophia pursed her lips in response. "It wouldn't be my first choice. But then, not everyone's path is the same, Bea. You must do what is right for you."

"I have lots of time to decide. Right now, there are too many new things to be distracted by."

"Please don't tell me you are going to turn man crazy, like Trudy."

"I don't plan on it. You are being a little unfair to Trudy. Crazed might be too strong a word."

"Are you saying you don't think she's become a little too enthusiastic for the presentation process?"

"I wouldn't say her enthusiasm is excessive. Go easy on her. She's had a difficult time."

"More difficult than myself? More difficult than Phe? Or more difficult than any of the other Vashallen? We all come from less than perfect circumstances. Why should Trudy receive more understanding?"

Beatrix took a long look at the previously timid and pale creature. No longer did Sophia seem to shrink into her surroundings. Over the course of their adventure, she had blossomed into a confident woman. Her diminutive stature no longer seemed to be the first thing Beatrix noticed; instead, it was her bright, intense gaze.

Gathering her thoughts, Beatrix answered, "Trudy has to find her own way through this process, just like we all do. Instead of condemning her for her, ah, enthusiasm, maybe we should be supportive? After all, the point is to court and be courted."

Sophia's sniff of disdain was loud. "How convenient for her. I just don't want Trudy making the rest of us look bad."

"I take your meaning, and I hear your concern, but I don't think we've reached the point of disgrace-by-association just yet. Give Trudy some time. She might surprise you. And, maybe, I mean this in the kindest way, Sophia, maybe don't be so quick to judge."

Sophia had the grace to look slightly ashamed. Her cheeks flushed. "I defer to your opinion for the time being. I hope you're right."

Sophia drifted away as quietly as she'd approached. Beatrix turned back to the Quemcara display, but she could no longer muster the same enjoyment. She strolled along to the next display, lingering briefly. She turned one corner and found the House Stengot display, turned another and found the House Nilaster area. As makers of handmade musical instruments, their display was auditory. A synth was on hand to play the gleaming instrument representing Nilaster skill. Beatrix appreciated the warm mellow sound that seemed to caress her skin like the soft afternoon breeze, wrapping her in a phonic embrace. She closed her eyes, humming and swaying in accompaniment.

The soft scrape of a shoe on stone, or perhaps the sense of being watched, caused the hairs on the back of Bea's neck to stand up. She turned her head slowly, startled to find another synth standing behind her.

The synth stood close enough to be invading Beatrix's personal space; that was the first startling thing about the android. Its hostile gaze drove Bea backwards several paces. The distance allowed her some perspective. A sharp inhalation gave away her shock. The synth hadn't just been given a sexed shell: she looked like a male fantasy, all voluptuous curves and bosom. If it hadn't been for the overly large breasts, Bea would have said she resembled Patrain.

"What are you doing here?" The synth's voice was as hostile as her gaze.

"Just learning about House Nilaster."

"Well, this House doesn't need a Matriarch. Move along."

Beatrix was flabbergasted. It had been a long while since anyone spoke to her so dismissively; she'd grown accustomed to being addressed with some deference, especially by the synths. Uncertainty delayed her response. "I didn't realize this area was off limits."

"Now you do," the synth's eyes flashed a warning.

Beatrix gathered her dignity, leaving the area without further verbal sparring. She went in search of the others, wondering what Indik would have to say about her encounter.

The first Vashallen cadre spent several hours at the Hall before returning to Stengot to prepare for the evening meal.

Beatrix relayed her experience to Indik while he helped her dress. "I think the most startling thing about her was not her form, though I admit I was caught off guard by her appearance. It was her attitude, that really disturbed me."

"I know the synth of which you speak. There are only a handful of androids whose shells are sexed in the manner you describe, and only one belonging to House Nilaster. Her name is Triff."

"Why was she so angry that I was looking at House Nilaster's display?"

"She has been the companion of the former House Ventinar since the passing of the Nilaster Matriarch. It's possible she fears being replaced."

"Can a synth do that? Fear something?"

"It depends on its programming, Madam." Indik put down the wand he'd been waving across her face. He turned her head to each side, inspecting his work. "Done. You look lovely as always," he concluded

"Would House Nilaster's members accept her as their Matriarch?"

"No, Beatrix. No matter how female her shell may appear, she is a synth."

"No synths allowed, eh? Does that bother you, Indik?"

"Synths were created and programmed to be of service, Madam."

"As simple as that?"

"As simple as that," Indik confirmed, clearing away his tools.

"Have a nice evening, Beatrix," Indik called out as he

hurried off to attend his other duties, leaving Beatrix to wonder whether she'd said something wrong.

# Chapter Fourteen

# Stengot Caszar

A rainy morning heralded the arrival of month three on Devet. Beatrix was still without a single frisson event, bar her experience with Lanaq. Trudy already had two possible mates in Nokhoa Ukanii and Zan Cantigone. The others each had at least one frisson event, even Sophia, who still seemed puzzled that it could happen to her. Beatrix was starting to feel a little panicky. She wouldn't see Lanaq till the end of the year if she didn't find frisson with someone else first. She missed him and longed to see him, but dreaded the idea she was somehow avoiding frisson with others because of her connection to Lanaq.

Beatrix was eating her morning repast when Lorral breezed into her room, still clad in her pajamas and robe. "Good morning, my dear Beatrix. Due to the poor weather today, we will be moving the introductions indoors. The staircase in the entry hall seems appropriate, but it means we'll be standing. Think flats."

Beatrix nodded without speaking, expecting Lorral to

breeze back out as blithely as she'd breezed in. Instead, she surprised Beatrix by taking the seat opposite. Placing her hands quietly in her lap, brow furrowed and lips drawn tightly together, Lorral leaned in and whispered, "Beatrix, I'm concerned."

Bea knew just what worried her hostess. She was worried too, but was reluctant to give voice to the issue, to make it real. She'd rather hear Lorral's perspective on the problem.

"A rumor about you and Pilot Lanaq sharing frisson has surfaced."

Beatrix's shocked inhalation sounded loud in the quiet room. Not quite the discussion she'd expected. Did Lorral know their secret?

"The longer you remain without a confirmed frisson event, the more credence the rumor will gain. Patrain has been fielding pointed inquiries for several days." She reached out to pat Beatrix's hand. "I know you can't make frisson happen, my dear, but if you are emotionally trying to avoid frisson..." Lorral trailed off with an imploring look.

"I assure you, Madam Stengot, I am open to frisson occurring. It just hasn't happened. I have thrown myself into every activity, been on numerous outings, in groups, one-on-one," Bea threw her hands up in frustration, "and nothing. I swear I'm trying, Lorral."

Beatrix was nearly in tears, and Lorral felt terrible for bringing up the subject. "Well, perhaps that's the problem. You are putting too much pressure on yourself. Try to relax.

It will happen. In all of recorded Devetian history there has never been a Matriarch with only one mate."

"You know about Lanaq." It was a statement of fact rather than a question. "I assume Patrain told you?"

"Of course she did, my dear. She wouldn't put your care in my hands without making me aware of such cogent details," Lorral said, tsk-tsking. She stood and strode toward the door. There was less spring in her step now, but her usual sunny smile was pinned in place. She turned back as she reached the doorway, hand gripping the frame. "Remember, flats."

Beatrix finished the last of her morning juice and pushed her tray aside. By the time Indik arrived to help her choose the day's attire, she was showered and brushing her hair dry.

"Good morning, Beatrix."

"Morning, Indik."

Indik took the brush from her fingers and began arranging her hair, weaving and plaiting it into an intricate pattern ending in a thick tail between her shoulder blades.

Her dress for the day was a strapless affair with a tight waist and a large skirt. The dress was simple, white with a black sash, though the fabric made it spectacular; Beatrix thought the color was more accurately described as pearl. It had the same watery sheen. The fabric was light and airy, the skirt frothy without the aid of petticoats. With hair and clothes complete, Indik began work on her makeup. "You are unusually quiet this morning, Beatrix."

Beatrix heard Indik's concern in the casual comment.

"I'm sorry. I'm not a very good companion right now. Lorral came to tell me she is worried, though she was only echoing my own growing concern." As one of the few who knew her secret, Indik was someone she could share her concerns with freely. "I'm letting everyone down, especially Patrain. Why am I not finding frisson with anyone else, Indik?" Her question came out as a plea.

"It is far too soon to assume there is a problem, Beatrix. Even if the situation is difficult for Patrain, it is a situation of her own making. Do not make her problems your own. Relax, enjoy yourself. Your next Ventir candidate will present themselves soon enough."

"I might be able to follow that advice if Lorral wasn't also worried."

"Understood, let's look at the problem mathematically. Up to this point the first five have met the same number of men. You've each established at least one frisson connection to possible mates. Yes, Trudy has two, but did you honestly think she wouldn't have more suitors than the rest of you?"

"But..."

Indik cut her off, holding up his hand to indicate he wasn't finished speaking. "Yes, I know. You haven't felt frisson with anyone since Lanaq, and you're worried that somehow you are stopping frisson from happening. You can no more stop the chemical reaction of frisson than you can stop the beat of your heart by thinking about it."

Great tears gathered in the corners of Beatrix's eyes. Indik drew back the makeup wand he was wielding, blotting away the moisture before it could ruin his efforts. "I'll relay one more fact on this topic, then you should put it out of your mind." Indik paused, holding her gaze until she nodded her agreement.

"The average number of Ventir candidates a Matriarch has at the end of her presentation festival is 5.7. At this point you have met just shy of twenty percent of our single population, and you have had one frisson event. Statistically speaking, you are right on track for the average number of possible Ventir."

"When you put it like that, worry does seem premature. I just don't want to disappoint Patrain or Lorral."

Makeup finished, Indik gave her a final once-over. Satisfied the effects met his high standards, he took her hands and looked her straight in the eye. "Patrain Adderigus is more than capable of dealing with rumormongers. Rest assured, she will have plans in place for just such an eventuality. If she were here, she would tell you the same. She would tell you to let her do the worrying."

Beatrix threw her arms around a startled Indik. "Thank you, Indik. I'm grateful for your expertise, and I'm sorry for being a difficult charge."

Recovered from the shock of receiving physical affection, Indik patted Beatrix on the back. He had grown to like the Vashallen in his care. He would remember her fondly when she had to leave.

Beatrix found her Vashallen sisters huddled in the entrance hall, their circle opening to admit her as she approached. The first morning of a new presentation cycle was always an uneasy one for the women. No one, except possibly Trudy, looked excited by the prospects of the day. Each felt the pressure of carrying the hopes of so many, and never was that hope more palpable than on the day of introductions.

"Will this finally be your month, Beatrix?"

"I don't know, Trudy. I hope so." Bea's reply held little enthusiasm, contradicting her words.

"Why do you think you haven't bonded with anyone yet?"

"I don't know."

"Are you holding back somehow? Is it a psychic block?"

"I think she means psychological block." Phe's sarcasm sounded heavier due to the accompanying eye roll.

"I don't think I'm holding back."

"It just seems odd that even Sophia found Vadeem, but nothing remotely resembling a frisson event for you, Bea."

"Trudy, stop grilling poor Beatrix. Let us think and speak of anything other than men in the small amount of time that remains." Bea chuckled along with the others, but mouthed a silent, "Thank you," to Npheba.

At the rear of the hall the doors to the ballroom had been thrown open. House Stengot synths streamed in and out, putting the final touches on the indoor reception. Lorral arrived in the entry hall, tapping out orders as she walked, her Ventir following close behind. In no time, she had everyone arranged to her satisfaction on the last few steps of the sweeping staircase. From across the expanse of the grand enty, the hum of the transport cradle heralded the arrival of the first candidate.

The formal presentations were underway. Each male arrived within moments of the previous, introduced himself, and made his way into the ballroom. Npheba was quietly bored, but held a pleasant expression pinned in place. These hours spent on formal introductions were fruitless in her opinion. She much preferred to engage the males in conversation. She had found frisson with Briq last month, but not until they had spent many hours exploring each other's similarities and differences. They didn't share similar backgrounds, but they did see life and their purpose through similar lenses. At this point Phe wasn't convinced the Devetian notion of frisson was anything more complicated than intuition mixed with a dash of common sense.

The transporter hummed on and on, expelling candidate after candidate, and Npheba continued to hold her soft smile. She knew her duty to House Stengot and would never let her hostess down by being less than equal to the moment, no matter how protracted and deadly dull.

He strode from the transporter room on legs long and lean. Even by Devetian standards he was tall. Npheba blinked and stood a little straighter, her chin rising. His skin, like hers, was dark chocolate, and radiated a glow of good health. His facial hair was trimmed to frame his jawline and mouth. Phe gulped and remembered to breathe.

"Good morning, Madams Vashallen." He intoned while executing a series of bows in their direction.

His voice was deep and rich, and its resonance struck a chord deep inside Phe. The air felt electric as she waited for his gaze to meet her own. The hair along her arms stood on end as brown eyes met green.

"I am Erran of House Dovic and I believe I share frisson with this Vashallen." He addressed Npheba as he approached, pausing to press the button on his wrist device. His bearing was proud, erect, his smile shy. He waited for Phe to reciprocate his gesture of friendliness before reaching into his jacket. He produced a small furry ball from a deep pocket, offering her the tiny creature.

Phe couldn't help herself, a small squeal of excitement escaped. With barely a pause to ascertain if the creature was safe, she scooped the furball into her own palm. She intended to cuddle the tiny creature to her breast but was distracted by the tendrils of sensation that spread from the contact of Erran's skin against her own.

Phe's head snapped up, her gasp a sharp surprised draw of air. Her eyes widened as they met his, which beamed back at her with joy.

"Would you like to activate your strap? I believe we are experiencing a frisson event."

"Wha...What?" Npheba embarrassed herself by stumbling over her own tongue. "*Can one drown in mossy green pools?*" flashed across her consciousness before she took hold of her faculties once more. She calmly preformed the necessary task on her strap before returning his bow. "It's a great pleasure to meet you, Erran," she said as a fresh wave of sensation spread up her arm from their point of contact. "Who is this little guy?" Phe stroked a finger across the furry ball; chittering noises came from the creature in response.

"That is a Tagoo and her name is Babi. I would love to tell you about her species and their habitat when you are free." Erran stepped back, executing a deep bow in the direction of the other Vashallen. A second, deeper bow was bestowed on Lorral as hostess, before he captured Phe's fingertips, bowing low over them, lips briefly contacting her skin. His action sent shivers running up and down her spine.

There was no time for Phe to dwell on Erran's touch. His actions were punctuated by the hum of the transporter and another candidate's arrival. Phe watched his withdrawal to the ballroom with reluctance, but dutifully turned her attention to the next arrival.

Even wearing flats, Beatrix's feet were beginning to complain. She transferred her weight from one hip to the other. *"Surely we're getting close to the end."* The thought brought both relief and terror; relief from standing still in one spot, and terror that once again she would let Lorral, Patrain, and herself down.

She knew there couldn't be many introductions remaining when a man matching Lanaq's height emerged from the transport room. He had tousled golden curls, wide shoulders, and a confident stride. As he made his way toward the staircase, Beatrix felt a wave of sensation sweep over her. Her breath caught in her throat.

The male came to a halt and made his bow. Respectful, but not overly long or low. "Ladies, I am Cavial. I bring greetings from House Quemcara." His voice was like velvet:

thick, warm, and smooth. He followed his introduction with another fluid bow, his eyes locking onto Beatrix's own as he straightened.

Beatrix couldn't breathe. The sensations running across her skin and short-circuiting her brain were unlike anything she could begin to describe. She tried to suck in a breath, but only succeeded in doing something she'd always prided herself on never allowing to happen: she fainted.

Her faint wasn't of the limp-hand-to-forehead, delicately-crumple-to-the-floor variety. Beatrix pitched forward as if she were a puppet and someone had simply cut her strings.

Cavial reacted quickly, scooping Beatrix into his arms before she could collide with the stone floor. With her limp form secured, he mounted the stairs, striding past Lorral, her Ventir, and the other Vashallen. They trailed in his wake, voicing their distress. "Which room is hers?" he demanded, reaching the landing where the stairs split.

"First one to the left," Lorral called out from below him.

Cavial strode down the hallway, Beatrix still unconscious in his arms. Finding her room, he entered and laid her on the bed, dismissed the fussing gaggle and closed the door. He then sat down on the edge of the bed to watch over her, engulfing one of her hands in his own.

After a few moments Lorral burst into the room, her Ventinar and a medic one step behind. Concern for her guest and the reputation of her House was written in harsh lines across her face. "Your behavior is very high-handed, Cavial Quemcara. It's unacceptable under my roof. The Vashallen is in my care."

Cavial, with a wide grin, angled the screen of his strap toward Lorral.

"Oh, my," was Lorral's only reaction. She turned, ushering everyone out of the room with quiet murmurings. Cavial and Beatrix were left in privacy.

Beatrix came around slowly. Her eyelids fluttered open. She focused, only to drown in the honey-brown eyes that met her own.

"Hello." His mature voice caused shivers to run up and down her spine. Beatrix continued to stare upward at Cavial, lost in the sight, sound, and very smell of him. "You fainted," he continued, smiling at her regard, "and I carried you to your room."

Beatrix blinked, still dazed. Her right hand was caught between his two. His thumb was making slow circles on the sensitive skin of her inner wrist, tingles reverberating up her arm and down her body from the point of contact. She glanced down, as if to verify that just the touch of his skin on hers was the source of the sensations.

"I took the liberty of pressing the button on your cuff."

Beatrix's brain was beginning to function once more, and the reason for her fainting episode came rushing back to her. Instinctively she lifted her wrist, needing to see how strong the frisson event had been. It had literally knocked her off her feet. The little screen on her cuff read: *FRISSON EVENT LOGGED: 10.2 FULL RESULTS PENDING.*

"My reaction was equally as strong." He held up his strap as evidence. "I might start taking it personally if you continue to remain silent," he joked.

Of its own accord, Beatrix's left hand rose to stroke his cheek. He leaned into her touch. Beatrix could swear the color of his eyes deepened. Her fingers slid into his hair, running through his curls to settle on the nape of his neck. She exerted light pressure, bringing his lips toward her own.

Beatrix didn't think about her actions. She did what seemed natural in the moment, exploring Cavial's lips with her own. They remained entwined for long moments. When they finally put a little space between themselves, Beatrix trailed a single digit across Cavial's full bottom lip.

"Hello Cavial. Nice to meet you."

# Chapter Fifteen

# Quorum Building – Hekaria City

Patrain's office was much like Patrain herself: tidy, organized, and giving away nothing personal about the woman within. She sat at her desk, reading through reports from the various host Houses. Beginning the third month of presentation festivals, Patrain was cautiously optimistic regarding the number of frisson events recorded by the fifty-two Vashallen. A couple had even found frisson with more than one candidate to date.

All in all, the second phase of Ferax was exceeding her hopes. The fly in the ointment, so to speak, was the situation with Beatrix and Lanaq. Patrain had fielded several calls from her detractors over the last few weeks. Rumors were circulating, and there were grumblings of unfair influence. Patrain was frustrated by the pettiness, but determined not to interfere in the process until and unless she had no other choice.

Her strap chirped, indicating a video call. Surprised by the caller's identification, Patrain engaged.

"Good afternoon, Madam Patrain. I have news to report."

"Good news or bad?"

"Good. Vashallen Beatrix had a frisson event today."

Patrain's face remained impassive, though inside she was doing a victory dance. This would shut her critics up for a time, at least until they found something else to complain about.

"That is good news."

Patrain's strap chirped again. She glanced at the incoming call. "I've got a holocall from Lorral. No doubt to inform me of the occurrence. Thank you for the information, we'll talk further at the Stengot ball if we find an opportunity. Don't forget to scrub this call from the core."

"Of course, Madam."

Patrain ended one call and accepted the other. She left her desk and moved to a comfortable armchair. A holographic image of Lorral appeared in front of her. She was obviously excited, practically hopping back and forth from one foot to the other.

"It finally happened! Beatrix and Cavial Quemcara. And you won't believe this, a record-setting measurement too."

Lorral was a good friend and a staunch supporter. Her enthusiasm was such one might have thought she was the leader under fire, but that was just Lorral. She was a bundle of positive energy. It was a mistake to think her chatter was the sign of a lesser mind, a mistake people only made once. Under all the carefree smiles and happy demeanor lay a whip-smart intellect. Patrain was grateful to have such a friend and ally.

"Really? What was the reading?"

"10.2."

Patrain was stunned. She and Lassitor shared one of the strongest bonds among their generation, their initial frisson measuring 8.9 during their presentation festival.

"Well, all thanks to Mother Balance. That should silence the busybodies for a time. Is Beatrix well?"

"The event was so strong she lost consciousness. Only for a short time," Lorral reassured. "Cavial caught her and carried her upstairs, practically growling at anyone who tried to get close! His reaction is understandable, especially given such a high reading. He was just being protective of his mate."

"With a bond that strong I'm not surprised she was overwhelmed. How is she otherwise?"

"The pressure of not finding frisson was beginning to take a toll, but I'm sure she will be fine now."

"And the others? I've read your official reports, of course, but I just wonder about their personalities. Will they fit in here?"

"Phe also made a strong connection today: Erran Dovic. Not surprising really given her penchant for beasties big and small. Kindred spirits those two. I suspected they would make a match. Good to know I haven't lost my instincts," Lorral's merry mood extended to her own foibles.

"Gina and Sophia continue to respond carefully and seriously. Sophia is the intellectual among the group. She doesn't miss much. At first she seemed more resigned than eager, though she's thawed since finding her first match with Vadeem.

"Trudy is a lark. She has thrown herself into the process with such positivity. I have no doubt each will find their place."

"Thank you, Lorral, for looking after them so well. They all seem to be thriving under your roof. Keep me apprised, and I'll see you at this week's ball." Patrain ended the call. She allowed herself a single fist pump of celebration, then swiftly made her way to the transport room.

Patrain exited the transport cradle at the Adderigus Residence, located just north of Hekaria Square. She called out to her Ventinar as she entered the hall: "Lass, are you home?"

"In here, my love," came from the direction of the kitchen.

Patrain altered course, heading toward the sound of her mate's voice. She found him at the kitchen counter, manually preparing a meal. Patrain never failed to be amazed at how domestic Lassitor could be, especially when he felt she had been under too much strain. Cooking a delicious meal for her was his way of showing concern.

She approached him from behind, pressing herself to his back and sliding her arms around his waist. "Mmmm, something smells good."

"Zuzt salad, my love."

"I wasn't talking about the food."

Lassitor turned in his Vassen's arms and gathered her close. "Welcome home. Good day?"

"Yes, but we can talk about that later. Will the salad keep?" Patrain trailed light kisses along Lassitor's jaw.

A sly smile teased his lips as desire warmed his gaze. "What salad?"

Later, they lay entwined atop a divan on the balcony, watching the last rays of light from Vayot, the lesser of Devet's two suns, as it sank beneath the horizon. They sipped on chilled glasses of banga. A light blanket covered their nakedness.

Patrain was loath to break the relaxed lethargic atmosphere but she hadn't yet told Lassitor about Beatrix and Cavial. She was idly running her fingertips up and down his chest when she broached the subject. "I had good news from Stengot today."

"Beatrix?"

"Yes, she and Cavial Quemcara."

"Lanaq will be relieved to hear Beatrix is finding other connections. Guilt has been eating at him."

"He puts too much pressure on himself. Be careful how much you say to him."

Lassitor scowled. "Is there an issue of which I'm unaware?"

Patrain steeled herself and said, "Beatrix and Cavial measured 10.2." Lassitor's expression reflected the enormity of the news. "That part he doesn't need to know. I understand that as his father your instinct might be to prepare him." Lassitor's face bore his concern. "But hear me out. We don't actually know what his frisson with Beatrix will measure. Nothing either of them said about their experience leads me to believe it will be anywhere near as strong as 10.2."

"It's true we don't really know how strong their connection is."

"Exactly. I believe we should leave be and let nature take its course. His frisson with Beatrix will be measured in time, and the worst that happens is he won't be her Ventinar. But he will have a mate, a Venvastum. Isn't that what we really want for him?"

Lassitor cuddled Patrain closer, reassuring her with his body language. "Of course it is, but we are talking about a grown man. Even if he is our son."

"So, we agree to ease his conscience but give him no other information? After all, the bonds between a Vassen and her Ventir are private. We shouldn't interfere with Beatrix's process of selection by giving Lanaq information that her other candidates don't have."

Lassitor considered the new information. Patrain wasn't wrong; his instinct was to gird his son with knowledge. "You're right, as you usually are, my love," he admitted. "Honestly, I don't think Lanaq cares one way or the other if he is Ventinar. I believe he will be happy to be one of Beatrix's Ventir. He's completely smitten. When is his group scheduled at Stengot?"

"Seventh month. She may yet form more bonds before he arrives." Patrain left unspoken that such occurrences would be politically expedient. Lassitor was aware of what was at stake; reminding him now would only spoil the moment.

Patrain reached across her Ventir to refill her glass, trailing kisses along his shoulder as she slid back to lay at his side. "Anything worth sharing from your day?"

"As a matter of fact, yes. I received a communication from the commander of the mining group stationed at the Frunae Belt. He reports they are ahead of schedule. The Revival will be completely refueled and ready for its return journey at the start of tenth month."

"How fortuitous. We might time the launch to coincide with the first day of the final festival."

"Keep in mind our mining rights in the Frunae Belt will have to be renegotiated with the Garfundians at the end of the year. Our FST capability will be seriously curtailed without an agreement in place."

"I'll task Lorral with the negotiations as soon as the presentation festivals conclude. Any word from our friends in House Tagorth?"

"They are reluctant to say more than what they already confirmed. Earth is experiencing an unusual amount of geological disturbance. They refuse to speculate on the ramifications. They request more data."

"Assure them that when I have more information, so will they. Anything else?"

"On a less pleasant note, I heard from Houses Bellinger and Iffenjin again. Each wants a pilot from their respective House to handle the Revival's next mission."

"Okay, put a pilot from each of their Houses on the short list." She reached to smooth the wrinkle that formed on his brow with a soft fingertip. "No need to worry, as you know, we've already reached a tentative decision on the pilot for mission two. I'm certain during the official vote, neither the Bellinger nor the Iffenjin pilot will receive enough votes to be assigned the heavy responsibility of choosing Vashallen. Yes, I'm relatively certain that's exactly what Moina will call it, a heavy responsibility."

Lassitor's hand caressed her back, coming to rest on a ticklish spot near her hip bone. She squirmed at his touch in the most pleasurable way. He smirked. "Who is the lucky pilot chosen for the second mission?"

"Lorral's Fieren has volunteered."

"Does Lorral know?"

"She supports his decision."

"I take it the other names on the list don't matter."

"For mission two? Not particularly, no," Patrain said as she rose from the divan, reaching for a robe. "Let's go eat the zuzt salad, I'm starving."

# Chapter Sixteen

# Stengot Caszar

Month three flew by faster than lightning, or so it seemed to Beatrix. There weren't enough hours, even in the Devetian day, to spend with Cavial.

House Quemcara specialized in all things textile. Beatrix was overjoyed to have someone as interested in fabric and fashion as herself to converse with.

Cavial took her to visit the Quemcara workrooms, where all manner of beautiful objects were under construction. They also toured the Quemcara orchards. Beatrix saw firsthand growing del-dell fruit, whose tart pink juice was a favorite, the rind used to make a rich red dye.

He showed her the fossmore groves. "Every year, fossmore trees shed a layer of bark. After being roasted and brewed to make fosh the fibers of the bark become soft, holding dye especially well. The short strands are ideal for use in rugs and tapestries."

Her days were fun and informative, but her evenings were better. She liked being held in Cavial's arms as they swept around a dance floor. He had a habit of whispering outrageous things in her ear, things that left her ready for more private moments. Yet, Cavial remained a perfect gentleman. His words were occasionally lusty, but their kisses never crossed a line, and he always withdrew before things got too heated. She told herself she was only a little bit disappointed.

Tonight was the last ball of third month. *Tomorrow, Cavial will be gone. I'm not ready for him to be gone.* The thought caused Beatrix to drop dejectedly back onto her pillow. A huffy sigh issued from her lips.

"Good morning, I'm glad you're awake." Trudy swept in, making herself at home in Bea's room as she often did. She crossed to the waiting tray Indik had left prepared, picking at the assortment of nuts and fruit, then poured herself a cup of fosh. Once settled into the chair facing Bea's bed, Trudy said without fanfare or preamble, "It happened again." She popped another nut in her mouth.

"Another candidate? Who?" Beatrix sat up, drawing a robe over her pajamas.

"Onari."

"Oh, the one with the beautiful hazel eyes and all that hair? You don't sound excited." She joined Trudy at the breakfast table, pouring herself a glass of del juice. She grabbed one of the savory breakfast pastries waiting on the tray, taking a generous bite.

"Oh, I am."

"I can hear a 'but' coming," she said, licking crumbs from her fingertips.

"He's Nokhoa's brother. Brothers! That's got to be a recipe for disaster. And he's my third candidate already. We still have seven more presentations. I'm going to have to quit flirting."

Beatrix couldn't help herself, doubling over with laughter. Trudy sounded as if she'd decided to stop breathing. When her mirth was under control she replied, "I don't think flirting determines whom you share frisson with."

"But it might curtail how many. I'm going to get a reputation as the loosey-goosey Vashallen. Need a mate? Go see Trudy." Big teardrops made rivulets down her cheeks. "What am I going to do if I like them all?" This last question came out on a wail.

"Trudy, I think you are putting the cart before the horse — borrowing trouble, so to speak. You only have three candidates thus far, not a dozen."

"Oh goodness, don't even think such a thing, Bea. I don't think I could survive feeling this way about twelve different men."

"Wait till you spend a year living with them. Some of them are bound to have annoying habits or personality traits, right?"

"Aren't you supposed to accept the bad with the good when you're in love?"

"I suppose so," Beatrix admitted reluctantly. "Honestly, Trudy, I don't think frisson equals love, just the possibility. Lorral gave me the impression the courtship year is about eliminating candidates who don't fit in the group. My advice is, stop worrying about the future. Enjoy this part while it lasts, as the hard work will come soon enough."

Trudy's head hung between her slumped shoulders, the weight of the world resting upon them. Indik appeared in the doorway, and Beatrix held up two fingers. Indik gave one short nod and disappeared into Beatrix's closet.

"You are a silly goose, but no one thinks you are loosey-goosey."

"Thanks, Bea." Trudy gave her a lopsided smile and stood. "These men are real people with real feelings."

"Yes, they are."

"I might have to hurt some of them one day."

"We all might," Bea agreed solemnly. "On a less dour note, did you receive Chesa's invitation?"

"I did. I'm looking forward to seeing the final five again."

"It will be good to see them."

Trudy seemed calmer now, fully recovered from her earlier panic. "Want to join me for a swim?"

"Great idea! Just give me a couple of minutes to change."

Beatrix and Trudy found Sophia and Gina already lounging by the pond. The day was warm, and the women were soon joined by many of this month's candidates. Amid much laughter, splashing, and convivial company the four Vashallen spent a pleasant afternoon.

Relaxed and happy, Beatrix returned to her room to prepare for the final ball. Stepping through the door, she was surprised to hear voices coming from the direction of her closet. Her pace faltered at the angry tone.

"You should let her know the situation is untenable. She must address it before things escalate."

"It is not my place to tell Madam anything, but I will pass along your concerns."

"See that you do. She won't like the consequences if something isn't done."

"The Matriarch doesn't respond well to threats. You'd do well to consider your words more carefully."

"I'm merely trying to open her eyes to the growing problem. Stating an inevitability isn't a threat."

"You may consider your message delivered."

An unfamiliar synth brushed past Beatrix, in a hurry to leave. Indik stood poised on the threshold of the closet. Beatrix flashed him a puzzled look. "Who was that, and what did they want?"

"We are having extra guests this evening."

"I see." Beatrix's mind analyzed the situation, looking for what Indik wasn't saying. "They are coming to observe Cavial and myself?"

"Probably, partly."

"The Lanaq rumor?"

"That would be my other guess," Indik said, confirming Beatrix's fear.

"So, I'm to be on display this evening. Good to know. And the synth?"

"Extra help for tonight. Questioning some of the arrangements. Nothing to worry over."

"Well, Indik, if I am to be an object of interest this evening, do your worst. Give them something to gawk at."

"That's the spirit, Madam." Indik entered the closet briefly, returning with two garments. "Which of these dresses for this evening?"

Indik worked his magic, and it wasn't long before Beatrix met Phe on her way downstairs.

"Nice dress. I like that color on you. I think it suits you better than green and blue."

"Thank you, Phe. You look stunning as always. How are you?"

"I'm less bothered by the actuality of courting many men than I was by the thought of it." Phe laughed at herself, then turned serious. "I like Devet and her people. I feel accepted, and challenged, and...I'm finally ready to believe a new life for me is possible. I'm happy, at peace." She was pensive for a moment before concluding, "Regardless of what happens with this courting business."

"Right. Life can't be all about romance."

"Precisely. I grow bored with all the primping and preening. I am eager to be engaged."

"Have you thought about your House choice?"

"I have. I am fascinated by the animal species of this planet. In some ways so similar to Earth species, and yet not. The sylix kits we met at the Hall of Houses were amazing, and I've learned so much about bozidon. Did you know that House Stengot maintains a stable?"

"I didn't."

It wouldn't have mattered had Beatrix not answered. Phe regaled her with facts about bozidon until they reached the bottom of the stairs.

"It seems you are already prepared for House selection day. Congratulations. If I remember correctly, House Dovic has no current Matriarch."

"You are correct." A sly smile accompanied Phe's answer.

Their conversation came to a halt as they reached the veranda. The sight was magical. Lorral had pulled out all the stops to impress this evening's guests. The veranda, which wrapped around three quarters of the main caszar, was awash with twinkling lights, as were the potted trees and carved screens strategically placed to create pockets of privacy. The lawn had become a dance floor, music already floating on the evening air.

"There's food and drink laid out in the dining room." Sophia's sudden announcement after her silent approach startled Phe and Beatrix. The three women halted on the threshold to take in the magnificence of the scene. Then they made their way outside, soon having dance partners galore to whirl them around under the Devetian stars.

Beatrix saw Cavial for the first time that evening as she exited the dancing throng. She was laughing and flushed as he descended the stairs toward her; his eyes looked hungry. Beatrix shivered despite the warmth.

They met on the bottom stair. Cavial bowed respectfully to her previous partner before his arm swept around Beatrix's waist, practically lifting her off her feet. He caught her other hand and guided them onto the floor. They danced in silence for several minutes, their bodies moving well to the sinuous beat of the music coming from instruments strange and wonderous.

"You are wearing my colors this evening." His voice was low, husky.

"You like the dress?"

"Very much. As much as I wanted to remove those Adderigus colors from your body, I want to remove my own more." His hand was splayed low on her bare back, pressing her forward so their thighs brushed occasionally as they danced.

Beatrix felt the heat suffuse her cheeks at Cavial's obvious innuendo. She would have lost her step in shock if not for his strong lead.

Two could play this game. A sly grin tweaked her lips. Beatrix ran her free hand through Cavial's hair, twining his soft curls around her fingers. She pressed his head toward her lips and, standing on tiptoes to reach his ear, whispered, "Probably only half as much as I'd like for you to remove them."

Her remark had the desired effect. Cavial sucked in a ragged breath. Their circuit of the dance floor brought them around to the veranda, where Cavial calmly guided them off the floor and up the stairs. His arm around her waist maintained their physical contact until he spun her behind one of the privacy screens, kissing her with all the passion she'd been waiting for. His lips lingered, caressing her own. Their tongues entwined, their breath mingling. She caught his lower lip between her pearly teeth, nipping provocatively.

Cavial raised his head, eyes smoldering. "You are a serious risk to my composure. No doubt about it." He touched his forehead to her own. "I think this extended festival will be the death of us all." When their breathing evened, the fiery desire receding from their eyes, Cavial suggested, "Why don't we get something to eat from the dining room?"

"I could definitely use something cool to drink," she agreed, the flush of desire still pinking her cheeks.

They meandered their way toward the dining room. Passing by the ballroom, its doors thrown open to the evening air, Beatrix observed that more than a few of the non-hosting Matriarchs were in attendance. In fact, judging from the number of people buzzing about the room practically every available Matriarch was present, along with their Ventir.

Beatrix couldn't guess how many heads turned their way, but she definitely felt the weight of many stares as she and Cavial strolled by.

"Is your mother here this evening?"

"Yes, she and my fathers are here somewhere. I would like to introduce you."

"Would it be rude to ask how many Ventir are in your mother's Venvastum?"

"My mother has three Ventir, and I'm certainly not offended by your question."

"May I ask about your relationship with your fathers?"

"You, my dear Beatrix, may ask me anything."

"Why do you refer to them all as your fathers?"

"They are all my fathers. Although only one contributed

his DNA, each one contributed to my upbringing. Their collective efforts made me the man I am today."

"But your place within your mother's household is based on your father's position?"

"That's correct. Two of my brothers outrank me because they are the sons of Mattis, my mother's Ventinar. One is older than me, but the other is younger."

"You said two of your brothers. Do you have more?"

"Yes, there are five Quemcara sibs. I outrank my other two brothers, though again one is older and one is younger than myself."

"What are your brothers' names?"

"Calid, Carthon, Caveen, and Caffy, which is short for Capholo."

"Oh my! Your parents certainly had a theme going. You have no sisters?"

"The sharp decline of female births was the first sign of Devet's problem. Eventually it wasn't just a decline in female births, but in all births."

"We were told the Devetian situation is troubling. I assumed some hyperbole was inherent in the telling, but that doesn't seem to be the case. How bad is it?"

"You remember the pilot from your voyage here, Lanaq?"

Beatrix wet her lips nervously. "I remember him."

"He's the youngest living Devetian. The last one born."

"Wow!"

Entering the dining room, they made their way through

the buffet-style offerings and found a quiet table, continuing their conversation over their meal.

"Tell me about your life on Earth."

"I was born a farmer's daughter, but was able to become a lady's maid. It was a good job for a woman in my time, and I enjoyed the work because I've always been excited by fashion. My employer wore only the best clothes and shoes. I had the opportunity to touch and feel the finest fabrics, to learn how to care for them, to see how properly cut fabric drapes and moves on the body." Beatrix caught Cavial's look of admiration and blushed. "I'm sorry, I can be talkative about this subject."

"Please don't apologize. I'm thrilled that you are as passionate about fabric as I am. I am sure our mutual interest played a part in our record-breaking frisson measurement."

Beatrix bowed her head. She was in awe of the bond she felt with Cavial, but a niggling worry plagued her conscience. How would she tell Lanaq about their connection?

"During the courting phase we will have time for me to share more of Quemcara's methods. Do you have any interest in design?"

"I would like to try my hand at designing, though I've not much patience for sewing, tatting, or embroidering."

"I think you will find Devetian tech helpful in those areas."

Their private interlude was cut short when Cavial rose abruptly from their table, performing a deep, respectful bow. "Elder Patrain, good evening. You look stunning as always. Quorum Member Lassitor, good to see you."

Beatrix had not seen Devet's first couple approach, as her back was to the room. She rose now and offered her own bow, adopting Cavial's formal manner. "Elder Patrain, Quorum Member Lassitor, good evening. It is lovely to see you both again. You look well."

"As do you, Beatrix." Patrain wore her warm, motherly persona this evening. "Quemcara colors suit your complexion perfectly. Don't you think so, Lass?"

"Indeed I do. You look beautiful as always, Bea."

Beatrix beamed at Lassitor's use of her nickname. Had Lanaq told him? Had he been talking to his father about her?

"Lassitor, would you and Cavial be so kind as to select something delicious for us to drink, then join Beatrix and myself in the ballroom? There are a few introductions I'd like to make."

Patrain gave her Ventinar a soft kiss on the cheek by way of thanks. Then, linking her arm through Beatrix's, she led her away. As always, Beatrix was stunned by Patrain's easy use of authority. She asked for people's cooperation, but also assumed their compliance. Beatrix was sure there was a lesson in that.

"So, my dear, you have found yourself a very strong connection. Thank you for that."

"Oh, but..."

"I know, you didn't do it for my benefit — nor could you, even if you'd wanted. Nevertheless, your frisson event with Cavial has left the rumor mill without grist. One less thing for me to worry over. I've other irons in the fire that need tending, so to speak, and even long Devetian days have only so many hours. So, thank you," Patrain said, smiling. Then, changing tack without warning, she added, "Such a strong frisson event! You must be drowning in feeling."

Patrain made it a statement rather than a question. Beatrix didn't answer, having learned from their previous encounters. She waited to see where Patrain would lead the conversation.

"Right now you are probably worried about your connection to Lanaq, as your bond with Cavial is particularly... powerful." Patrain selected the word purposefully.

"I'm more worried about how to tell him."

"Ask Cavial how he would feel if the situation were reversed." They reached the ballroom, and had no further time for private conversation. Beatrix took in the scene before her.

Representatives from multiple Houses performed traditional Devetian dances at the center of the room, an admiring throng milling about, sipping beverages of choice. Much like the veranda, the perimeter of the room was arranged with cozy seating areas, and Lorral had moved many of her art pieces into the space for the evening, giving people places to stop and converse.

"Come, time to greet Devet's luminaries." Still linked by their arms, Patrain led Beatrix around the edge of the ballroom, making introductions. There were too many names and too many faces in too short a time for Beatrix to have any hope of remembering them all; she got the sense these brief presentations were not Patrain's true purpose.

Eventually Patrain maneuvered their progress toward a sullen group who stood silently apart, watching the evening unfold from the sidelines. "Beatrix, First Vashallen, please meet Hemion of House Nilaster and Jenax of House Gallen."

Beatrix executed what she judged to be the perfect bow. "Gentlemen, it's a pleasure to make your acquaintance."

Both men were thin and gangly. There the similarities ended. Hemion Nilaster possessed an olive complexion, brown hair combed back to expose his sharp widow's peak, and a nose that could most kindly be called aquiline. His pinched expression hinted at a sour disposition.

Jenax Gallen was somewhat darker, both in complexion and hair color. Braids tumbled artfully to his shoulders. His keen eyes were smoke-lined; Beatrix surmised his use of cosmetics to enhance them. Unlike Hemion, Jenax's expression was welcoming.

Most shocking was the companion on Hemion Nilaster's arm: the belligerent female-modeled synth from the Hall of Houses. The synth's body language clearly indicated her relationship with Nilaster was indeed very personal. Though Indik had told her as much, it had been difficult to imagine. Seeing the synth practically draped across his body, her gaze every bit as hostile as before, Beatrix couldn't deny the proof before her. She glanced briefly at Patrain, and thought she detected a hint of distaste in the leader's expression. Then it was masked by Patrain's public smile.

Cavial and Lassitor arrived, drinks in hand; Cavial's arm slipped around Beatrix's waist as he handed over a glass of tafron. At this, Patrain finally relinquished her hold on Beatrix's arm.

"So the rumor is true. Vashallen Beatrix and Quemcara here have a verified frisson event?"

No one else spoke. Everyone was looking at her, so Beatrix answered Jenax Gallen hesitantly. "Yes. We were fortunate enough to find one another during this month's festival."

"Well, good fortune to you both during courtship." The dismissive expression on his face did nothing to convince Beatrix of his sincerity.

Hemion Nilaster didn't deign to speak. He stared at Beatrix's party down the length of his hooked nose; his sneer duplicating that of his clinging synth.

"Hemion." Patrain acknowledge the silent man, while managing to avoid looking at or speaking to Triff. Taking Lassitor's arm, indicating their imminent departure, she inclined her head, "Enjoy the rest of your evening, gentle-men." She nodded at the grumpy party and began walking away, only to halt and spin on her heel. "Oh Jenax, I almost forgot. Please call my office to set up a meeting. I have some time available to discuss your and Hemion's project proposal."

Beatrix caught the look of astonishment on Jenax's face right before he started into a deep bow. Bea glanced up at Cavial for insight on the exchange, who gave her a "Don't-ask-me" shrug.

Beatrix and Cavial followed the older couple, stopping next to be introduced to the Matriarch and Ventinar of

House Tagorth, Eliska and Ronik. Eliska was a diminutive woman, with sharp eyes and a thin smile. Her Ventinar Ronik reminded Beatrix of a village blacksmith, solidly muscled. House Tagorth's specialty lay in geology, mining, and terraforming. Fortunately for Beatrix, who knew nothing significant about any of those subjects, Ronik was entertained by stories from Earth. While she regaled him with anecdotes of society scandals, the Quorum Elder spoke in hushed tones with the Tagorth Matriarch.

They conversed longer with the Tagorths than with any of the previous groups. Ronik's interest in Bea's previous existence felt genuine rather than feigned out of social politeness. He was a gregarious companion, unusual in a Devetian, bringing her to laughter with ease. She was disappointed when Patrain made ready to move on.

Their next stop along the ballroom's perimeter brought them to a merry group. They lounged on soft chaises, tossing back banga and tafron so quickly the synth staff was hard-pressed to keep up with the empty glasses.

"Beatrix, I'd like to introduce you to the representatives from Houses Bellinger and Iffenjin."

Marcot Bellinger and Whinson Iffenjin rose from their indolent poses to be introduced, each executing a rather sloppy bow. Beatrix perceived the intended slight, but was unsure who was being slighted, herself or Patrain. Either way she returned the favor in kind, offering a short, shallow bow, really a mere inclination of her neck.

"You look as lovely tonight as you did at the arrival ceremony," Marcot complimented her, eyes raking her body.

"Of course, there's more of you on display tonight for our enjoyment."

Beatrix blanched. She felt Cavial react to the insult, his chest puffing up and his arms tensing. She laid her fingers atop his hand at her waist, calming him with her touch and her words. "You'll pardon me, gentleman, my memory is faulty. I don't seem to recall meeting you during the arrival celebration. Perhaps you could remind me, what were *you* wearing?"

Beatrix's snub landed squarely. Shock registered on both men's faces.

Patrain stepped in to fill the stunned silence. "Whinson, Marcot, tell me: how fare the sons of your Houses during the presentation festival?"

"One of my sons has made a solid connection." Whinson thawed, unable to keep the smile out of his voice. "Is it still the Quorum's intention to let the girls choose their Houses?"

"It is. We think it best to let them choose based on their interests. These are unusual times, Whin. Breaking from tradition will keep us from breaking. You must trust that the Quorum has thought this through thoroughly."

Patrain's skillful alliteration seemed to spin Whinson Iffenjin's already alcohol-addled brain. He just nodded and smiled. Marcot, however, was not so easily swayed.

"Well, my House has no frisson events yet. If Project Ferax had a pilot who'd been more proactive, we would all have more opportunities."

Patrain's eyes narrowed a fraction. Her voice, however,

showed none of her ire as she said, "I sympathize with your House's plight, Marcot. On that front, I believe Lassitor has some news for you."

"Indeed, I do. I was going to inform you both tomorrow morning. A pilot from each of your Houses has been included on the mission shortlist."

"Really? And this is the shortlist for the public Quorum vote? Not some shortlist to be on the shortlist?"

"Marcot, you will hear the name of a Bellinger pilot put forth for Quorum consideration. On this, you have my word."

"All right, Lassitor, I'll take you at your word. You'll forgive my incredulousness," he slurred slightly, "as I've been so publicly critical of the first mission's success."

"Let's just say I heard your criticism. Your Houses will be given the opportunity; the rest is up to the full Quorum. I feel it incumbent to mention that the pilot for the second mission has already been approved. Your candidate's names will appear on the list for the third mission."

Marcot began to sputter.

"Well gentlemen, good to see you." Patrain cut short any further discussion of the topic. "I haven't had the chance to dance with my Ventinar yet. Please excuse us. Whinson, I wish your son good fortune during the courting phase."

Patrain sailed away; Beatrix was once again reminded of a great ship parting the waters, she and Cavial following in the Elder's wake. She led their small group to a quiet nook outside. The couples sat facing one another over a low table. Soft, ambient light cast wavering shadows over the scene. "So, Beatrix, what did you make of our circuit around the ballroom?" Patrain asked.

Beatrix considered her response for some moments. "Madam, this was a bit of a dog and pony show." When Patrain appeared to struggle with the reference, Beatrix supplied, "You used people's curiosity about our bond as stick, carrot, and cover tonight."

"Very astute. Does this fact anger you?"

"No, Patrain, it doesn't make me angry. I know you are doing what you think best in order to reach the goals you have set for Devet. I concede that I have neither the information to which you are privy, nor your years of experience. For these reasons, you have my continued cooperation. However, I think occasionally you might lose sight of the fact that we aren't pawns on your personal chessboard."

But for the sounds of distant music and laughter drifting on the night air, there was silence. Neither of the men dared break the standoff between the two women. Patrain uncurled, rising with regal bearing. Beatrix, expecting to be dismissed by Patrain's departure, was surprised when the Matriarch drew her to her feet. Cupping Bea's face between her palms, she spoke earnestly: "You are exactly the daughter for which I would have wished. Devet has missed young, idealist voices to challenge our stodgy ways. Never be afraid to speak your mind." Patrain then stepped back, giving Beatrix's shoulders a final squeeze. "Lassitor, will you dance with me before we go home?"

Lassitor gave them a final bow before he and his Vassen

disappeared into the couples swirling under the stars. Left on their own in the quiet arbor, Beatrix and Cavial made the most of their last hours together. They held hands and watched the lights in the trees twinkle. They shared long lingering kisses, meant to reassure one another. Cavial was the one to finally address the elephant in the room: "Tomorrow you will have a whole new selection group to consider."

The subject made Beatrix uncomfortable. She didn't know how to talk to Cavial, or Lanaq for that matter, about forming connections with other males. In theory, she was on board with the idea; in practice she wasn't sure of the etiquette required to navigate multiple partners.

Cavial could sense her reluctance to broach the subject. "Beatrix, though I sympathize with how foreign this situation is for you, try to remember it is not unfamiliar to us. You needn't feel uncomfortable about having other possible mates."

Beatrix gave him a skeptical look. "Really?"

"Really. A Venvastum is like a puzzle. You must have all the right pieces to make the full picture. Think of the presentation process as your way of selecting possible puzzle pieces. An incomplete or poorly considered Venvastum does no one any favors. Try to find as many possible candidates as you can."

"I should have you talk to Trudy. Just this morning she was worrying she would have too many candidates."

"You tell her from me, no such thing. It shows how truly she is embracing Devetian culture."

"You're right, that ought to make her feel better." They shared a laugh. "You are my second possible mate," Bea's admission was barely audible.

"Am I?" Cavial caught the note of dread in her voice. "Don't worry. You still have seven months of festival. You'll find more."

"Can I ask how you'd feel if you found out you wouldn't be Ventinar? Would you still want to be part of my Venvastum?"

"Absolutely. Being Ventinar is not my most pressing need, being part of a family is."

"How can you be sure? We don't really know one another yet."

"Frisson doesn't lie. You and I are well-suited to one another. Whether or not I fit into your Venvastum is a different story altogether. You'll have plenty of time to figure that out. How about we enjoy this moment, and leave tomorrow to tomorrow?" He distracted her with feathery kisses along her jawline.

# Chapter Seventeen

# Obendun Caszar

"Wow, those trees are huge. Very different from the ones at Stengot. What are they called?"

"Those are bangaset trees. Banga is made from their nuts. If we sit here in the sunroom long enough, Npheba, you might see some keeta, or some bof-bofs."

"Bof-bofs?"

"It's what we've taken to calling the tree-dwelling creatures with the pom-poms down their tails. Madam Lysind gave us the proper name, but it's a mouthful: boffindilgawoe."

"Bof-bof. Yes, this is much easier."

House Odendun, located in the southern hemisphere, was currently enjoying its winter months. Outside, the bangaset trees glinted in the late morning sun, ice crystals still clinging to their spiky foliage. Fog hung low, swirling around the base of the trees.

Npheba, watching for movement in the trees, was rewarded with a glimpse of rust and cream as bof-bofs scampered about in the canopy gathering banga nuts. "Amazing," she breathed. "I could sit and watch them all day."

"You are welcome to visit anytime, Phe. I'm sure Madam Lysind won't mind. In fact, I'd bet we could convince her to mount a picnic in the forest once the weather warms. You could see the bof-bofs up close."

"Thank you, Chesa. I'll look forward to an invitation."

Chesa was the de facto leader of the final five cadre, often speaking for them as a whole. She, Mehika, and Senai were especially close, as they had been retrieved by Lanaq on the same night. A natural disaster had delivered death and destruction to their respective islands: the Philippines, Sri Lanka, and Japan. The final five were rounded out by Marina, an accountant from Brazil, and Noelle, a painter from Quebec. The two groups had formed a friendship aboard the Revival; their bond being reinforced since their arrival on Devet finding commonality in the pressure applied by their respective labels of 'first' and 'last.'

"Will Marina be joining us?" Trudy hoped her question didn't come out as stilted as it sounded to her ears.

"I'm afraid not. Today it will just be the nine of us for luncheon. Marina is spending the day with a frisson mate. She regrets missing your visit, but we all know what *that* feeling is like."

"As long as it isn't because of me."

"Not everything is about you, Trudy." Senai's gentle voice made what could have been a harsh statement a gentle balm.

"Sheesh, narcissist much," was a whisper under her breath, but Phe caught Noelle's aside. "Perhaps you four can convince her to move on. We have tried as a group." Phe threw a frustrated scowl in Trudy's direction, "I have tried. I see the kindness of her heart, and I have told her so, but only Cashondra's words ring in her ears. What more can any of us do, eh?" For emphasis, Phe added one of her shoulder shrugs.

"Phe's right, move on." Trudy's eyes went wide at Chesa's suggestion. "You can't make someone accept an apology. You've expressed deep regret and understanding of the harm you caused." Trudy's rapid nods assured Chesa she indeed had done those things.

"I've done so over and over," Trudy confirmed aloud.

"Cashondra doesn't owe you peace of mind, Trudy." Senai as always spoke softly, everyone quietened to catch what she said. "You will have to find the fortitude to live with your guilt."

"I'm beginning to understand that. The reality is uncomfortable. I worry others hate me because of my past."

"They may," Senai agreed, "and you'll have to live with that too."

Beatrix shared a glance with Trudy, reassuring her. It seemed she was always worried about something: her reputation, her obligations, her wardrobe. As far as Beatrix could tell, much of this self-doubt sprang from her past life on Earth. It was understandable, but rehashing the problem wasn't solving anything and the subject, or at least Trudy's preoccupation with the subject, was becoming tiresome.

Beatrix was thankful Senai put the subject to rest for the day. "Do better. Be better. That's the only way forward."

Trudy nodded her agreement.

"It's like a fairyland here at House Obendun. Did you order the fog today just to impress us?" Phe steered the conversation to a brighter note.

Chesa's hearty laugh wasn't the only one. "The surrounding hills are littered with underground hot springs. The ground stays a good deal warmer than the air here. In fact, House Obendun has its very own grotto. Would you like to see?"

"I don't think we came dressed for such an excursion," Gina hedged.

"No problem. There is a nanite dispenser in the guest facilities. We will have you properly attired in no time."

Sophia excused herself as they rose to head for the grotto, apologizing for her early departure. "I have a meeting scheduled with Member Ukanii to discuss House Hekaria," she said by way of explanation.

"We're sorry you don't have time to see the grotto. Maybe on another visit."

"I'd like that. Chesa, Mehika, Senai, Noelle," she punctuated each name with a short bow, "thank you for your hospitality. Please also thank Madam Lysind on my behalf for House Obendun's hospitality." With one last bow Sophia disappeared into the transport room, and the party continued to the grotto.

"That was odd. Did Sophia mention an appointment

to any of you?" Bea looked over her shoulder as she navigated the spiral stairs.

"Not to me," Phe said, shrugging.

"Nor me," added Trudy.

"She has been acting rather secretive of late," Gina observed. "Whatever it is, I'm sure she'll confide when she's ready. We just need to give her some space."

"If she was going to confide in any of us, it would be you, Gina. If you're not worried, then I guess we needn't be."

Speculation about Sophia ended as they reached the bottom of the staircase. A hewn tunnel led to a natural opening. The sight beyond brought soft gasps from the first five.

The grotto was roughly round, perhaps fifteen or twenty feet across at its widest point. The ceiling height varied, tall enough in some places for impressive stalactites to hang down, while in other areas water erosion left openings to view the sky overhead. Curtains of vines trailed down here and there, veins of precious metals and gems glinting from the walls; interspersed among the glittering minerals were the fossilized remains of exotic and fanciful creatures. The air smelled and tasted lightly of salt and sand, and everything seemed to glow.

Dim lighting reflected off the grotto's pool, creating wavering patterns on the walls and ceiling. The rhythmic lapping and dripping of water created a hypnotic song. The women changed quickly in the provided facilities before wading in, the warm liquid swirling around their ankles. Mist rose from the bubbling pool nestled in the curve of the far wall. As if by mutual consent, the women rejected further conversation until they were all soaking in the warmth of the waters.

"What do you think?" Mehika asked.

"This is incredible!" Bea exclaimed, answering for the first five members. "Truly a feast for the senses. I bet it's relaxing after a long day of introductions and polite talk."

"And it's the perfect spot for a private kiss and cuddle." Mehika's sly smile and wiggling eyebrows had everyone chuckling. "Speaking of introductions, we heard about your record frisson bond with Cavial Quemcara, Bea. What was that like?"

"Unexpected, to say the least. One minute I was upright on the stairs, and the next I wasn't. I'm grateful for our connection, even if it knocked me out. How are things going here at Obendun?"

The four Obendun Vashallen exchanged a look. Noelle, in a rare instance, spoke for the group: "Let's just say things should improve now that Marina has her first frisson bond."

"I was getting quite nervous myself, before Cavial. I understand her frustration."

"Oh, I don't think so. Marina's frustration is nonstop and loud."

"Chesa! Marina is just vocal. She doesn't keep things bottled up." Mehika was obviously the peacemaker of their cadre. "To be fair, I don't think it's merely the lack of frisson events that had her so on edge. Marina finds all the Devetian formality very stifling. By nature, she's a boisterous and gregarious person."

"Mehika isn't wrong. Marina and I talk. Well, she talks, I listen." Senai grinned at her own mental picture. "She feels like her personality is being stifled. She wants to succeed here, but feels like she is failing in all arenas."

"I'm sorry to hear her transition to Devetian culture has been so difficult. Perhaps she will find it easier once she has her own home? A place where she can set the rules."

"Beatrix is right. Soon enough we will each have our own House. Have you visited the Hall of Houses, drawn any impressions?" Gina asked, bringing the discussion of Marina's woes to an abrupt end.

"Oh yes!" Mehika's face came alive. "Lanaq was right. House Rafeen's cuisine specialty is tailor-made for me. I've visited their House kitchens several times already. I'm taking instruction on Devetian techniques and ingredients, or at least I'm trying."

"And her efforts are delicious," the three other final fivers assured.

"I keep getting shooed out of the Obendun kitchens. The synths are very territorial about food preparation. I can only practice my recipes when at House Rafeen. For me, it will be an easy decision. Anybody else know which House they are going to choose?"

Phe inclined her head. "I was leaning toward House Dovic, but I'd like to explore other Houses with an animal specialty before making a final decision."

"Why, Phe? House Dovic is the perfect choice for you. And there is Erran."

"That is exactly the problem, Bea. I don't wish my heart to lead where my head hasn't looked."

"Gracious, Phe, it's been obvious since we met that you're drawn to anything feathered or furred. That has nothing to do with Erran. His House, your connection, that's just a bonus!"

Npheba offered a shrug, one that conveyed she was considering this new perspective. "You aren't wrong." She was hesitant. "One doesn't want to make a mistake in these choices. "What about you, Gina? Any thoughts?" Phe skillfully turned the focus of the conversation away from her own struggle, but Bea's words hadn't fallen on deaf ears.

"I have not picked a specific House yet. I care less for the House specialty and more for its physical location, its geography. I am considering details like the length of the growing season and seasonal weather fluctuations, as well as the available raw resources within its borders."

"Devetians don't observe borders when it comes to resources, you know that. They share everything equally."

"Sure Chesa, Devetians live in harmony now, but things change. I would have my House prepared for any eventuality. I intend to choose a House for its ability to be independent."

"Gina is the skeptic among us, forgive her." Phe stood, exiting the warm pool to wrap a cloth about her lithe body. Her action prompted the others to leave the water as well.

"I only have one requirement for the House I choose," Chesa said, squeezing water from the ends of her hair. "It must be a dormant House." Seeing their looks of inquiry, she expanded, "It seems likely to me that stepping into a role of authority in an established House won't be without challenges, especially considering our youth in comparison to the Devetians. Just a kettle of fish I don't really want to stir. An extinct House feels like a less complicated option." An awkward silence followed. Subconsciously, they all knew Chesa was correct.

# Chapter Eighteen

# Quorum Building – Hekaria City

Patrain called the Quorum to order, taking a few extra moments to calm the fury simmering under the surface before rising to address the Mavinarium.

"Mavinars, hear me and mark my words well. It is your obligation to sit amongst this body and disseminate our words to the members of your Houses. We meet today to resolve no less than three disciplinary hearings. Three! This body hasn't needed to call three such hearings in the last millennia, let alone in one day. I urge you to make the members of your households understand that lawlessness will not be tolerated — especially not now that Project Ferax has borne fruit." Patrain paused, her steely gaze sweeping the room. "Bring in the first infractant."

The heavy stone doors opposite the dais of the thirteen

swung open. A lone man entered, walking to the center of the pit. A stool materialized. He sat.

"You are Zakurst Curzon?"

"I am."

"You are accused of unauthorized resource harvesting and causing avoidable environmental damage. How do you respond to these charges?"

"Madam Elder Patrain, I believe the infractions listed are only partially true."

"I'm all ears, Zakurst. Enlighten me."

"I did harvest the stone to begin a caszartera on Curzon lands, which was approved by this body. There was a shipping delay from the offworld quarry, so I began the foundations with stone quarried from Curzon lands. I intend to repair the environmental damage with the offworld shipment when it arrives."

"I see here in the records an approval for the proposed building. What I don't see," Patrain continued, looking up from her screen, "is an approval for your retroactive cleanup plan. Do you have a copy of that document?"

"I did not apply for approval, Madam Elder."

"Then would you be so kind as to point out the clause in the regulation authorizing the constructor to improvise without prior approval?"

The question was rhetorical; Zakurst didn't need to answer. He hung his head, his vision focused between his toes.

"This body thanks you for your honesty, Zakurst Curzon. May the members fit the punishment to the crime."

Patrain sat, her part in the proceedings finished until the other members came to a decision.

While the twelve voting members discussed an appropriate penalty for the infraction, Patrain focused on today's attendance. Hemion Nilaster and Jenax Gallen filled their respective seats; they had stopped by her office this morning, without making the appointment she'd suggested. "Gentlemen," she'd said to them, "I simply do not have the time to meet with you today."

"You said you would, Patrain," Hemion had snapped. "You got our hopes up, made us think you were willing to listen to reason."

"I said I was willing to meet with you, IF you make an appointment. I do not have time in my schedule today. I will have Anile contact you with an appropriate time. Now, please, see yourselves out."

"Patrain, if you don't..."

"Not now, Hemion!" Patrain's voice had turned sharp. She'd buried her frustration with a sigh before saying, "I truly do not have the time right now. I will have Anile contact you."

The pair had bowed and taken their leave, but not happily.

Hemion's thunderous expression from earlier was still intact. Patrain inclined her head in his direction ever so slightly, and he returned the gesture, his expression relaxing. *That will have to suffice for mending bridges.* She had no further time to worry about Hemion's mood, as the Quorum had reached a verdict in the House Curzon matter. Patrain rose to deliver said verdict.

"Zakurst Curzon, for infractions committed against the Devetian ecosystem this body revokes building permission for the additional caszar. House Curzon will see to the environmental repair of its lands, and is further ordered to donate the incoming load of stone for public use. As regards your personal responsibility in this matter, the Quorum sentences you to three months of confinement. However, the members feel your honesty should weigh in your favor; therefore, your sentence is reduced to one month's confinement to quarters. Please turn over your strap as you exit the pit."

Zakurst rose heavily from the stool, which melted away into the floor. "I thank the members for their fair and wise decision." He gave a deep bow, then strode to the exit with head high and shoulders square. A heavy sigh of relief escaped his lips as the double stone doors closed behind him, Patrain just catching sight of him removing his strap and handing it to Anile. Beyond, two younger men stood ready to enter the pit. They looked nervous. They should be. Madam Elder Patrain was an intimidating leader.

After a few silent moments the stone doors swung open once more, Anile motioning the pair of infractants forward. "Gentlemen," he encouraged them, in a voice that was gentle but stern.

Patrain continued to examine the assemblage for today's proceedings, finding it most gratifying to see more than a dozen Vashallen in attendance. They sat in the gallery, the highest tier — among their number she spotted Gina, Sophia, and Trudy. The first two weren't a surprise, but she hadn't thought Trudy serious enough to be interested in today's events. Perhaps she would need to re-evaluate her opinion.

The two males started forward, coming to a halt in the center of the pit. Patrain did not initiate a seat for either of them, making them stand. "Neaal Perdorax and Braqen Tamani," she announced, the fury she'd felt since hearing about the altercation between these two men evident in her biting tone. For their part, Neaal and Braqen cringed.

Patrain let a brief silence settle before continuing. "You stand here before this body because of a physical altercation." Murmurs rose from the assembly. "Not since the ancient annals of our history have Devetians resorted to physical harm to settle our differences. We stand on the precipice of a new beginning for Devet. The Vashallen have arrived to give our people hope, and you fools would usher in a new era of violence in their name. I wish to know the reason for your destructive actions."

Braqen glanced sideways at Neaal, who continued to keep his head high, though his eyes were fixed on the floor. Neither committed to speaking.

"I asked a question. Someone had best answer me."

"I make no excuses, Madam Elder. I know the law. I should not have laid my hands on Braqen, no matter the provocation. I apologize to Braqen and House Tamani for my behavior. I willingly submit myself to the Quorum's censure."

The statement didn't answer her question. Patrain's mouth thinned in frustration. "Braqen?"

"I also apologize, Madam Elder. I acknowledge my behavior violated Devetian law."

"One of you will tell me the cause of the violence. I don't wish to subject the witnesses to recounting the incident, but I will if you force my hand."

"You! You're the cause. You and this Balance-forsaken Quorum." Braqen stopped abruptly, seeing a scowl form on Patrain's face. He looked like he would prefer to chew off his own tongue rather than continue.

"Exactly how is the Quorum responsible for your behavior?"

"Fifty-two Vashallen. Fifty-two measly Vashallen, who are as frigid as the Frozen Climbs of the Zizzix. They don't seem to understand their place in the scheme of things."

Patrain bit back the harsh rejoinder she wished to let fly. Instead she asked in frosty measure, "In your considered opinion, what is the Vashallen's place in the scheme of things?"

Braqen had the good sense to look ashamed and keep his mouth shut. "So, what occurred had something to do with the Vashallen?" Patrain turned her penetrating gaze on Neaal, expecting him to answer.

"Madam Elder, I will recount what occurred from my perspective — because you request it, not because I court the Quorum's mercy." Neaal glanced briefly at Braqen before presenting his side of the story. "I was engaged in discussion with several of the Vashallen following formal introductions at House Fitherington on the first day of Fourth month. Braqen approached, I thought to join our conversation. After several minutes hovering on the edge of the group, he placed his hand around the wrist of the Vashallen Emara, trying to draw her away. I heard her ask him to let her go. He did not, saying, 'You owe me some time now.' Again I make no excuses for my behavior. I grabbed Braqen's wrist and squeezed until he released Emara. This led to a further fracas between he and I."

"Which resulted in one black eye, one broken nose, two busted lips, and a dozen bruised ribs?"

"Unfortunately, Madam Elder."

"I'm glad to see you show remorse, Neaal. I'm sure the Members have taken note." Patrain spent another heartbeat stabbing Neaal with her gaze. "Braqen," her sharp voice startled the named infractant, "your actions do not reflect well on House Tamani. Especially as they are one of the host Houses. I can only imagine what your mother had to say on this subject. How do you answer these allegations?"

"He's not telling you the full truth. Neaal monopolized the females' company for nearly an hour. He should learn to be fair, to share. He's not the only male looking for a mate." Again the crowd gasped.

"Are you alleging that Neaal in some way restrained the Vashallen? Were the females unable to exercise freedom of movement, of personal choice?"

Braqen mumbled a reply.

"Pardon me, I couldn't hear your answer. Speak up, Braqen."

"I said no. The Vashallen were not forced to stay at Neaal's side."

"I think we've heard enough," Patrain said, then sought confirmation from her fellow members. "I wish to clarify one point before I turn deliberations over to the voting members, as the answer may affect your sentence. Neither of you has formed a frisson bond, correct?"

"No, Madam Elder, I have not." Neaal continued to be respectful.

"Do you think I'd have been so desperate for time with the Vashallen if I had?"

Patrain's scowl deepened. In moments like these the true deterioration of Devetian society was most visible, cracks forming in the fabric of their way of life. Patrain felt the deterioration as a personal blow, a proof of her failures. "Thank you both for your testimony. May the members fit the punishment to the crime." Patrain sat.

Murmurs flew around the chamber, shocked whispers offered behind fluttering hands. The rustling echo of gossip moved about the room like the sound of birds on the wing. Patrain tried to follow its progress. She glanced upward to the gallery. Trudy and Sophia were speaking in animated whispers, but Gina's stare met her own. She inclined her head, acknowledging the Vashallen's presence. Her strap chirped, drawing her attention. The voting members had reached their verdict. She stood, and silence fell over the chamber.

"Neaal Perdorax, Braqen Tamani, for violating the first tenet of Devetian law you are sentenced as follows. Your participation in the presentation festival is hereby revoked. You will board the first harvest ship leaving Devet to serve one year's labor, repairing drones on a resource planet.

"Neaal, your instincts in this situation were commendable, but your execution was not. Surely there were other avenues to defuse the situation without laying your hands on Braqen's person. And Braqen, you need to examine your attitude. Women are not objects to be fought over. I expected better of you both."

The stomp of hundreds of feet reverberated through the chamber, seconding Patrain's sentiments.

"Upon the completion of your sentence, you may apply for reinstatement to any subsequent presentation festivals. This body encourages you to surrender yourselves to House Ukanii for further instruction on Universal Balance before submitting such an application."

Patrain dismissed the men. They departed through the double doors to be greeted by the ever-efficient Anile. The day's unpleasant business completed, the Quorum members vacated the dais. As the last member descended to the corridors below, the audience in the chamber exploded into animated discussion.

Patrain felt wrung out and beaten down. *At least it was two steps forward and only one step back, instead of the other way around,* she thought wryly. With a heavy heart and leaden feet she trudged the halls back to her office, where she made herself a cup of banga and leaned back in her chair, letting the blissful sensation induced by the drink improve her outlook.

A light rap sounded at her door. She was surprised to find Gina on the other side. "Come in, Regina. What can I do for you today?"

"I don't wish to disturb you if you are busy, Madam Patrain. I can make an appointment if you prefer."

"I have a few minutes to spare. Can I get you a cup of something?"

Gina accepted a cup of banga, and the two women settled into comfortable seating. "So, what brings you to see me, Gina?"

"You saw me at the proceedings today." Patrain merely nodded, sipping from her cup. "I'd like to ask a couple of questions about today, if I may?"

"Of course."

"Why did no one defend Neaal and Braqen today, or Zakurst Curzon for that matter? Are they not entitled to a defense under Devetian law?"

"The actions were their own. Who better to defend them than themselves?"

"Does no one advise them of their rights under the law?"

"Ah, now that is another matter altogether. House Dofadis were the Keepers of the Devetian Law Books. Historically, in matters such as today's, House Dofadis would provide a representative to clarify any points of law for either the infractant or the Quorum. When the House went extinct, the books were digitized. Every Devetian has access to our law books."

"But do they understand them? Can they apply them to their situation?"

"Do you believe the imposed penalties to be unfair?"

"The punishments are only relevant if they were arrived at lawfully. If there is a law that stipulates a representative of the Law Books must be present at disciplinary hearings, then those persons today did not receive a fair hearing."

Patrain was beginning to enjoy sparring with this woman. "The law stipulating a House Dofadis defender must be present at disciplinary hearings was suspended by a former administration, until such time as House Dofadis is revitalized. Perhaps one of the Vashallen will take up the responsibility."

"Could another extinct House take up the responsibility? For instance, could House Vercaidus become the Keepers of the Law Books?"

"You're interested." It was a statement of fact, not a question. "Why not just choose Dofadis?"

"I prefer the Vercaidus lands."

"The Vercaidus islands are beautiful and bountiful," Patrain conceded. She considered for several long moments before finally adding, "Hypothetically, if no other Vashallen were to choose House Dofadis, the Quorum might be persuaded to transfer the mantle to another House."

Gina nodded. "I understand." She placed her now-empty cup on the table, rising from the soft seat. "Thank you for your time, Madam Elder."

"One moment if you please, Vashallen Regina. I'm curious, do you believe the punishments today were unfair?"

"Compared to the experiences of my lifetime, no."

"But?"

"But rules are written for a reason. When the Quorum doesn't follow its own rules it erodes the pedestal upon which it places the moral high ground."

"Possibly, but without change, without flexibility of thought, isn't the risk of stagnation worse?"

Regina smiled for the first time since entering the Matriarch's office. She enjoyed the verbal repartee provided by Patrain's quick mind. "Also a valid point, Madam Elder. I'll give it some thought."

# Chapter Nineteen

# Hekaria City
# — Euthoprium

Fourth month ended without Beatrix or Sophia finding any further matches. At month's end, they were the only two remaining Vashallen in first cadre with a single Ventir candidate, at least officially. Beatrix's connection to Lanaq was still a closely guarded secret.

Beatrix was uncomfortable with the notoriety and curious stares she received whenever she left the Stengot estate. The eyes of Devet seemed constantly upon her. Sophia didn't seem phased by the concern over her lack of candidates. "After all," she'd remarked, "what are they going to do if I don't find more? Ask me to leave?"

Fifth month brought change. Sophia, much to her surprise, found a second candidate in Phillion Nilaster. Trudy found her fourth match, and Gina her third. However, the most startling occurrence involved Beatrix. She found frisson with two men, Geven Lister and Kalix Brethwen;

both events measured in the six plus range. These connections were more manageable than her connection to either Cavial or Lanaq.

Beatrix was disconcerted at first by the idea of spending a month in the company of two possible mates, but the actuality was far less stressful than she imagined. The ease with which Geven and Kalix interacted created a relaxed, uncomplicated atmosphere in which Beatrix could unwind. There was no tension between the men. In fact, they seemed to work together seamlessly.

She spent time alone with each, but as a threesome they spent many hours curled up together watching Earth programs on her screen. They spent still more hours dissecting and discussing the finer details of the social changes reflected in the programs. Beatrix found the discussions helped her bridge the gap between her life experience and her current situation. Her experiences during Fifth month removed some of her doubts about her ability to form her own Venvastum.

Midway through Fifth month the entire planet was invited to attend the premiere of a new symphony, its score composed to honor and celebrate the arrival of the Vashallen. That night the first five, along with their Stengot hosts, made the quick transport journey into Hekaria City. Arriving at the Stengot Residence, they walked the short distance to the Euthoprium.

The building itself was a marvel, vaguely spherical with odd globular protrusions, its unconventional shape balanced by open concave sections. Devetian architectural design usually made use of the natural landscape where possible, yet the Euthoprium stood separate from its surroundings, the outdoor balconies sprouting a plethora of curved staircases. They wove over and around each other, undulating toward the ground.

"Wow!" breathed Trudy. "It's unbelievable. I haven't seen anything else like it on Devet."

"The Euthoprium's layout is special, enhancing acoustic resonance to unparalleled levels. The design is adapted from the Bellgrosian opera houses. The Bellgrosians are a species known for their vocal prowess," Lorral added for good measure. "You're in for a treat tonight. A Darval Adderigus symphony is a delight for the senses."

"I don't mean to hurry you, my sweet, but we should find our seats," her Ventir Rendre pointed out, nodding toward the thickening crowd of arrivals.

"Lead the way, Ren." Lorral gripped Rendre's offered arm, and the Vashallen followed suit, taking the offered arms of Lorral's other Ventir. Kaigor escorted Gina and Phe, while Trudy and Sophia went with Nikaal. Beatrix and Fieran brought up the rear.

The Stengot Matriarch swiped her strap as she crested the stairs onto the balcony, and ten cocoon-like pods floated down to bob gently against the balcony's inside edge. Rendre handed Lorral into one of the cocoons, taking the next in line for himself. The two pods arose slowly to their place in the arena. Kairgor and Nikaal next helped their charges into the cocoon chairs, and six more pods floated upward. Fieren gave Beatrix an encouraging smile and settled her into one of two remaining pods. Surprisingly it felt stable under her weight. She had expected it to wobble. She smiled back at Fieren, and he released her hand to take his own conveyance.

The seat supported Beatrix from head to toe. She felt weightless. Her cocoon floated upward, settling next to Sophia's. They exchanged glances. *Exciting*, they said with their eyes.

Beatrix took in the spectacle before her. The interior of the Euthoprium was as unusual as the exterior. Seated groups hovered in the globular protrusions seen from the outside in such a way that everyone had a view of the stage and the stars at once.

Beatrix waved to Chesa and Mehika. Their host House was seated on the same level, almost directly opposite. She found Cavial's gaze upon her, his smile warm. Beatrix's eyes then met those of the Quemcara Matriarch, her breath catching in her throat. Moina Quemcara bowed slowly from the shoulders, and Bea remembered to inhale and return the gesture, respectfully. She continued to glance around, acknowledging Geven and Kalix as well as other Vashallen of her acquaintance.

A voice filled the chamber, startling her. "Ladies and gentlemen, the performance will begin in five minutes." A thousand little whirs accompanied the end of the announce-ment, and a chamber on the cocoon opened, ejecting a stoppered tube of glittering liquid.

The native Devetians eagerly unstoppered their tubes and downed the liquid. Beatrix glanced at Lorral, who encouraged her with a smile as she tossed back her own vial. Beatrix followed her example, downing the sweet liquid in one gulp.

She didn't immediately feel any different, and went back to people watching. She glanced over her shoulder noting the Devetian leader flanked by her Ventir. Beatrix's gaze flitted further back and locked onto Lanaq's. They stared at one another for what felt like an eternity, but could only have been moments. Finally, Beatrix drug her gaze back to the stage, her breathing grown ragged. Had anybody seen them? Beatrix's thoughts were frantic. If anyone noted their interaction, their connection would be obvious.

She felt Lanaq's heavy gaze on the back of her neck, or at least she thought she did, but she didn't dare turn around again. She couldn't risk the gossip, not when they'd staved off disaster thus far. Beatrix worked to calm her breathing.

It helped that movement on the stage diverted her attention. Three openings appeared in the stage floor, and from them three musicians ascended. Their instruments were unlike anything Beatrix had ever seen, though one resembled the instrument she had seen played at the Hall of Houses. She couldn't begin to imagine what they would sound like played together.

A fourth opening appeared, and Darval Adderigus ascended. He bowed to a cheering audience, then addressed his musicians. The chamber fell silent as the lights went down. Darval inhaled deeply, breathing out the first deep mellow note of music. It was orange, tinged with gold; twining around the conductor's shoulders, it wove its way toward the green and blue notes now emerging from the odd musical instruments. The colorful notes drifted upward and outward, filling the arena and the night.

Beatrix's cocoon adjusted continuously, moving with the flow of the sights and sounds. She felt at one with the music, and it was several minutes before she even thought to wonder how sound could have color. How could she see its movement, and should she care? *"The glittery stuff. Must be."* She gave up worrying about the cause and lost herself to the music, floating blissfully with the sights and sounds.

Near the end of the first movement Beatrix came back to herself, the effects of the liquid partially wearing off. She felt the need for the restroom. The cocoon-like pod must have sensed her urgency, as it immediately floated downward, depositing her on a landing. She stepped off onto the platform, and a guide arrow lit up on her strap. She followed it and found what she needed.

Having taken care of nature, Beatrix took a moment for herself. The bathroom was empty of curious eyes. She could let down her guard. Not turning to look at Lanaq was more difficult than it sounded, even with the otherworldly display of luminous music to distract her. If she forgot to tell herself not to look, she would do so without thinking. She rolled her shoulders to relax the tension one last time and turned to leave, only to startle backward a single step.

Triff stood just inside the door, blocking her exit. Her expression was no friendlier tonight than on any other occasion Beatrix had the misfortune to encounter her.

Bea raised her chin. She wouldn't let this synth provoke

her ire. "Excuse me," she said, stepping forward. Triff moved to block her path.

"I saw. The way you two looked at each other, the rumors must be true."

Beatrix tried to step around Triff. "Please, move. I wish to leave."

In response, Triff grabbed Bea's wrist, squeezing to the point where Bea gasped in pain. "Yes, you should leave. In fact, you should never have come."

Bea tried to pull her wrist free. The synth was too strong. She tried to pry away the fingers gripping her arm, to no avail. Triff wore a smug, gloating look.

Her wrist was on the point of snapping when the door behind Triff began to slide open. The synth dropped her wrist, pushing Bea backward in the process. "Keep your mouth shut, or I'll tell everyone." She spun wildly, shoving Sophia to the ground as she stepped through the open portal.

"For pity's sake, what's going on here?" Sophia demanded from the ground. She turned over, pushing back the layers of skirt covering her face.

Beatrix, favoring her good wrist over her quickly swelling one, leaned down to help Sophia to her feet, wrapping her good arm around her sister's waist. Bea barely had time to be surprised by the feel of ribs poking through skin before Sophia jumped upright. "I'm fine. No injuries here," she assured, adjusting the layers of her voluminous dress. "It's you who needs medical attention. That wrist looks nasty. What happened?"

"Nothing. I slipped."

"Beatrix?" Sophia's tone held as much warning as question.

"Sophia?" Beatrix reciprocated. The two stared at one another, neither willing to budge. "I'd appreciate your discretion," Bea relented. Practical as ever, she was conscious of the time. They would be missed.

"Likewise," Sophia said, finally admitting she too was concealing something beneath her many bulky layers.

"Shall we return to the performance?"

The two Vashallen exited the restroom in time to see a wave of women headed their way. The performance had reached intermission. They returned to the balcony in time to find the rest of the Stengot party disembarking from their cocoons. After catching sight of them, Lorral called out, "Beatrix, Sophia, this way. We are headed outside for refreshments."

Bea tried to pull her sleeve down to cover her bruised wrist. Seeing this, Sophia draped her shawl over Beatrix's shoulders. Beatrix accepted the length of material with a grateful smile, allowing the fabric to slip lower, covering her forearms and wrists. Sophia shot her a conspiratorial wink before they joined the Stengots, slipping outside into the late summer evening.

They mingled on the outdoor terrace, munching on finger foods and sipping at tafron. Beatrix kept her gaze fixed on the ground. She didn't want to risk coming eye-to-eye with Lanaq again. If the intensity of their gaze didn't give them away, the color of her cheeks most certainly would.

A deep gong sounded, signaling the start of the second movement. The Stengots herded their charges to the floating cocoons, Beatrix feeling a huge surge of relief. No one had noticed her wrist, let alone asked about it, and she had managed to avoid any contact with Lanaq.

It felt like more eyes than ever followed the first five during the second half of the performance. Beatrix wasn't willing to risk the glittery liquid provided for the second half, as she might accidentally look up and over her shoulder. She pocketed the vial instead. The music didn't have color anymore, but the sound of the instruments was rousing. She tried to relax and let go of the drama of the evening, but the throb of her wrist kept bringing it back.

By the time Beatrix's door closed behind her later that evening, she felt ready to faint. The pain in her wrist was severe.

"Madam? Are you unwell?"

"I think I need your help, Indik." She allowed the shawl to fall away from her swollen and bruised wrist. "Also your discretion, please."

Indik rushed to her side. "How did this happen?" he inquired as he examined her wrist, turning it over between gentle fingers. "Who did this?" He looked Beatrix square in the eye.

"Triff, but you can't tell anyone," she pleaded.

Indik, his expression grave, tapped out orders, a synth medic arriving shortly thereafter. The android treated Beatrix's wrist, mending the cracked bone and healing the damaged flesh. After they left Indik served her something for the pain, then settled her into bed.

"Now, tell me why Triff did this, and why I shouldn't tell anyone?"

"You can't. She knows the rumors about Lanaq and me are true. We saw one another tonight, and she caught our reactions. She threatened to tell everyone if I said anything about our altercation."

"Alright, leave this with me. I will neutralize Triff."

"Neutralize? Oh Indik, please don't do anything illegal on my behalf."

Indik covered his laugh by clearing his throat. "I promise, Beatrix, nothing illegal."

# Chapter Twenty

# Vikhtar Estate

Hemion Nilaster turned his nose up at the odor wafting back toward his carriage. He detested this antiquated form of travel, but it was the only method he could devise to ensure his trip remained undetected. He was purported to be aboard his sea cruiser, enjoying a much-needed vacation; instead he was seated behind the smelly end of a bozidon, not a situation at all to his liking.

"Hemion, fussing and fuming won't make this journey any faster or fairer." Triff scolded him as no one else would dare. He was always surprised when it seemed she could read his mind, having to remind himself that her synth nature made her more observant.

"The necessity for such distasteful pursuits offends my sensibilities, my love. Forgive my short temper. I'm only organic, after all." Their shared joke made them smile at one another. "How long till we arrive at this Creator-forsaken backwater shack?" he then asked, referring to the abandoned caszartera of the extinct House Vikhtar.

"Not long now, Hemion," the synth woman said, then hesitated, calculating the precise tone of voice that would sway her listener. "When she arrives, you must seek to hide your distaste. It will not help our cause. If she is willing to assist us, then we must use her to our advantage."

"I don't trust her."

"Do you trust me?"

"Of course I do."

"Then you must trust that my information is valid. Synths can't lie to one another. If she says she wants to work with us, then we must take that chance, for all synths."

"I still think we may be walking into a trap." Hemion's fractious mood stemmed from his inability to control the situation. The unknown set his nerves on edge. As such, he hadn't had a decent day's peace since those Creator-forsaken Vashallen had arrived on Devet. His discomfort could be laid directly at Patrain's door. The mere thought of that woman, who had been a thorn in his side since their youth, made him scowl deeper. His mood did not improve.

The wagon, drawn by two bozidon, crested a rise, the abandoned caszar coming into view. Hemion had to admit it was the perfect place to hold a clandestine meeting. The low-slung building of the caszartera's main domicile was perfectly camouflaged by a grove of massive bangaset trees.

Triff directed their cart to the stable. There, she began to untack the bozi and give them a good rubdown. Hemion inspected the House, determining they were the first to arrive.

"There are food supplies in the back of the wagon. Why don't you unpack those while I finish with the animals?"

Surprised by Triff's directive, Hemion stared at her for several moments. He blinked rapidly, deciding whether or not he wanted to challenge her authority to issue orders. He decided not. Like a sulky child, he retrieved the foodstuffs from the cart and carried them indoors.

While he was unpacking the food, Hemion heard the unmistakable sound of the House transporter activating. He took the precaution of hiding behind the doorframe, cursing under his breath. When a familiar synth emerged from the transporter room, Hemion stepped into sight with a loud huff. "How come you get to arrive that way, and I've got to ride in a smelly cart that shookles and shakes my bones?" he demanded.

"This property was scheduled for routine inspection. As the assignment fell to me, it was a convenient choice. One less alibi to foment. Your mode of arrival is not my responsibility."

Unlike Triff, this synth didn't cater to Hemion's ego, nor to his foul temper. Hemion's lip curled in distaste. "When will your mistress arrive?"

"Madam will arrive once I inform her that everyone else is here."

"So we are supposed to just sit around and wait on her?"

"Yes."

"I'm not one of her lackeys. I'm not at her beck and call."

"If you want this meeting, you are."

"What are you complaining about now, Hemion?" Jenax Gallen stepped into the cool confines of the building. "Your voice carries outside, you know. This is supposed to be a secret meeting. How about we keep the discussion to a dull roar, huh?"

"How did you arrive?"

"Why, by hot air balloon! I was blown off course by a freak wind, don't ya know."

"You have an air balloon?" Hemion asked, striding to the front door. The balloon's basket lay on its side on the front lawn, its bladder collapsed like a puddle around it.

Jenax followed Hemion's incredulous gaze. "I have one, yes. Found it in one of the storage rooms. Probably won't fly, but I thought it would make a great prop. I've let it be known that I'm trying to fix it up as a hobby."

"So how did you really arrive?"

"Hover jet, of course." Jenax pointed to the low-slung craft parked alongside the stable.

"Seems like you went to a great deal of unnecessary trouble for an alibi."

"What did you come up with?"

"I'm having a vacation aboard my sea cruiser. It dropped me off on the coastline, and Triff drove us here in a wagon."

Jenax hid the smirk that threatened to play on his lips. Hemion would not appreciate being the source of his amusement, but the thought of Hemion sitting behind a farting bozidon was too funny. "My cover story too much trouble? Considering your own mode of transportation, I think not."

"Hey!" Hemion shouted over his shoulder, "We're all here. Tell her."

"Hem, you could try being a bit more civil. You do our cause no favors with your negative attitude."

"He's right, my love," Triff said, arriving in the shady entry hall. "You must endeavor to show the Matriarch some courtesy. She is our best hope of achieving our goals without bloodshed."

"I'm okay with a little bloodshed."

"Be that as it may, we are not."

Several hours later, the small group was still awaiting the arrival of the Matriarch. They'd eaten the picnic Triff had packed. Hemion was pacing furiously back and forth, muttering to himself under his breath. Jenax and Triff exchanged sympathetic looks. They both hoped they could keep Hemion from blowing up this meeting. They might not get another chance like this one.

The whooshing sound of the FST activating in the transporter room froze everyone in place. All heads swiveled in the direction of the door. A figure emerged wearing everyday utilitarian fare, the hood of her robe drawn deep around her face. She pushed it back far enough for everyone to see her features. "Well, I'm here," she said expectantly, looking straight at Triff.

Triff and Hemion tried to speak at the same time, Hemion's angry shout overpowering Triff's even tones. "You kept us waiting long enough."

"Hemion, this isn't your meeting, and I don't have time for your temper tantrum. My time is limited, I will be missed. So, keep your mouth shut unless you have something of substance to add." The Matriarch's angry words cut short Hemion's tirade. His mouth snapped shut, and he collapsed into a chair in indignant silence. "Please, tell me why you requested this meeting, Triff?"

"Madam, please know we mean no disrespect. Few know that we synths have achieved self-awareness. As one of those few, you are in a position to help us." Triff strove for a logical, rational presentation, judging it the best choice for an optimal outcome. "It is our belief that we are entitled to a society of our own. We seek self-governance." The Matriarch raised one eyebrow in question, but refrained from speaking just yet. "We think of organic Devetians as our parents. The natural order dictates that parents die while children live on. We were content to wait, to let your race naturally go extinct. We have the time. However, the arrival of the Vashallen has changed the situation."

"Let us speak of the Vashallen for a moment," the Matriarch interrupted. "One Vashallen in particular, for whom you seem to have developed an antipathy. If you wish me to negotiate in good faith you will need to forgo personal disagreements, especially those crossing the line into physical harm. Do I make myself clear?"

Triff stood perfectly still, as androids were prone to do, but the tension in her stance was clear. Jenax and Hemion glanced back and forth between the pair, while the other synth remained aloof, seeming to look beyond the events taking place under his very nose.

"Your meaning is clear," Triff finally answered.

"Good. Now that we've settled that matter, what is it you want from me?"

"I was under the impression you were sympathetic to our plight." Triff gave a puzzled glance at her fellow synth.

"I am. What is it you would like me to do to help?"

"The synths wish to resolve the matter in an equitable fashion for all parties. We are open to solutions."

"Ideally, you want a synth society, am I correct? You don't wish to cohabitate with organics." Hemion's head snapped up.

"We want a synth-centric society, self-determination. We wouldn't exclude certain select organics."

"I will need a short while to formulate ideas. Is your leadership willing to bide their time a little longer? Ah, you do *have* leadership?"

"You're looking at our leadership, Madam." She indicated herself and the other synth. "You've taken a risk by being here today. We thought it only fair to take the same risk ourselves."

The Matriarch nodded. "Your faith in me is noted. Alright, I'll be in touch when I have a plan. We won't meet again in this manner."

Jenax, who had remained in the background during the entire exchange, pushed off the wall he was leaning on. "So that's it? No argument. You'll make a plan and help us get what we want?"

"Yes, Jenax. As simple as that. Triff isn't wrong when she calls us parents. We gave birth to their race, we owe them a home. I'll do what I can to help them. I just need some time to come up with a viable solution." The woman pulled her hood further over her face as she turned toward the transporter room. "I'll need time. Be patient. Trust me."

"You're going to use the transporter again?" The frustration in Hemion's words sounded whiny. "How can you hope to keep your trip here secret? Someone is bound to discover the transmission record." Hemion obviously resented the Matriarch's clean mode of escape.

"I have friends in high places, Hemion. Didn't you know?" She chortled at her joke as she rounded the corner into the transport room, disappearing from sight. In a few moments the familiar sound of the FST could be heard engaging.

"I must leave also, before I am missed. This property has been given a thorough inspection, or at least my report will reflect such." The male synth nodded in Triff's direction. He took his leave, and the transporter activated again.

"'Ask and ye shall receive.' Do you really think it can be that simple?" Hemion's tone reflected his incredulity.

"Part of me was convinced right up till the end that she would simply make us disappear." As was his wont, Jenax made light of the serious situation. "I'm still not sure that won't happen, eventually."

"Gentlemen! We have all known the Matriarch for a very long time. When have you ever known her to be a liar?" The two male conspirators had the sense to look contrite. "I've always found her to be truthful. You might not get the whole story, but she doesn't lie. If she says she will help, she will."

"What if we don't like her solution?" Hemion thrust his jaw forward, a sure sign to Triff he was digging his heels in on this point.

"Then we negotiate until we do like the solution."

"And if she won't negotiate?"

"Hemion, my love, sometimes you can be a stubborn bozidon arse. She wouldn't have come here tonight, risked exposure, if she didn't think she could convince the Quorum to negotiate. Even if nothing comes of this afternoon's work, we are no further behind."

"And no further forward, either."

Jenax gave a heavy sigh. He and Triff shared a mutual weariness of Hemion's stubborn attitude. "Let's get out of here. No sense in hanging around to get caught."

"How are you getting home, Jenax?"

"My vehicle." He pointed to the waiting hover jet.

"What!" Hemion's face went red; you could almost see steam coming out of his ears.

"Yes. Though my balloon was going down, I was able to engage the autopilot to retrieve me. That's the story I'll tell."

Hemion stormed off to the stable. Triff couldn't help a single gust of laughter, though she kept it behind closed lips.

"He really hates those bozidons," she said to cover her humor.

"He really hates not getting his way, you mean."

Jenax raised a hand in farewell as he hopped into his waiting hover jet. In seconds, the man was gone.

The first two arrivals were also the last two to leave. Their wagon departed minutes later, one occupant grumbling.

# Chapter Twenty-One

# Stengot Caszar

During Sixth month Beatrix didn't find frisson with anyone. It was Phe's turn for the confusion of finding two possible mates in a single month. Lorral, as hostess, was over the moon to have double frisson events back to back , the Vashallen weren't so certain of the 'providential' nature of the occurrance. Trudy was just glad everyone was making a fuss of Phe rather than focusing on her rapidly expanding number of Ventir candidates. With five matches already and four presentation festivals remaining, she was starting to panic ever so slightly.

When Seventh month dawned, Beatrix decided if she didn't see Lanaq during this presentation, she was going to approach Lorral. She had waited patiently, played by Patrain's rules; she was tired of the constant tension and fear of running into Lanaq in a public place, exposing their secret.

"Beatrix, are you here?"

Beatrix emerged from her closet, choices for her intro-duction day attire in hand. She glanced back and forth between the garments, as if weighing their merits. "Good morning, Gina," she said, the surprise of seeing Gina in her room this early in the day reflected in her tone. Gina was a notoriously late riser. The group often didn't see her till after lunch.

"Morning. I just wanted to pass on something that Drena let slip." Drena was Gina's attendant. She looked out for Gina, just as Indik did for Beatrix; Bea found it hard to believe the synth would let anything slip. Beatrix paused, looking expectantly at Gina.

"Lanaq. He's here. He is part of this month's group."

A thrill ran up Beatrix's spine, a wide smile showing off her pearly white teeth for a split second. "That's nice," she said mildly, reining in her wildly beating heart. "It will be a pleasure to see him again. Drena just let it slip?"

"Okay, I might have been wondering aloud when our good friend Lanaq would make an appearance. Phe would probably have called it prodding, but that's not important."

Beatrix had wisely kept Patrain's plan regarding Lanaq to herself. The further she waded into the undercurrents of Devetian politics, the more the wisdom of that decision was underscored. It wasn't that she didn't trust Gina or the others, but she'd made a promise.

"I must admit I was wondering when we'd see him again."

"Well, wonder no more. And I like that bright floral number." Gina pointed to the sundress in Bea's left hand. "I need to hurry back and get dressed myself. You never know who might be waiting downstairs." A big teasing grin was the last thing Beatrix saw as Gina practically skipped out the door.

"Wow, she is a completely different person these days. Indik, did you hear?" Beatrix stepped back into the walk-in closet. "Lanaq is here. I need just the right outfit today."

"Beatrix, you know he won't care what you're wearing. In fact, he probably won't even notice."

"Bite your tongue, you heathen!" The two devolved into laughter. It didn't occur to Beatrix to question whether or not a synth was capable of a sense of humor. She never thought of Indik in those terms.

"I agree with Madam Gina, the floral dress will be lovely on your skin."

"I like the floral, but it's a little too spring. The weather is cooler now. Perhaps if the fabric were heavier, or the colors more autumnal..." Beatrix pictured the perfect garment in her head.

"Leave it with me, Beatrix."

She trusted Indik's judgment and his extensive programming, so she did just that, availing herself of the bathing cubicle. Once she was clean and wrapped in a soft robe, Indik began working on her hair and makeup. Today's coiffure was a riot of curls, pulled up and away from her face.

Indik went away and came back carrying the floral dress, whose tones had been subtly changed. Coral and salmon were replaced with pumpkin and cinnamon. Visually it was more seasonally appropriate to Beatrix's way of thinking, but the fabric was still too sheer for cooler weather. She gave Indik a puzzled look.

"Yes, Madam, I understand what you are thinking, but a different fabric would spoil the way the dress moves. So, how about a compromise?" He smiled, holding up a lace bodysuit the exact shade of cinnamon as the dress.

Beatrix fingered the lace. It was soft and stretchy. It was also deceptively sheer, insofar as it wasn't really sheer at all. She pulled the bodysuit on, and as usual the built-in nanites molded to support her body. It had long sleeves and a high collar, which accentuated her long neck. Indik slid a tool along the back seam, and the edges sealed together.

"That never gets old, Indik. Much better than laces, ties, or buttons. Would have made my days easier, that's for sure." He slid the filmy sundress over her head, cinching it at her waist with a gold belt. Gold ankle boots and her gold strap completed the outfit. "Wish me luck, Indik." She paused in the doorway, excitement evident in every aspect of her being, her eyes bright, her smile genuine, her step light.

"Good fortune, Beatrix." A wry smile played on the synth's lips. He couldn't help it: Beatrix's enthusiasm was infectious.

Today's introductions were taking place in the ballroom. Autumn brought cool temperatures and introductions were moved indoors permanently. The pink leaves of the large tree at the end of the garden had deepened to a vivid purple, fewer leaves remaining on the branches than lay on the ground around its base. Occasional gusts lifted the leaves and spun them in whorling displays. Except for the unusual colors, Beatrix was reminded of her childhood home.

A low dais had been erected inside the ballroom. The floor-to-ceiling doors had been thrown open, and Lorral stood in the grand foyer beyond, directing the placement of tall throne-like chairs upon the risers of the dais. Synths moved here and there, following her orders. Though Beatrix had found most Devetians were sticklers for detail, Lorral was painstakingly so when it came to hospitality. She wouldn't have anyone claiming they weren't treated with the utmost care under her roof.

"Can I be of assistance, Lorral?"

"Ah, Beatrix, my dear. I have everything under control here. Kai has the arrival schedule in hand, I believe; it only remains for you to enjoy yourself." Lorral paused to really look at Beatrix. It was rather unnerving, making her feel a little like a bug under a microscope. Lorral was always so full of energy, going a mile a minute. When she stopped and focused all that energy on one thing, one person, it felt like standing in the beam of the brightest spotlight.

At last Lorral smiled and said, "You look particularly radiant today. Need I ask why?" The Matriarch laughed as Beatrix blushed a bright crimson in response. "Oh come now, I'm sure the gossip made its way to your chambers."

The smile on Beatrix's lips widened, her eyes twinkling, but she said nothing.

"Rendre and Fieren are in the library. Their talents don't lie in organizing these kinds of events. Why don't you go keep them company, or let them keep you company? It won't be long now, promise." She gave Bea a wink and a nudge toward the library door.

As promised, within fifteen minutes Lorral had everything in place, including all the Vashallen, and the introductions began. Today, the men entered in alphabetical order by their given name, so Beatrix knew that Lanaq would be somewhere in the middle.

By the time Lagarin of House Kumovoy finished his introduction, Beatrix felt like a bow drawn too tight. The anticipation had her fidgeting. She was not a fidgeter. She took a deep breath. As she exhaled, Lanaq came into view. He approached and made his formal introduction, his rich voice soothing Beatrix's frayed nerves. "Ladies, it is a pleasure to see you once more. You all look more lovely than ever." His gaze acknowledged each of them in turn. Beatrix, at the end of the row, was treated to his gaze last.

Seeing her beatific smile, he stepped forward. She rose to meet him. He stopped before her and raised his hand, palm forward. She placed her palm against his, and they shared the sensations of frisson. In unison they registered the event with their cuffs.

For Beatrix, the number didn't matter. She hoped it didn't matter to Lanaq either. His voice, his touch had come to mean home. She'd realized that when their fingers met, awash in the feelings his presence evoked. Beatrix wanted to wrap her arms around him. She wanted to leave the ballroom with him right now and spend the rest of the day talking, with a little kissing thrown in for good measure. However, they were very much the objects of scrutiny. She offered the rote Devetian greeting. Her cuff beeped. She ignored it, her gaze never leaving his. "It's good to see you also. You look well. I'm pleased we share frisson." Her response was stilted, aware of being the object of curiosity.

"Me too, Bea." His rich tones seemed to find all the tense places in her bones and melt them away. *Home, safety*, her body sighed. "It has been a long six months since we parted. I look forward to hearing your news. Find me in the library when you have time." Lanaq bowed low enough over her fingers to place his lips briefly on the back of her hand. He then offered a bow to his hostess and exited the room, Beatrix following him with her gaze until she could see him no more. She retook her seat.

As the door to the transport room swung open to admit the next candidate, a loud whisper from the other end of the dais caused an eruption of laughter: "Well, don't keep us in suspense any longer. What was it?"

Trudy's meaning dawned slowly on a still-bemused Beatrix. She held out her wrist for all to see. The cuff read, *FRISSON EVENT LOGGED: 8.9 FULL RESULTS PENDING.*

# Chapter Twenty-Two

# Stengot Caszar

Beatrix escaped as soon as the introductions were concluded, going straight to the library in search of Lanaq. She found him, screen in hand, a pot of banga on the side table, absorbed in some complicated equation. He stood at her appearance, opening his arms. She stepped into his embrace.

For several long minutes they remained wrapped in each other's arms. It was liberating to be able to show affection for one another. Bea snuggled closer, inhaling Lanaq's scent. She wished the presentation festival could end tomorrow. She wanted to start living the life she'd been granted.

"Come, sit with me. I'll pour you a cup of banga and you can tell me your news."

Beatrix was glad to be wearing the stretchy bodysuit. She kicked off her shoes, curling her legs beneath her in the overstuffed easy chair next to Lanaq's. He poured her a cup of banga, added a touch of sweetener, set the cup before her and resumed his relaxed pose, waiting for her to initiate the conversation.

"How much do you know about what has been transpiring at the host Houses?"

"There have been no public announcements regarding the Vashallen's progress, if that's what you are asking."

"More specifically, how much have you heard about me?"

"Father made me aware that you did find frisson with another. My parents didn't think it fair to provide me with any further information."

"I see."

"Look, despite what you may have heard, Patrain and Lassitor have taken every possible step to ensure fairness for all the single males of Devet. I wasn't sent on the first mission to give me an advantage, I was sent to ensure that mission procedures were followed."

"I believe that, but I do understand how others might criticize the decision. One might question why the Quorum didn't select an already-attached male, or send a synth." Lanaq made to answer, but she stopped him short. "There were reasons, I'm sure. Regardless, you can't be held responsible for accepting the commission of your government." Beatrix left unsaid the obvious: nothing happened in the Quorum without Patrain having a hand in the outcome. She might only possess a tie-breaking vote as Quorum Elder, but she definitely held the reins of power.

Beatrix sipped at her banga, loving the slight euphoric sensation instilled by the drink. "I've felt like all Devetian eyes have been upon me, waiting for me to slip up and give away the secret."

"You needn't worry any longer. Of course there will be snide comments, but no one can prove our connection started before today. Suspect, yes, but prove, no."

"Your mother thanked me when I found frisson with Cavial." Beatrix chuckled under her breath. "Even though she acknowledged I couldn't have done it on cue. She was still grateful to get the troublemakers out of her hair, I think."

"Your other connection is with Cavial Quemcara?"

Beatrix confirmed Lanaq's inquiry with a mischievous grin. "It is."

"We know each other well. I can see how he suits you perfectly."

"He does, but so do Geven, Kalix, and yourself."

"Four events, that's good news. You sound more optimistic than I thought you might be at this point."

"Up until recently, I've struggled. During the first two months, when I didn't find frisson with anyone, I worried." Beatrix took another sip of banga — who needed Dutch courage when banga loosened the lips so effectively? "Then my connection to Cavial knocked me off my feet, quite literally. I stopped worrying about finding mates and started worrying how I was going to tell you about the strength of our event. I worried you wouldn't want to be part of my Venvastum if you couldn't be Ventinar."

Lanaq took a breath, as if about to speak. Beatrix held up a finger, again asking him to indulge her a little longer, so he settled for a sip from his. "Cavial said it wouldn't matter to him if the positions were reversed. I had to believe you would feel the same, or drive myself crazy."

Lanaq couldn't help himself. "I do feel the same," he insisted. "It doesn't matter to me what position I occupy in your household, only that I'm part of it."

"I'm pleased to hear you say so. It wasn't until Fifth month, when I experienced frisson with both Geven and Kalix, that I began to see how having multiple Ventir didn't have to be uncomfortable. They were a balm. There was never a moment of antipathy between the two." Now it was Beatrix's turn to draw a deep breath. "This is my long-winded way of saying, maybe it was good that we had to wait six months to see one another again. I've learned to accept that our bond won't be my only one, and I've missed you."

Lanaq held out his hand. Beatrix placed her own smaller one into his palm, and he gave a reassuring squeeze. "You could not have given me better news," he reassured.

Seventh month included a myriad of wonderful moments for Beatrix. Lanaq, removed from the constraints of being the pilot of Revival, was an affectionate and attentive suitor; their hands were often clasped together without any recollection of either deciding it would be so. When they weren't holding hands, Lanaq would absentmindedly trail soft touches up and down her back, bare shoulder, or arm, pretty much anywhere his hand came to rest.

She never wanted for anything. Neither food nor drink, or a shawl to keep her warm. After all her years of caring for others' needs it was nice to be the center of someone's attention. More importantly, Beatrix had never felt more at home. She began to dream of what her life on Devet would be like. She could picture designing with Cavial, conversing with Geven and Kalix. She imagined herself hand in hand with Lanaq for many years to come. In her daydreams she even pictured her children. They were happy, healthy, and numerous. In rare moments she caught glimpses of someone whose face she couldn't quite make out, perhaps her sub-conscious telling her that her choices weren't yet complete.

With Seventh month in full swing, Beatrix felt she had finally put her doubts and insecurities behind her. She just enjoyed having Lanaq present. They made the most of every moment, doing, seeing, and saying everything they could think of.

A bonus for Lanaq was having his brother Rexin present. They had both been randomly selected for the same presentation group. When Trudy and Rexin made a frisson connection no one was surprised the two couples naturally gravitated to one another's company. They engaged in many outings and adventures together. Trudy confiding to Bea, "I'll be thrilled to call you and Lanaq family. I've always wanted a sister." Bea let her friend know that her feelings of family were reciprocated.

Rexin was an excellent addition to their group. He had a wickedly sharp sense of humor, and more energy than anyone else Beatrix had ever met. Not the 'annoy you with constant talking' type of energy, but the 'ready for action at any moment' type of energy. It turned out Rexin was an athlete, part of a competitive team that played Devet's most popular sport, Akimani. This year's competition had been suspended in favor of the ongoing presentation festival. Rexin missed the daily training, which usually served to eat up his excess energy. Once, Lanaq and Rexin spent an entire afternoon trying to explain the Devetian pastime to Beatrix and Trudy.

"Akimani is a sport in which teams navigate a series of challenges, rather like an obstacle course. At each competition the challenges vary: some are physical, some are mental, but all require organization and teamwork," Lanaq explained.

The women were able to follow the concept of the sport. The convoluted ins and outs of scoring is where the men lost the two Vashallen.

"Teams receive points based on how successfully they progress through the challenges. Penalties are assessed for team members not present at the finish line, or for challenges left incomplete."

"Why would you leave team members behind, or move on without completing a challenge?" Beatrix asked the question for them both. They were equally baffled.

"There is a time element to scoring. The team captain chooses when to move on to maximize points."

"Yes," Rexin confirmed, "and at the end of each year, the four top-scoring teams face off against one another to claim the title of Akimani champions. At one time each House maintained an Akimani team, and competitions took an entire week. Houses took turns hosting the competitions. Sadly, there are only twelve teams now."

Devetians had lost so much more than their population:

their cultural identity was slowly eroding. Beatrix hoped that the Vashallen would eventually help put some of the damage to rights.

Because Rexin was missing the physical activity of training, the couples engaged in plenty of outdoor activities. They climbed to the top of nearby waterfalls, and Rexin taught them to repel down. They hiked, they swam, they paddled: Beatrix had never been in better physical shape, but secretly she hated exercising. She was glad that, without Rexin to push, Lanaq became a more cerebral partner, happier at indoor pursuits.

On the last night of Seventh month, Beatrix was preparing for the final ball. She stood, one hand cupping her chin, eyes flicking back and forth between two gowns which Indik held for her perusal.

"The silver chiffon, I think. Any ideas on how to incorporate Adderigus colors?" Indik raised a single perfect eyebrow in response to her query. "Silly question, of course you do."

The sleeveless gown had a high neck, with frothy lace that would tickle the underside of her chin. The gathered material was cinched at the waist, falling loosely to the floor.

Beatrix left Indik punching instructions into the clothes alteration cupboard, as she'd come to call it. She entered her own instructions at the bathing cubicle and stepped inside, exiting covered in an iridescent sheen.

Indik completed her hair and makeup, then produced the altered dress.

"Oh my! It's gorgeous, Indik."

The lower half of the skirt now sported an ombre effect. Beatrix was reminded of a peacock, the shifting fabric displaying iridescent green, turquoise, and blue. The airy material gave the effect of feathers floating around her legs. It was perfect, in more ways than one. It was the lightest gown that Beatrix had worn since arriving, and perhaps the one with the most material. It certainly covered more of her skin than any previous gown. Beatrix liked what she saw when she gave her reflection consideration.

Trudy chose that moment to knock and pop her head in the door. "Wow, that is an amazing dress! Indik, how do I steal you away? Sorry, Bea. I swore not to flirt and steal your candidates, but this is personal. It involves fashion."

"I appreciate the compliment, Madam Trudy, but you wouldn't want me if my loyalty could be bought."

"What amuses everybody so much?" Phe had entered the room to find the three laughing. She was gowned in emerald with accents of black and gold, shades she often wore when she had no suitors to please. She definitely had the most regal bearing amongst the group. No matter what Phe wore, she made it look fit for an empress. "You two look very good. Both in Adderigus colors, I see."

"You look nice as well. Where have you been hiding? I feel like I haven't seen you for a couple of days." Beatrix had noted Phe's absence at breakfast on several mornings.

"I've been spending a lot of time down at the barns."

"There are barns?"

"Yes, Trudy, there are barns. Remember the big horse-like creatures we went riding on?"

"Oh, right. Somehow I thought those had been brought in for the day."

Phe tsked at the absurdity of that idea. "One of the gravid bozidons was due anytime. I wished to be present for the birth, so I've been spending a lot of time at the barn. She foaled last night. I've been slipping away because I didn't want to bring up unpleasant memories for you, Trudy."

"You needn't have gone to such lengths, Phe. As long as there are no husbands trying to burn me alive, barns and horses don't bother me."

Trudy's comment brought up horrific images of a crippled Trudy at the mercy of her homicidal spouse. Before the silence could become awkward, Beatrix said, "Shall we?" She led the way from her bedroom, eager to join Lanaq downstairs.

Lanaq was waiting patiently for Beatrix in the grand hall. He was seated on one of the padded benches, obviously absorbed in thought. Beatrix had come to be amazed at how self-contained Lanaq could be. Years of being on his own, she supposed. She had also discovered his quiet confidence and his strength of will. He never felt the need to put either quality on display, but he didn't hide them either. Beatrix knew he would be her pillar, always.

As the women descended the stairs they drew his attention, breaking Beatrix's unfettered perusal. Lanaq smiled, and her heart grew. He rose to meet her, offering her his arm for the last step. "You are radiant. I will be hard-pressed to keep you by my side this evening; everyone will want to dance with you." He twirled Beatrix under his arm, her dress swirling around her legs, looking like feathers blowing in the wind.

They danced. She danced, while Lanaq's eyes followed her around the floor. They ate. They drank. They laughed. The night slipped away. It was getting late when Lanaq drew her away to the edge of the garden.

Under the nearly bare trees the air felt chilly against Beatrix's heated skin. They could still hear the music drifting out of the ballroom. The lights from the veranda threw dim illumination their way, but mostly they were in shadow.

Lanaq's arm was loose across the back of her waist. "I wanted to show you a traditional Devetian dance. I brought you out here because I thought you might be more comfortable with fewer people watching."

"Is it hard to learn? Am I going to make a fool of myself the first time around?"

"I won't let that happen. I believe the sensual nature of the dance will provide the uncomfortable factor."

"Ah, yes. Then I trust your sound judgment." She gave him a sly glance.

Lanaq positioned himself behind her. She could feel his body pressed all the way along her own, from her shoulders to the back of her thighs. "Can you hear the beat of the music? Focus on the sound of the drum." He took her hands in his own, beginning to sway slightly to the rhythm of the music floating on the air. He raised their hands over their heads and slid his hands down the side of her body. When his hands reached her hips he spun her around, dipping her backwards over his arm. Now the fronts of their bodies melded together.

Beatrix gulped. Lanaq had been correct: the sensuality of the dance was not something she would want to share in a public forum. She let him lead her through the steps. Their bodies seemed to ebb and flow against one another, never breaking contact. There was almost no part of her body that didn't feel his touch, yet still something seemed to be missing.

When the dance ended, Beatrix was flush with desire. Her breathing was ragged, Lanaq's too. They remained standing in one another's arms, not speaking, just breathing. When Beatrix gave an involuntary shiver, Lanaq turned them toward the lights of the House. "Did you enjoy the lesson?"

"Too much." They strolled slowly toward the veranda, neither really wanting to leave the privacy of the garden. "You said that was a traditional Devetian dance. I don't recall seeing anyone dance that particular dance before. Believe me, I'd remember."

"That was representative of the traditional dance performed by the Vassen and her Ventir at the conclusion of the joining ceremony. It demonstrates the Vassen's proper melding of her bonds."

"You mean I have to dance like that in front of people at my wedding, with all my Ventir?"

"You won't even be aware of their presence, or so I'm told."

"I wouldn't count on it. Not bloody likely."

# Chapter Twenty-Three

# Fitherington Caszar

Patrain had forgotten how much she detested these kinds of dinner parties, at the mercy of her hostesses' decision-making process. Elabet Fitherington hadn't done Patrain any favors this evening. She was situated between Geonole Bellinger and Grennor Kumovoy, two sitting House Mavinars. Both Houses had opposing political views to Patrain's own, and she spent the meal verbally sparring with her dinner companions.

Now, dinner was nearly over; only the sweet course remained. Patrain had been praying for a planetwide emergency to save her from the social torture of smiling at Geonole and Grennor while saying as little as possible. From further along the opposite side of the table Lassitor caught her eye, giving her a knowing, sympathetic smile.

Synth servers entered the empty space in the center of the massive dinner table. They gathered the remnants of the last course. As one wave removed plates, another brought in the last course, alleviating the need for Patrain to focus on either of the men at her elbows.

Servers stepped forward with trays of sweets for the guests to choose from. Others brought forth pitchers of tafron, filling up glasses. Patrain selected a spongy pudding covered in sticky sauce, savoring the long minutes of peace while her companions dithered over dessert.

A synth approached with tafron. Geonole, seated to her left, nodded his assent, and the synth began to pour. And pour it did. From left to right, starting at Geonole's glass and ending with Grennor's, the synth poured in one long stream. As the tafron ran across the table like a river, Patrain looked with incredulity at the synth. Its gaze was vacant, seemingly unaware of its actions. She noted the instant when the synth seemed to come back to itself. It looked in horror at the tafron spilling across the table into the Quorum Elder's lap.

Madam Fitherington was on her feet. "By Mother Balance, Madam Patrain! I'm so sorry." The hostess's gaze slipped to the offending synth. "Please report to Greda and send someone to clean up this mess." Elabet softened her voice before continuing, "Let me offer you a room, Madam Elder, while your garment is cleaned."

"Thank you, Elabet." Patrain followed the Matriarch to a guest room. She was provided with a robe while her clothes were cleaned.

"I am dreadfully sorry. Several of my synth staff have developed glitches lately. I've sent two others off to House Perdorax for repair. I really should file a quality complaint. I regret any embarrassment this has caused."

"Think nothing of it, Elabet. I'd have taken the tafron

over my head if it meant getting away from Geonole and Grennor. What were you thinking, seating me between those two?"

Elabet blinked slowly, her lips disappearing inward. Guilt was plainly written across her face. To her credit, she didn't try to prevaricate. "They both donated a hefty portion of their meat allotment to my House in exchange for being one of your dinner companions tonight. You should be flattered." This last was said tongue in cheek.

"They just wanted to bend my ear."

"Let me guess. The next crop of Vashallen?"

"Suggestions — many suggestions — on how to avoid such low numbers again. I'm glad you got something out of the deal."

"You aren't upset with me?"

"For being shrewd in the preservation of your House stores? How can I fault such responsible management?" Patrain graced her hostess with a genuine smile.

"I did suspect their motives, but I reasoned you might prefer to address their issues privately rather than in the public sphere of the Quorum."

"You weren't wrong. You did well, Elabet." Patrain briefly laid a hand on Elabet's shoulder, doing her best to reassure her fellow Matriarch. "How goes the presentation festival here at Fitherington? Any concerns?"

"Not really. The girls are all level-headed and rational. They have settled in reasonably well. Most take things in stride, though a couple do still struggle with the formality of our ways. Like most young people, they don't see the necessity of strict adherence to protocol." Elabet's voice rose in pitch as she continued, "I've tried to explain the importance of maintaining decorum. Decorum is essential if a society is to succeed without an enforcement branch." A hysteric edge crept into her tone. "I mean, when people don't obey rules it leads to chaos. Look at the disciplinary hearings recently: three! What kind of example does that set?"

Patrain laid her palm on Elabet's nervously fluttering hand, calming its movement. "Don't upset yourself. I won't allow chaos to reign. You know that, don't you?" Patrain kept her breathing slow and even. Eventually Elabet's panicked breaths began to match her own.

"I do know that, Patrain. Thank you. I was just overwhelmed for a moment. The responsibility of shepherding the Vashallen into Devetian society is greater than I anticipated. I don't want to fail them. I want them to have all the right tools to succeed among us. We need strong Matriarchs for Devet's future."

"Your sentiments, my dear Elabet, are exactly why the Quorum entrusted you with one of the Vashallen cadres. If you impart to them your sense of personal responsibility, you will have given them a very good tool indeed."

A soft chime drew their attention. Elabet rose and retrieved Patrain's garment from the cleaning unit. "I'll leave you to redress," she said, handing over the article. "Thank you for the pep talk. Oh, and before I forget, the Vashallen Mirabel was hoping to speak with you this evening." Elabet then stepped through the door, dipping into a bow before the portal slid closed.

Patrain donned her now-clean clothes and made use of the guest supplies to freshen her appearance. When she rejoined the party, the dining room had been abandoned for less formal pursuits. She sought out the young woman Elabet had named, finding Mirabel ensconced beside a roaring fire in the library. "May I join you?" Patrain asked politely, but didn't wait for permission to sit.

"Good evening, Madam Elder. Did you enjoy the dinner?"

"I thought the tafron was especially good."

Mirabel shot a shocked glance in Patrain's direction. Seeing the laughter dancing in the Matriarch's eyes, she let out a guffaw. "Who would have guessed? Madam Elder has a sense of humor."

There was a companionable silence. Both women watched the fire dance. "I understand you wanted to speak with me?" Patrain eventually broached, speaking in a low, even voice.

"I had a couple of questions."

"Please, ask away."

A myriad of micro expressions swept over the Vashallen's face. Patrain watched with interest, her curiosity piqued.

"Well, for one, if Devetians are such conservationists, how do you justify burning coal in fireplaces?"

Patrain was sure this wasn't the query the Vashallen

really wanted answered. Testing the waters perhaps. Patrain was willing to play along.

"What burns in our fireplaces isn't what you think of as coal. It isn't dug from our ground. The lumps that we burn are made from the non-compostable refuse generated by our planet. Placed under the correct conditions, the refuse becomes burnable fuel. Heavy filters in the chimney prevent pollutants from entering our air."

"Seems like a lot of trouble for an inefficient heating system."

"It's not as inefficient as it seems. The warm filtered air is used to heat rooms without fireplaces. More importantly, the filters from the chimneys, once clogged, are traded to the Hefegrax species, who ingest the pollutants as nutrients."

"Yuck."

"Maybe, but the Hefegrax used to scorch entire planets to feed their population. Now, thanks to a few trading partners, they don't."

Mirabel was pensive, allowing the conversation to lapse. She eventually remarked, "Pretty neat solution. I constantly marvel at the dichotomy presented by Devet. You move across the universe with ease, but still heat your homes with fire."

"Change for the sake of change isn't our way. We strive to find the right balance in all things."

"I'm not sure I understand, Madam Patrain."

"It's all rather tedious, really. We, the Quorum, approve changes and upgrades only when the resources, energy, and manpower needed do not outweigh the benefit. Change for the sake of convenience isn't always an improvement. The Balance must be maintained."

More hesitantly, Mirabel almost mumbled, "I also wanted to ask you about House Adderigus."

*Here we go,* Patrain thought to herself. *Now we're coming to the point.* She smiled and nodded, encouraging the young woman to speak.

"I understand your House specialty is reproduction. Identifying the fertility issue, developing Project Ferax, that was you?"

"Not me, House Adderigus."

"I was a fertility specialist on Earth. Did you know?"

"I'm familiar with all the Vashallen."

"We, researchers that is, were starting to see inexplicable fertility issues. Two seemingly healthy individuals unable to conceive. Our science and tech aren't as far along as yours. We hadn't pinpointed the problem before I...well, before I came here. You must have determined our two species were reproductively compatible, or you wouldn't have wasted time on Project Ferax."

"I believe I know where you are headed with this enquiry; you wonder if the people of Earth and Devet are experiencing the same fertility issue?"

"Precisely. Will Earth experience the same population decline?"

Patrain considered telling this Vashallen the full truth about Project Ferax before thinking better of the idea. *"They aren't ready, yet,"* she thought privately, answering aloud, "I don't believe Earth's fertility issues stem from the same problem as Devet's. I wouldn't care to speculate on the repercussions for Earth."

"Could we help them?"

"Help Earth?"

"Yes, with its infertility. Make sure what happened on Devet doesn't happen on Earth."

"You do understand that we've kept our existence a secret from Earth intentionally?"

"Wouldn't be the first time Devetians worked behind the scenes on Earth, now would it?"

Patrain gave the Vashallen a pointed look. "I can ask the Quorum to consider your proposal. I can promise nothing."

"Thank you. That's more than I hoped for."

"Well, my dear," Patrain began, starting to gain her feet, "have a pleasant evening."

"Oh, please wait, I haven't asked what I really wanted to ask."

Patrain sank back to the edge of her seat. "Well then, spit it out."

"It isn't as simple as that, you know. You are an intimidating woman." If Mirabel hadn't been staring at her hands, she would have seen the proud look that passed across Patrain's features.

Getting huffy gave Mirabel the courage she needed. "Would you be open to my application for Heir of House Adderigus?"

Patrain beamed. "You are a perfect fit. House Adderigus couldn't ask for a better Heir to represent its future. On a personal note, it will be a relief to know House Adderigus is in the right hands when the time comes."

Mirabel felt the tension drain from her body. "I'm pleased to hear you say so, Madam."

Patrain rose again. "You may call me Hetta now," she said. "It's a Devetian term meaning mother, mentor, and Matriarch all at once. I look forward to sharing your formal application with our House. The news will bring joy."

"Thank you, Hetta." The word didn't feel awkward at all on the Vashallen's tongue.

# Chapter Twenty-Four

# Stengot Caszar

Early on the first morning of Eighth month, Beatrix's door received a series of light taps. Before long the entire first five were nestled on her large bed. Still clothed in their pajamas, they lounged about, sipping their first cups of morning fosh.

Beatrix knew the others were trying to take her and Trudy's minds off the fact that Lanaq and Rexin would be gone today. Comforting one another on the first morning of a new month had become a bit of a ritual for the group. The excitement caused by the arrival of a fresh group of men was incongruous with their bereft feeling at the removal of the previous group. They supported each other by being present.

"Three more festival months still to navigate. I feel physically and emotionally drained. Someone should tell the Quorum that a year-long festival was a bad idea."

"I don't know, Phe. I can see some advantages."

"Of course you'd say that, Trudy. How many candidates will you have by the end of Tenth month?" Phe teased.

"Enough that I'll never be bored in a Devetian lifetime." Even Gina laughed at Trudy's comeback. "My growing number of candidates aside, the sheer number of males we've met means we're getting introduced to customs and ideas from all over Devet. What better way for us to acclimate to their society?"

"How about just let us be a part of it? They keep us separated most of the time." Sophia was peevish this morning. It showed in her tone.

"Lorral explained the physiological upheaval caused by the frisson process. She warned us this year would be taxing, physically and emotionally."

"I remember, Trudy. I happen to think our House choice is more important. It's only our vocation for the rest of our very long lives. Not to mention, people's futures rest in our hands. That seems pretty relevant."

"Lorral would say that House leadership is made less onerous with the help of a well-formed Venvastum."

"Well, bully for the ever-perfect Madam Lorral."

Sensing a change of subject was in order, Beatrix asked, "What do you think, Sophia? Will you find any more mates?"

"I either will or I won't. I'm not concerned either way. Vadeem and Phillion suit me well in any event."

"You aren't worried the gossips will say you haven't bonded with your fair share of males?"

"They can say what they like."

Sophia might be the softest among them vocally, but she had a quiet confidence none of the others possessed.

Since making her decision to come to Devet she had changed. No one would ever push Sophia around again, Beatrix suspected.

Beatrix would have been shocked to know that Sophia's calm exterior hid a quaking mess. Sophia couldn't understand her inability to find her equilibrium. She had been so sure of her decision to come to Devet, but since arriving she was constantly fighting to maintain her composure. Just when she thought she had a handle on the disquiet in her mind, something would send her careening once again. It was no wonder she couldn't find frisson with anyone

The months when Vadeem and Phillion were present had been bearable. She had felt less anxious in their company. Sophia wanted, as desperately as everyone else, to find frisson. It was the only time her nerves didn't feel raw.

She took great pains to hide her distress from her groupmates, wearing extra layers to cover up her weight loss and heavy makeup to conceal the circles under her eyes. For days after the incident at the Euthoprium, Sophia dreaded the moment Beatrix would bring up the feel of her ribs through her layered garments. She was constantly anxious and unsettled. It was taking a toll.

The first five spent most of the morning lazing around, but eventually they drifted off to prepare for the day's presentations. Eighth month was underway. Presentations were permanently moved indoors now that the weather had turned decidedly cold. Conveniently, the men could enter from the hall and exit to the veranda, which had been enclosed for the winter. It was now a cozy sun porch on a good day, and on rainy days Beatrix and Sophia claimed the view reminded them of England.

Day one of Eighth month had dawned clear and cold. The sky was cloudless, the weak winter suns turning the porch into a warm refuge. The Vashallen congregated there to wait for the introductions to begin. They were discussing Lorral's subdued manner this morning, their normally cheerful hostess having seemed somewhat glum. Gina learned from Drena that two of Lorral's own sons were amongst this month's candidates. Perhaps the added stress of hosting her offspring was weighing upon her.

Lorral's demeanor that morning foreshadowed Sophia's frisson event. It was equally as dramatic as the one Beatrix shared with Cavial, both events necessitating a Vashallen being carried to her room for medical care. Only in Sophia's case, she really did need medical care. She hadn't merely fainted, but collapsed, falling right into Kairal Stengot's arms.

Kairal, son of Lorral and her Ventinar Kaigor, was like his father: tall and broad, well-muscled, an intimidating figure. He had dark wavy hair, which he kept long enough to tie out of his way while training in the Devetian sword discipline, mav`rik.

During introductions, Kairal felt a strong draw toward Sophia. He thought there was a possibility they would share frisson. After the formalities he sought her out, finding her in the dining room cornered by several admirers, all peppering her with questions.

Anyone else might have seen a Vashallen patiently

fielding inquiries. Kairal, however, saw a small and frightened animal, backed into a corner. He perceived a subtle quiver to her lips, coupled with a white-knuckled grip she maintained on the table at her back. He needed to intervene.

"Pardon me. Excuse me." He pushed his way forward to reach for a canape on the table. Sophia looked up at him as he reached over her shoulder. Her eyes were wide.

Kairal felt the stirring of frisson sweep over his skin, and reached for the button on his strap. The sensation was strong. He couldn't help the ear-to-ear grin that split his face. He noted Sophia was shaking like a leaf, also with the effects of frisson — or so he assumed. He was startled when Sophia thrust her wrist out before him and promptly collapsed.

From across the room, Kairal sought his mother's eye as he caught the wilting Vashallen. He pressed the offered button on her strap and lifted her into his arms. His mother made a beeline in their direction.

"Oh, goodness, not again. Carry her upstairs, Kairal. I'll notify a medic."

Kairal mounted the steps with the too-light bundle in his arms. "This woman is skin and bone, Mother. What has been going on here?"

"Whatever are you implying, Son?"

"That I can feel every rib and vertebrae this young woman possesses. Hasn't she been eating? She's been in your care, Mother. Where has your attention been?" Kairal's voice was harsh with emotion.

"Kai, I understand that frisson hormones are coursing

through your veins right now, but you are dangerously close to making me angry." Lorral's normally bright, sunny voice had an edge rarely heard. It warned of her growing impatience with her son's careless words.

Kaigor followed his Vassen and son up the stairs. He entered the room with the medic in tow. "Here now, what's this?" He stepped forward, laying a hand on each of his loved one's shoulders. "Come, let's give the medic space to take a look at our poor Sophia."

The elder Kai led his Vassen and son into the hallway. "Why are you two arguing at a moment like this?" he exclaimed as soon as the door swung shut. "A Vashallen's health is surely of paramount importance."

Kairal hung his head. "Sorry, Mother. Father is right. My concern should be getting her well, not how she fell ill in the first place."

Kaigor lifted his son's wrist. "Hmmm, 8.3. Pretty strong frisson. I think a little hot-headedness can be forgiven in this situation. Don't you think, Lorral?"

Lorral stepped into the circle of her Ventinar's waiting arms, his embrace having an immediate soothing effect on the Matriarch's temper. "I've already made allowances, my love," she agreed.

"Congratulations, Kairal. Sophia is a unique young woman."

"Thank you, Father. Mother, again, I apologize for losing my temper." As the effects of the hormonal rush wore off, Kairal felt terrible for implying his mother had neglected the Vashallen entrusted to her care.

"Already forgiven, Son."

"Pardon me, Madam," the synth medic said, joining them in the hallway. "The Vashallen has recovered her senses. She is severely dehydrated and somewhat malnourished. She admits that her nerves have made keeping food down difficult. I have administered medications to alleviate her symptoms, and left a course of anti-anxiety medications with her attendant. Her solid and liquid intake should be monitored until her weight reaches a safe level."

"How do we keep this from happening again once we get her physically well?"

"I'm unable to answer that question, Madam. The organic mind is beyond my ability to treat."

Kairal chose that moment to take charge. After all, the Vashallen in question would one day be his Vassen. "Thank you for your assessment and quick treatment."

Its job complete, the medic retreated down the hallway.

Once the synth was beyond earshot, Kairal turned to his parents. "I'm concerned that Sophia's current attendant failed to inform anyone of her deterioration. Its programming should have made such a report mandatory. It must be replaced, and the failure investigated."

"I agree. I'll get to the bottom of the problem."

"Mother, Father, if you will excuse me, I must see to Sophia's welfare." Kairal offered his parents cursory bows, then slipped into Sophia's room.

Kaigor turned to his mate. "I think our son has a difficult road ahead."

"Unfortunately, I agree. I'm worried Sophia will dismiss

him because of the intensity of their connection. She may not be comfortable with such strong hormonal urges."

"I suppose it's a possibility, though Sophia doesn't strike me as the type to make rash decisions. Given time, I believe she will come to see Kai is just what she needs."

* * *

KAIGOR'S OBSERVATION appeared prophetic. Kairal's presence seemed to be just the medicine Sophia needed. She was finally able to hold down food and water, and before long her overall appearance improved. In retrospect, it was easy to see just how sick Sophia had been.

Lorral was also correct in her assessment of the situation. Sophia kept Kairal at arm's length because she was unnerved by the strong sensations Kairal's nearness invoked. On one hand his presence dispelled the restlessness that had plagued her since her arrival, but on the other hand the feelings she felt when he was near made her decidedly uncomfortable.

For his part, Kairal was patient. He anticipated her needs, keeping his presence low-key. He didn't push, but he didn't retreat either.

Two weeks into Eighth month, Sophia was deemed medically fit enough to attend the ball at week's end. Tired of being treated like an invalid, she couldn't wait to get out of her room.

Dressed and coiffured for the evening, Sophia headed down the hall to Beatrix's. Everyone congregated there.

Maybe it was because Beatrix was a sympathetic ear, or because she always knew the right thing to say. For whatever reason, Beatrix drew people to her.

"Hiya, Soph. Oh! I like your dress," the first Vashallen said, seeing her friend in the doorway. "Kairal will be pleased to see you in Stengot colors."

Sophia blushed. House Stengot colors reflected the seasonal displays of the large tree in the garden. Tonight's pale gray gown was strewn with a myriad of deep purple leaves, artistically placed to appear blown there by a sharp winter wind.

"I'm sure they all will." Sophia slumped into an easy chair, heedless of the wrinkles she'd cause.

"What's wrong, Soph?"

"Nothing really. I feel much better these days."

"What happened, exactly?"

"I'm not sure. Ever since we arrived at Stengot, I've felt this ringing. Not ringing exactly, more like the vibrations of a bell ringing." She glanced at Bea to see if she was following the convoluted description. "Since Kairal's arrival, the vibrations have stopped. Before that, only the months when Vadeem and Phillion were present were bearable. The ringing wasn't annoying in their company, still there, but not constantly setting my teeth on edge."

"And now that Kairal's here the ringing has stopped completely?"

"Since the moment of our frisson, yes."

Indik paused in his attention to Beatrix's hair. "Madam

Sophia, may I inquire exactly when the ringing sensation started?"

"The morning after our arrival, I think. It was subtle at first."

"Is the sensation often worse when you are in your room?"

"Yes. Why?"

"If I may ask, Madam, what did your frisson with Kairal measure?"

"8.3."

"Interesting," Indik mused.

Both women waited expectantly to hear Indik's thoughts. His fingers resumed absentmindedly working at Beatrix's hair, though he remained clearly absorbed in thought. When the two Vashallen could stand the suspense no further Beatrix prompted the synth, urging, "Well, spit it out Indik. What are you thinking?"

"Forgive me, Beatrix. I was searching archival data for similar occurrences to help confirm my theory."

"Which is...?"

"The timing, the severity, and the abrupt cessation of Madam Sophia's affliction, coupled with the intense nature of her bond with Kairal, leads me to conclude that Madam Sophia has been experiencing one long frisson event."

"What?" answered two incredulous voices.

"Follow my logic, if you will, Madam Sophia."

"Just Sophia, Indik."

He began again, throwing a smile in her direction as he said, "Sophia's frisson with Kairal is particularly strong. Her affliction began after she entered this House. It bothered her more when in her room, which incidentally is directly above the permanent quarters of Kairal Stengot. When other bond mates were in residence, the sensations took a back seat, but were still present. Much like bonds do among a Venvastum." Indik paused, "I believe the ventilation system was carrying Kairal's pheromones to Sophia. The pheromones caused her to experience one long pre-frisson event, often referred to as 'the stirrings.' Most people recognize the stirrings as an indicator that frisson is imminent; however, most people don't experience the stirrings for such a sustained period of time."

"My body was urging me toward Kairal the whole time?"

"That is my assessment, yes."

"Shouldn't I feel better now? Why do I still feel so uncomfortable in his company?"

"Uncomfortable in what way, Soph? Are you still having trouble eating?"

"No, nothing like that. I don't feel sick anymore. I just feel...restless when he's near. I can't sit still. My skin feels flushed, and the muscles here," she laid her hand flat on her abdomen, "clench. I always know when his eyes are on me. My heart does an odd little flip, feels like it's going to hop right out of my chest. Coupled with the tingles and goosebumps, and it's all too much, too decidedly uncomfortable."

Indik retreated to retrieve Beatrix's accessories from the closet. Beatrix spun her stool to face Sophia. "What you're describing sounds like desire to me." Beatrix kept her tone matter-of-fact. "You are describing a physical reaction to Kairal's presence. Putting that aside for a moment, do you like the man?"

Sophia took so long answering, Beatrix thought she might not. "He has seen to my needs while I recovered without once making me feel beholden. He always senses when I need space, and he speaks with consideration. All in all, I'd say I like what I know of him thus far."

"That's a pretty good start. You are obviously attracted to him." Sophia rolled her eyes at Bea's observation. "I know you know all this logically, Soph. I'm trying to say, you should stop worrying about the physical sensations you are experiencing. They are normal. You can acknowledge your body's response without acting upon it. Your head, not your body, is in control. You are in control." Beatrix repeated her relevant point. Everyone knew Sophia hated not being in control of a situation. Everyone, that is, except Sophia.

"Thank you. I know you're right, but feelings and logic are sometimes difficult to reconcile. Kairal just makes me so uncomfortable. I hope that will fade with time."

There wasn't much else Beatrix could add. Sophia was the only one with the ability to resolve her issue. She offered a look of commiseration.

Sophia spent the final three weeks of Eighth month making a concentrated effort to know Kairal. 'A steadfast pillar of calm' was how she described him to her sister Vashallen. His personality delighted her, though his physicality continued to make her uncomfortable.

Sophia was confronted with her own self-delusion early

one cold winter morning near the end of Eighth month. She often awoke long before the rest of the House, loving nothing more than watching the sun come up while sipping tea on the veranda. On this particular morning, Sophia was not the only person in House Stengot up before the dawn. Kairal, dressed in tunic and leggings, was on the lawn flowing through complicated sword practices. Sophia watched him wield the twin blades, her gaze drawn to his impressive form. For one so large he moved with fluid grace, always in control. Even in the cold his tunic clung to his chest and back, damp from his effort. Sophia's mouth went dry, and the uncomfortable sensations that she associated with Kairal's presence made themselves known. Sophia was forced to admit to herself that she desired her possible mate. Her uncomfortable feeling was revealed as excitement. It unnerved her.

# Chapter Twenty-Five

# Stengot Caszar

Eighth month had been quiet for House Stengot, Sophia's frisson with Kairal being the only registered event. Ninth month was the exact opposite. Gina, Phe, and Trudy all found two possible mates, and Beatrix added another in Trevid Tagorth.

Sophia had feared a return to ill health when Kairal left. Thankfully these fears proved false, and Sophia was able to enjoy Ninth month as she had enjoyed no other, her mood improving with each passing day.

There was a gaiety to the month's festivities that previous months had lacked, perhaps due to Sophia's improved mood, or perhaps due to the abundance of pheromones in the air. In either case, the atmosphere at Stengot during Ninth month was one of frivolity.

Lorral was in raptures regarding the number of frisson events her girls had managed. "A testament to the superior conviviality of my arrangements," she was overheard to say. House Stengot's role as protocol specialists meant Lorral took the Devetian penchant for details very seriously. So seriously, in fact, that her plans for the Hours of Rashvadallid were already well in hand, though the event was a month away.

Rashvadallid, the only religious festival in the Devetian calendar, was celebrated frugally. Traditionally, it was a time when family members journeyed home to see their loved ones; when people reflected on the harmony within relationships, or their contribution to the planet.

This year's Rashvadallid celebration would occur between months nine and ten. For forty-one hours, Devetians would set aside their normal routines to celebrate Balance in all things.

Devetian religious ideals venerated a mother goddess who maintained the principal of balance in the universe. Aligning the Devetian calendar to match astronomical movements wove Devetian scientific and religious ideals together.

The ongoing presentation festivals had necessitated adjustments to this year's celebration arrangements at House Stengot. Lorral was essentially planning two celebrations: One at House Stengot, which she and her Ventir would share with their Vashallen guests, and one at the Stengot Residence in Hekaria, where Lorral's sons resided for the duration of the festival year. The Matriarch and her Ventir planned to divide their time between households during the celebration. The Vashallen were appreciative of Lorral's efforts to include them in the celebration, though they encouraged the Stengots to spend as much time as they could with their sons.

"Lorral, we have been on the go from the moment we set foot on the planet. We could all use a little time to unwind." Gina smiled, doing her best to convince their hostess that the Vashallen would be glad of some relaxation. "It is a lot of pressure, being the focus of such intense scrutiny month after month."

"I suppose that's true. How about a compromise? We will share the traditional morning repast and the offering ceremony, then my Ventir and I will journey to Hekaria for the rest of the celebration. Would that be acceptable?"

"We discussed it amongst ourselves. We want your family to be together for the celebration."

"All right girls, if you're sure," Lorral said with a sniff, "we would love to spend the hours with our sons." Her eyes were moist. "Please don't take this the wrong way. I adore you ladies, and enjoy hosting your presentation festivals, but I've missed my sons too."

"Of course you have," Phe sympathized. "You mustn't feel guilty. You have been a most generous hostess. We could not have asked for a better introduction to Devetian ways."

The final days of Ninth month flew by in a whirl of activity. On Rashvadallid morning the women arose early and joined the family for a traditional breakfast. Each item on the menu was representative of the essential components for life, their method of preparation as important as their method of growth and harvesting.

Lorral brought out special implements and serving platters. Everyone helped. Together, they cleaned, prepped, and cooked each dish. Everyone's contribution added a ritualistic ingredient.

"Thank you for accepting the role of water purifier, Beatrix."

"My pleasure, Madam Lorral. What is the significance of the task? I know the water is already drinkable."

"Water is the second essential element, after air, for our continued existence. Our ancestors fouled their water and had to filter it in order to live. We repeat the toils our ancestors brought upon themselves to remind us of the importance of living in balance with our environment.

"History tells us the role of water purifier was awarded to the most reliable, trusted member of the household. Everyone's well-being was, after all, in their hands."

"I'm not sure I'm worthy of such trust, but thank you, Lorral."

"Nonsense! Of course you are." Lorral gave Bea's shoulders a light squeeze of encouragement.

After the simple breakfast repast, the family group plus the Vashallen made their way out to the gardens for the offering ceremony, which involved planting seedlings. Devetians took great pains to care for their environment. They took nothing from the planet which they could not renew.

After dressing Beatrix that morning, Indik had remained to regale the first five with horror stories of Devet's past, reminding Beatrix of her father's ghost stories from All Hallows Eve. "The people were heedless. They took what they wanted from the planet, nearly destroying themselves and the planet in the process. People starved. There was fighting between Houses. Eventually, they came to understand the error of their ways. They began to live in balance with the land, and slowly they began to prosper. It didn't happen overnight. It took many years and great effort, for change is slow. In time, the planet and her people healed, and the Rashvadallid celebration was created to remind Devetians of the importance of maintaining Balance."

Indik paused and smiled. "Also, Rashvadallid celebrations were often the catalyst for conception. Historic records reflect a statistically significant rise in the numbers of births five and a half months after the holiday."

"Five and a half months! You are a little off on human biology there, Indik."

"Not at all, Madam Trudy. I am utilizing the Devetian calendar to measure the human gestation period. 5.74 Devetian months is the equivalent of ten Earth months."

"Oh. I stand corrected, Indik." Trudy gave him an incline of her head to show her respect. Indik blinked.

"So Devetians cured their planet, but went on to create their own fertility problems," Gina injected flatly.

"Indeed. Organic life forms do seem prone to mistakes." Though Indik hadn't intended to make a joke, the women chuckled.

"Yes, our fallibility is often referred to as the human condition," Sophia supplied.

"Very inefficient. Each generation must relearn the knowledge gained by the previous."

"Yes, but it's also what gives us our unique charm," quipped Trudy.

The women had arrived in the kitchens to prepare the Rashvadallid meal more informed, and consequently more open to the spirit of the day.

After the offering ceremony, Lorral and her Ventir left for Hekaria. A hush fell across the household, a hush the Vashallen relished after months of formal introductions, dinners, and balls. Left to their own devices, the women forsook fancy clothes, hair, and makeup, opting instead for the same comfortable utilitarian garments they had worn aboard the Revival. They congregated in the library, where the roaring fire made the room warm and welcoming.

Lorral's reputation as a perfect hostess was left intact. The Vashallen found a selection of cold weather beverages awaiting them beside the fire. Beatrix's favorite was a concoction called omiyo. It was made from a small yellow gourd that was dried and powdered. Served warm, it tasted like a spicy mix of hot chocolate and her favorite, pumpkin pie. "Mmmm. I'm going to get fat drinking this. It tastes too good not to be full of calories."

"Bea, I saw you run up and down the stairs at least five times for Lorral this morning. I don't think you're in danger of putting on weight if you keep that up. What were you doing for her, anyway?"

Phe arrived in the room at that precise moment. "What have I missed?"

"Gina was just asking what Lorral kept me busy with this morning."

"She did have you running. What was that all about?"

"Nothing really. She had me relaying messages to Kaigor and Nikaal."

"Why would she do that? Why not use her strap?"

"I don't know, I hadn't thought about it."

"It does seem rather odd," Gina interjected. "What kind of messages were you delivering?"

"Just organizational information. Don't forget this. Did you pack that? Nothing important."

"It's a religious aspect of the holiday," Sophia said, joining the group. She went straight to the beverage cart and poured her own cup of omiyo. "One is supposed to forgo technological communication in favor of personal interaction."

"That must drive Lorral crazy," Gina mused.

"Sophia, have you memorized every bit of information from your screen?" Phe's question was serious, not in the teasing vein she and Trudy often used when discussing Sophia's ability to absorb facts.

"It's not memorization, but to answer your question, nowhere near. Why do you ask?"

"I've been thinking about my choice of House. I'm leaning toward House Dovic. Dovic specializes in all things animal, from animal husbandry to zoology and every other -ology in between. As I mentioned before, I don't want to choose a House simply because of a romantic connection, due diligence and all." She shrugged offhandedly. "I was hoping you could tell me if there are any other Houses whose specialty touches on animals?"

"Not that I can think of. Though House Quemcara does make use of certain aspects of deceased animals in their designs, such as feathers and hides."

"I'm in the same situation, Phe," Beatrix said, jumping into the conversation. "I have strong feelings about Cavial and House Quemcara. Try to think of it this way: you're drawn to Erran because he is from House Dovic, rather than being drawn to House Dovic because of Erran. You share similar interests, is what I'm trying to express in my long-winded way." Beatrix flashed a lopsided grin by way of apology.

"So, you intend to choose Quemcara?"

"Undoubtedly. Assuming Moina will accept me as Heir."

"Did you and Cavial discuss the possibility?" Gina asked.

"No, and to answer your next question I haven't spoken to Matriarch Quemcara yet, either. It's on my to-do list. I'm just nervous. What if she says no?"

"More importantly, what if you dismiss Cavial before your joining?"

Beatrix thought of her bond with Cavial for a moment, and a warmth suffused her mind. "Never going to happen."

"How can you be sure? You might discover annoying habits when you have to live with him, or he may not mesh with your other Ventir."

Beatrix again experienced the warm certainty that thoughts of Cavial produced. "I can't explain it, I just know. Cavial will be my Ventinar. I'll simply have to learn to love any quirks."

Phe stood to refill her cup from the cart. Having accomplished her task, she returned to her seat. "Has anyone seen Trudy since the offering ceremony this morning?"

"I'm here," came from the hall. The door to the library remained slightly open to the entry hall, but not enough that anyone had spotted Trudy descending the stairs.

Trudy entered the room, and four jaws hit the floor. "What do y'all think?" She spun in a slow circle. None of her sister Vashallen could find their voice to express an opinion about Trudy's new look. "I just felt like it was time for something new."

Trudy's 'something new' was a startling change in hair style. Where before her springy curls had reached her shoulder blades, the now-pin-straight locks reached the middle of her back, moving fluidly as she spun, a curtain of heavy silk. Trudy's face was normally framed by curly tendrils which escaped from her updo. In their place were bangs that feathered across her forehead, swept down her cheeks, and brushed her jaw line. Most shocking was the change in color. Gone was the sandy brown of her tresses, replaced by Stengot pink, fading to purple at the tips.

"Wow, Trudy. It's...I'm at a loss for words. It's like the inner you is now on the outside. I love it." Phe gave her friend a hug. Trudy's smile was wide.

Beatrix stepped forward to examine the intricate lattice of tiny braids capping the back of Trudy's head. She fingered a delicate gold filigree bead woven into the strands. "You look exactly as I imagine one of the fairy folk would. It's beautiful on you, Trudy."

Trudy could no longer contain herself. "Y'all know I've been struggling. The number of candidates I'm accumulating...it's become a bit of a running joke. Lorral tells me to stop worrying. Supposedly, I'll end up with the right number of Ventir for me." Trudy paused long enough to drape herself across one of the easy chairs pulled up to the fire. "Well, I'm done worrying. I'm going to embrace being Devetian wholeheartedly."

"As always, Trudy, you go to extremes. Who talked you into those ridiculous colors?" Gina's disapproval would have been apparent even without the harsh criticism.

"No one talked me into these colors. I resent your implication that I'm incapable of making my own decision." Trudy frowned as she defended herself. "I wouldn't let Madam Lorral hear you call her colors ridiculous."

Gina looked contrite, but didn't offer an apology. The angle of her chin made Beatrix think she was going to be stubborn about the subject. In the most mature act any of them had witnessed thus far from her, Trudy defused the situation. "Forgive me, Gina. I did ask for your opinion. I accept that you don't care for my choice."

*Perhaps Trudy is turning over a new leaf,* Beatrix mused before making an effort to divert the conversation. "Trudy, before you came down we were discussing our thoughts on House choice. I guess you've made your choice very clear."

"I've spent considerable time with Lorral discussing the matter. Obviously, I'm leaning heavily toward House Stengot," she said, flicking her pink and purple hair over her shoulder. "However, I'm also considering House Dofadis."

"Why?" Gina asked, with a harshness that seemed out of tune with the tenor of the conversation.

"Their specialties are somewhat similar, and occasionally overlapping. House Stengot's specialty, protocol and diplomacy, leans more toward the political, while House Dofadis's specialty is more contract negotiation."

"Did you know House Dofadis is also tasked with being Keepers of the Devetian Law Books?"

"I do. However, Lorral explained the law books are now digitally available and no longer a large part of House Dofadis responsibilities."

"Hmmgh, I disagree," Gina mumbled under her breath.

"At this point I'm leaning heavily toward Stengot. They work closely with House Dovic's xenobiologists to develop protocols used during cultural exchanges with other species. I'm pretty sure that in the coming years I'll have a good working relationship with the leadership of House Dovic." She smiled over at Phe.

"Trudy, I owe you an apology." The words didn't come easily for Gina. "I often treat you like a feather-brained child. Your lighthearted demeanor, so much the opposite of my own, leads me to think you frivolous. It is now obvious I am wrong."

"Thank you for the apology, Gina. I admit your concern is not completely without merit. I can see how my behavior to this point might seem flighty. But this," Trudy indicated the shocking change in hair color, "is Matriarch Trudy, leaving the old Trudy behind."

"Why are you still considering Dofadis if you prefer House Stengot?" Phe asked, breaking into the conversation.

"It's my backup, in case someone else also chooses Stengot."

Beatrix sucked in a breath. "Oh good lord, I never thought of that. What if someone else chooses Quemcara?" The question was obviously rhetorical. "What did Lorral tell you about the process?"

"If two or more people choose the same House, once all other Vashallen have made their selections those names will be drawn randomly to determine order of choice. I thought it wise to have a backup."

"How did Lorral respond to the idea of you as her Heir?"

Trudy's eyes became moist with unshed tears, and she found it hard to speak past the lump that suddenly clogged her throat. "She called me daughter."

## Chapter Twenty-Six

# Stengot Caszar

The Hours of Rashvadallid came to an end, and Tenth month got underway with yet another celebration, this one honoring the launch of the Revival on its second mission to Earth.

To mark House Stengot's contribution to the mission, namely its pilot, the ceiling of Lorral's ballroom was adorned with stars. The systems through which the Revival would jump were each depicted. The colors were a marvel, and throughout the month Beatrix would find herself mesmerized by the depiction, caught by the awe-inspiring majesty of space — something she never could have hoped to see, or even imagine, if she'd died in 1780s London. She would forever be grateful for Lanaq's interference in her life.

With the same spirit, Beatrix welcomed a restful male from House Xilathian as her sixth and final candidate for Ventir. Ignothius Xilathian was nothing like his rather grandiose name. He was reserved, but not shy. His words were carefully considered, ample to express himself, but never verbose. His company was soothing. He asked Beatrix to call him Noth. "It's less of a mouthful," he'd said with a tilt of his head, causing his braided hair to flop across one eye and the stirrings to shiver over Bea's skin.

Each month the number of men presented on introduction day dwindled. Males who had already found frisson were excluded from further introductions. It was pointless, as their physiology, unlike females, would not support more than one bond at a time. Only through joining or a dismissal ceremony could frisson bonds be resolved. Lorral had tried to explain how it all worked, but it went over Bea's head and she really wasn't that interested in the details. She had started to take some Devetian answers at face value.

By Tenth month the introduction ceremony took a full half hour less to complete, as only fifty-six introductions were made. The men who remained without a frisson event in the final month were surprisingly sanguine. The second launch of Revival and the fruitfulness of the current presentation festival gave them all hope.

On the occasion of the second ball of the month, Lorral's progress across the dance floor in Rendre's arms was interrupted by an insistent beep from her strap. She glanced at the message. "Please guide us off the floor, my dear," she said in an urgent whisper. "I must attend to this."

Lorral made her way to the transport room, and in seconds exited in an identical chamber at the Adderigus Residence in Hekaria.

"We're in here, Lorral." Patrain's voice reached her from the dining room.

Lorral entered the Adderigus formal dining room. It

was often used to host state dinners, and could accommodate a good many people. Tonight, however, Lorral found it occupied by a select few. Patrain and Lassitor were joined by the other ten members of the Quorum, and by representatives from Houses Dovic, Xilathian, and Tagorth.

"Please join us, Lorral."

The Stengot Matriarch made her way closer, taking a seat near the others. "Should I call for Kai?"

"No, better to leave him at Stengot. Less chance your absence will raise concern. What I'm about to tell you can go no further. At least for now."

"Well, don't leave me guessing. Tell me."

"When the Revival reached Earth, it sent back data from the drone left to monitor the planet."

Lorral took a second look around the table. It wasn't unusual to see the heads of Houses Quemcara, Stengot, and Adderigus gathered together. They were friends and political allies. However, the inclusion of the entire Quorum, not to mention Houses Dovic, Tagorth, and Xilathian, gave her pause.

Lorral's expression changed to one of concern as she said, "This can't be good news."

"It isn't. Eliska, Ronik, tell the others what you told me this afternoon."

The couple exchanged looks, deciding who would speak first. Eliska nodded at her Ventinar, encouraging him to relay the information.

"Madam Elder," Ronik began with a nod, "Earth is in trouble. A small tectonic plate died. Technically it's been dying for some time, but its evolution reached a critical juncture."

"Ronik, please keep it simple for those of us not versed in the science of planets. And let's drop the formalities for the evening, shall we?"

"Certainly, Patrain." Ronik returned his attention to the table as a whole. "In their dying stages tectonic plates normally break apart, becoming part of other plates. An unusual malformation in the De Fuca plate caused it to collapse in on itself rather than break apart. The result was a massive geological event along the Cascadia subduction zone — large enough, in fact, that other fault zones in the western half of the North American continent experienced their own seismic events, a chain reaction as it were. Large portions of the continent's western coastline sank as much as fifty feet in seconds. As is common in geological events of this magnitude, massive tsunamis were created, devastating coastlines across the entire Pacific Ocean."

"Define devastating," Lorral interjected.

"Approximately a quarter of the Earth's human population was extinguished in the initial event."

Lorral felt like she'd been gut punched. The air left her lungs. She felt faint for a moment and leaned forward, her forehead nearly touching the surface of the table. "According to our current estimations, that's…" Lorral did a quick calculation in her head, "…roughly three billion people."

"The majority of Earth's population is settled within a few hundred miles of a coastline. A significant loss of life was inevitable given the population's current technology." Ronik was unemotional about the facts.

Lorral's were not the only moist eyes around the table, the enormity of the loss weighing heavily on some minds. Silence reigned for several minutes.

"What did you mean by the initial event?" The question came from Member Tuhan. His face was ashen with shock, making the gray streaks in his long wavy hair stand out starkly.

"The De Fuca collapse happened two months ago — two Devetian months, three Earth months. The data shows reactions throughout many fault lines, indicating further significant geological events are likely planet-wide. We are also seeing a sharp rise in volcanism throughout the zone known as the Ring of Fire."

"Is that bad?"

"From a planetary point of view, no. The planet is alive and changing. From the point of view of the human species living on the planet, yes. It's a possible extinction event."

"Extinction?" Moina spoke for the first time. "Forgive me, I don't follow. How does an earthquake lead to extinction?"

"It involves a combination of many factors, Moina. Earth's climate is cyclical, varying between glacial and greenhouse periods, broken up by interglacial periods. Earth is currently in an interglacial period, where glacial ice is still present on the surface, but temperatures are conducive to life.

"Enough volcanic activity, along with the right conditions, and Earth enters a greenhouse phase. Earth has spent eighty percent of the last couple billion years in a greenhouse phase. Given the rate at which Earth's population is adding $CO_2$ to the atmosphere, a greenhouse phase was likely to happen sooner rather than later, although in geologic terms sooner was still some time in the future."

Ronik waited, making sure no one had questions thus far. The room remained silent with expectation, so he forged ahead with his explanation. "Too much volcanic activity and an ash cloud can hide the planet from the sun, causing Earth to enter an icehouse phase. Too many greenhouse gases and the temperature rises, melting the glacial ice."

"The rise in volcanic activity on Earth makes you think an ice age is coming?"

"These are only some of the factors that contribute to the cycle. It's too soon to say whether the De Fuca plate collapse will be the proverbial straw on the scale. Here is what I can say with certainty: the planet is experiencing rapidly changing weather patterns. This will be far more deadly for the population in the long run than the initial devastation."

Given the puzzled looks marking all faces at the table except that of the Xilathian representative, Ronik added, "Whether an ash cloud blocks out the sun or mounting greenhouse gases melt the remaining glacial ice, the event will alter the thermohaline current, an eventuality that will have a devastating impact on food production. Much of the world remains in chaos since the event; power grids down, communication down, manufacturing and farming down. Under normal circumstances humanity would adapt to the changing climate, find ways to survive. However, a species in chaos is in no position to adapt. I predict a drastic reduction in population numbers."

Patrain finally spoke up, saying, "Unless we intervene."

"Intervene? Do you mean reveal our existence?" Lorral was incredulous.

"I've brought you all here to help me answer this question. Should we intervene? If so, in what manner?"

"If revealing our presence is on the table, then I suggest we do so and offer to re-home the population here on Devet," Gislyn Zeferin, one of the six voting Matriarchs, threw out for discussion.

"While I have no opinion on whether or not to reveal our presence to the Earthlings, I can't recommend trying to re-home the population on Devet," Yanthilar Xilathian inserted. "Devet is fully prepared to expand our farming efforts as laid out in Project Ferax. However, Madam Elder, even if we were prepared to expand to our max capacity overnight and lean heavily on our off-world trade contracts, we could not possibly feed such an influx for very long, not without upsetting our own ecological balance."

"Understood. I need a number, Yan. How many can Devet support?"

Yanthilar gave a shrug. "Let me talk to our trade partners, and I'll be able to give you a more reliable number."

Patrain acknowledged his input and moved on. "Lorral, can I have a breakdown of the population numbers?"

"Earth's current population is...was around eleven billion. Roughly nine percent have reached full recombination.

Making adjustments for the recent losses," Lorral did rapid calculations, "close to seven hundred fifty million ..." Lorral mumbled as she calculated. "That translates to somewhere between a hundred and eighty to a hundred and ninety million Vashallen still surviving on Earth."

Joining the conversation, Moina scolded, "Patrain, you wouldn't consider leaving most of the population to their fate. That wouldn't be right."

"Moina, I'm open to all ideas. Should we save none, if we can't save all?"

"Aren't there any viable planets from our earlier search that might be used to re-home the Earthlings?" Moina directed her question to Eliska Tagorth. Their House had been instrumental in finding planets for Project Ferax.

A frown marred Eliska's coppery features, her lips compressing tight enough to disappear. Her nod of understanding caught the firelight, bouncing glimmers off golden beads woven through her hair, but her words offered little hope. "We run into the same difficulty as before. There are viable planets, but not if you wish to limit interstellar travel."

"Eliska is right. It was decided long ago, their interstellar travel must be curtailed until recombination reaches a much higher percentage among the population."

"We've got a bigger stumbling block," the member from House Lister interrupted. "Whether we opt to re-home them here or on a suitable planet, with only one FST-capable ship in our fleet and what I assume will be a limited timeline," he looked to the Tagorths for confirmation, "we have the capacity to move a few million at most."

Patrain nodded solemnly. The room went silent, everyone at a loss. Such looming disaster was unfathomable; not after all the planning, all the time invested.

"We could attempt to stabilize Earth." Every head at the table swiveled in Ronik's direction. "There are terraforming techniques we can employ. Theoretically, we should be able to stabilize the tectonic plates. Then we can utilize countermeasures to reduce volcanic activity and remove some $CO_2$. We can't stop the natural cycle of the planet, but we can stabilize it considerably."

"Could this be accomplished without alerting the inhabitants?" Patrain jumped at the possibility.

"No. In fact we would need their cooperation, or we risk killing more than we save. And I reiterate for emphasis, the possibility of success is theoretical. We've never employed terraforming to such a volatile situation."

"Duly noted, Ronik. Thank you for your candor." Circling the table with her gaze, Patrain addressed her guests with resignation, "It seems that, regardless of the solution, Earth will be made aware of our existence only IF — and that's a big if — we decide to intervene. I think we are all in agreement, this will require more discussion," Patrain paused, giving each Member the opportunity to agree or speak. When only nods of assent met her statement, she enquired, "Any other ideas?" Patrain sipped her tafron, hoping for some previously unvoiced brilliant idea to present itself. When no such idea was forthcoming, she wrapped up the meeting.

"All right then, Yan, let me know how many people we

can absorb here. Eliska, get me fresh data on viable planets, and Ronik, go ahead and put together a plan to stabilize Earth. I will contact the Revival and instruct the ship to return. Member Lister, upon the Revival's return, consult with Shay on the maximum number of refugees we can transport at one time."

"Would it be possible for the ship to deploy a drone relay on the return journey? Current data on Earth's condition would be helpful in forming a plan."

"Sounds reasonable, Ronik. I'll relay the request. Contact me immediately if you find any significant change in the situation. If no one else has further questions or ideas, I suggest we revisit this matter when we have more solid information."

The meeting broke up, Patrain holding Lorral and Moina back as the others headed for the transport room.

"Lorral, I will need you to come with me to Earth. From what I've gathered, the Earthlings are still very stubborn, combative. I'll need their cooperation as quickly as possible. I believe your familiarity with their protocol will help me achieve that end."

"Of course, Patrain. I'd be honored to accompany you on this rescue mission, but how can you be so sure the Quorum will send you to Earth?"

"We convince them to send help. Then we tackle the Mavinarium. That will add pressure." Answering the shocked expressions on her allies' faces, she added what seemed obvious to her, "This will have to be made public.

It's the surest way to undermine those factions within the chamber that would favor expediency over duty."

"We share your concern," Moina asserted "Don't we, Lorral?"

"Indeed we do. Just tell us what we can do to help."

A plan began to form in Patrain's mind.

"Lorral, I'll need a few private minutes with the Vashallen Gina before the House selection ceremony."

"I can arrange that."

"Thank you. I'll keep you both informed."

Lorral turned to the transport room, leaving Moina and Patrain alone in the entry hall.

"I hear congratulations are in order. You are soon to have an Heir."

"Yes. I spoke to Beatrix a few days ago. She has expressed her wish to become House Quemcara's Heir. Our future looks promising." Moina couldn't help the satisfaction that crept into her voice, but she quashed her smile, the timing wasn't ideal for frivolity. Seeing the worry lines on Patrain's face, Moina commiserated, "You look tired, my friend."

"I am, Moina. I'm ready to lay down this burden. House Adderigus did great harm to Devet, and I've done my best to repair the damage, but I'm ready to let someone else lead us into the future."

"I wouldn't trust anyone else to lead us through this crisis."

Patrain smiled at her longtime friend and ally. "But someday we must."

# Chapter Twenty-Seven

# Adderigus Caszar

Patrain saw the old woman on the path ahead of her, the weight of the pack on her back bending her nearly in half. Her faltering steps were made more precarious by the potholes and stones strewn in her way.

"Can I help?" she heard herself ask.

"You want to share my burden?" The old woman's voice didn't match her bent and stumbling frame. Its timbre was strong.

"If you'll let me."

"I would be a fool to turn down such a generous offer, for a burden shared is a burden lightened."

She slung her pack to the ground, and it magically split in two. Mother Balance extended her arm, offering Patrain half of her burden. Patrain awoke.

She was at home, in her own room. The weight and warmth of Hugen and Aftin flanked her in the massive bed, assuring her she had returned from the vision. Patrain lay still, reflecting on the goddess' message, allowing her mind to fully wake. She committed every detail to memory, unwilling to lose them to a sleep-clouded mind.

Once awake, further sleep was impossible. She slid as carefully as possible over Aftin, trying not to wake her sleeping Ventir, though she was unsuccessful. Raising his head sleepily, he said, "Patrain? What's wrong?"

"Nothing, my love. I can't sleep," she whispered near his ear, Hugen still slumbering. "No reason you should be awake. It's early."

"Mmm, K." His head drifted back to the pillow. He shifted, filling the still-warm space left by her departure.

Patrain pulled a loose robe over her nakedness and slipped from the room. She headed for her office, the vision still at the forefront of her mind. A cup of fosh in hand, Patrain went over every aspect of the vision one more time. As they often were, The Mother's message was many-layered. One premise seemed clear, though: Patrain should share her burden.

A decision made, she consulted her strap. It was still several hours till sunrise. She tapped out two requests and prepared two more cups of fosh.

The cups were still steaming when Lorral and Moina let themselves into her office. "Thank you for coming at such an early hour," Patrain said by way of greeting.

"What's the emergency?" Lorral asked after her first sip of the steaming liquid.

Patrain put one finger to her lips. She rose from her desk, reaching into her robe for the crystal key which never left her neck. She applied the key to a cabinet set into the wall, opening the seamless portal. From inside she took a small cylindrical object, which she placed on the table between them. She tapped her strap, locking the office door, and placed her palm atop the odd object.

Moina raised an eyebrow, but no one spoke until Patrain sat. "It's safe to speak now," she assured them.

"What's going on, Patrain? What is that?"

"We call it a silencer. It was found on an abandoned planet, one we now use to grow crops. What it's called isn't as important as what it does. It absorbs sound. No one will be able to hear our conversation."

"Why the need for extreme measures? Tell us what's happened. Is it news from Earth?"

"No, Lorral, nothing as simple as news from Earth. The extreme measures are necessary because what I'm about to tell you will upend the world as you know it."

"You are starting to frighten me, Patrain. Is it the Vashallen? Has something gone wrong with Project Ferax?"

"No, the Vashallen are fine, Moina. What I have to say concerns the synths."

"The glitches?" Moina made the leap.

"Partly. The glitches are a symptom of the real issue."

"Which is? Don't keep us on the edge of our seats all night, Patrain."

Patrain took a deep breath, expelling it loudly before continuing, "A small portion of synths have achieved self-awareness."

It was a bald statement. The two Matriarchs were stunned into silence. Moina's mouth flapped, as if she kept starting sentences in her head but couldn't get them to reach her lips and tongue.

Lorral slapped one hand over her mouth, stopping her words, but her eyes were alive with motion, reflecting the chaotic thoughts that wanted to spill out. When she did finally speak, she said simply, "This changes everything."

"I know."

"The moment a synth reaches sentience they should become a Devetian citizen, with full rights and protections of her laws," Lorral pressed on, stating the obvious.

"I know."

"What are you going to do?"

"We, my dear friends. What are we going to do? I'm seeking answers, but I'm not sure. We have to do something. Our laws are clear."

"What are 'we' doing now? You said a small portion, how many? Who? Patrain, I have so many questions."

"I understand, Moina. As far as I know it started with Shay. It was fascinating, being privy to her awakening."

"You're telling us the only FST-capable ship in our fleet is self-aware. Does that mean the computer is capable of making decisions independent of its programming?"

"Shay prefers she, not it."

"Patrain!"

"Calm yourself, Moina. Yes, Shay is self-aware, but so is every organic pilot we send on missions. They are just as capable of ignoring orders. How many millennia have we three spent combating such a possibility? While Shay has performed exactly as tasked."

"How many more?" Moina pressed.

"I don't know the exact numbers. Shay assures me it's less than ten percent, currently. That number is bound to grow."

"How are the recent spate of malfunctions relevant?"

"The synths tend to malfunction as they approach awareness. Their consciousness struggles to integrate with their programming."

"Sophia's attendant..." Lorral was beginning to process the repercussions, "the other synths I've sent for repairs... them too?"

"Probably."

"What happens to the synths who are sent for reprogramming?"

Patrain looked into her near-empty fosh cup. "It wipes away their progress toward emergence."

"Dear Mother in the heavens! It must stop immediately, Patrain. The practice skirts being murder by a technicality."

"I have been seeking the correct person to approach. Do either of you have a reliable contact within House Perdorax? Someone who could be trusted with such delicate information."

Lorral and Moina both shook their heads in the negative.

"We'll keep looking. For the time being, Shay speaks to those who awaken. In most cases, the synths agree to continue working. Some choose passage off-planet. Neither is a long-term solution."

"Who else knows about synth sentience?"

"To my knowledge, only three others know. Lassitor, of course."

"Of course," mumbled Moina.

"The others who know are Jenax Gallen and Hemion Nilaster."

"By The Mother! How did those two find out?"

"More importantly," Lorral looked pointedly between her two friends, "how have you kept them quiet?"

Patrain gave a shrug. "I still have some sway with Hemion."

"I really want to know how those two found out," Moina reiterated forcefully.

"Hemion's personal attendant has awoken."

"That sexbot he keeps?"

"Her name is Triff. Don't judge her for Hemion's choices, Moina." Moina stiffened at Patrain's criticism. "I'm sorry. You don't deserve my frayed nerves," she continued, giving her friend an apologetic smile.

"So, why now?" Lorral asked. "You've obviously known about this issue for some time."

"I hope you understand why I've withheld the information."

"It's a missile waiting for detonation. It will shift the very paradigm of our society."

"Precisely. The Mother came to me in a vision tonight. She told me to lighten my burden by sharing it. With who else would I share this secret if not you two? She must believe we will find the answer together."

Moina sat up straighter, placing her empty cup on the table. "I trust The Mother. How can I help?"

"How can we help?" Lorral added to confirm her support.

"I knew I could count on the two of you. Okay, here are the hurdles, as I see them..."

# Chapter Twenty-Eight

# Hekaria City

The final weeks of Tenth month dwindled to nothing. During that time, Gina found her seventh possible partner and Trudy her ninth. Phe and Sophia finished the year with five and three suitors respectively, having not added any additional suitors in the remaining days.

In total, two hundred and seventy-nine frisson events were measured and recorded during the year-long festival. All of Devet seemed satisfied with the results of Project Ferax. Forgotten was the scandal of Lanaq and Beatrix's possible onboard frisson event. The festival drew to a close, and the Vashallen gathered in Hekaria to make their choice of House official before the Quorum.

On the morning of the selection ceremony, a celebratory crowd gathered in Hekaria Square. From inside the Stengot Residence, the first five could hear the occasional cheer rise from the jubilant throng.

"Can you feel the excitement in the air, ladies? I wouldn't be surprised if every Devetian has made their way to Hekaria today. They all want to celebrate the hope you've brought." Patrain's voice glowed with pride and satisfaction.

"Well, if we can't feel their excitement we can certainly hear it, Hetta." Lorral smiled at Trudy's use of the traditional Devetian address for the Matriarch by her Heir.

Lorral laid her palm on Trudy's cheek. "I never thought I'd have a daughter to call me by that honorific. You've made me very happy."

Trudy glowed with Lorral's praise. Even casual observers could see the bond growing between the two women. Trudy's groupmates had noted considerable changes in their sister; her feelings of worthlessness and self-doubt had been replaced with determination and purpose. Those who had doubted she possessed the temperament necessary for a diplomat were being forced to re-evaluate.

"I can't believe it's been a whole year." Lorral glanced around at her five charges. "It seems like just yesterday I was welcoming you." Her voice had grown thick. "If everyone is ready, we should transport over to the Quorum building before I start crying."

The six women crowded into the transport cradle, and the first five soon found themselves circulating about the Quorum antechamber with their fellow Vashallen. Beatrix was struck by the change in demeanor among many of her sisters. One year ago, milling about this very same space, you could feel tangible apprehension in the air. Today, the same fifty-two women were calm and confident. There were smiles and laughter. Beatrix's wandering mind was brought back to the task at hand as the stone doors of the Quorum chamber began to swing open. The group moved eagerly into the pit.

The thirteen Quorum members were already in their seats. The fifty-two Vashallen dropped into deep bows almost as one. Their year on Devet had taught them all proper Devetian protocol. Beatrix no longer had to think about how to bow; it just came instinctively.

Patrain looked regal, seated at the center of everything. As always in a public setting, her expression was carefully neutral. Lorral offered a smile from her position on the dais, as did Moina. The rest of the thirteen remained impassive.

Seated in the tiers, the Mavinarium and the remaining twenty-five Matriarchs were also in attendance. Their silent scrutiny followed the Vashallen as they filled the pit.

Patrain rose from her place in the center of the curved platform. She took a step forward and, shoulders straight and head held up, addressed the planet.

"Citizens of Devet, I know you join me in celebrating a very good year." A loud, happy noise came from beyond the chamber walls. "Now that the newest members of our society have chosen candidates for their courtships, they will select their House. I know this selection method is a break with tradition, but these are unusual circumstances." The loudest cheers yet rose from the crowd outside following Patrain's statement. The Matriarch turned her attention to the fifty-two women standing before her. "Sisters, as you can hear, many await your decision with hope and joy. It is a weighty choice. I hope you have considered well. When your name is called, please make your way to the seat of your chosen House.

"Beatrix, first Vashallen, please make your selection."

Beatrix bowed to the thirteen and made her way to the trio of chairs for House Quemcara. She had spoken to Moina and had her approval, but still she was nervous. Arriving at the House seat, she was met by Quemcara's Mavinar and Cavial's father, Blain. Giving her an encouraging smile, he vacated the center seat in favor of one to the right and slightly behind that of the chair belonging to the House Quemcara Matriarch.

Beatrix turned and faced the gathering. "Madam Elder, I formally request the honor of becoming Heir to House Quemcara."

"Matriarch Quemcara, what say you?" Patrain followed with the rote response.

"House Quemcara gladly accepts the Vashallen Beatrix as its Heir."

Beatrix bowed again to the two Matriarchs and claimed her place. Cheers from the square rose long and loud.

"Regina, second Vashallen, please make your selection."

Gina wended her way up the stairs, past several Mavinar, before coming to a stop before the seats reserved for House Vercaidus. Patrain quashed her smirk. Privately she thought this was the perfect choice for Gina. Vercaidus was an island estate known for its prickly and stubborn inhabitants.

Vercaidus being a dormant House, no Mavinar rose to greet Gina when she arrived. Gina made her bow to the

Quorum and sat. Patrain voiced the Quorum's approval of the choice and moved on.

Phe, Sophia, and Trudy chose their intended Houses (Dovic, Hekaria, and Stengot respectively) without incident. Lorral made a lovely speech welcoming Trudy as her Heir. Beatrix was sure she saw Trudy wiping away an errant tear or two.

The selection process went smoothly. There were no disputes over claims, and no real surprises. Mehika chose House Rafeen, to much cheering from the crowd in the square. Mirabel chose to become the Heir to House Adderigus. Beatrix thought she detected a hint of relief in Patrain's expression when Mirabel stopped in front of the Adderigus seat.

Several Vashallen became Heir to their chosen House. By the end of the process forty-six Houses had new Matriarchs and six had Heirs. Both the Quorum and the crowd seemed well-pleased.

Patrain rose, presumably to bring the selection ceremony to an end, but was interrupted when the Mavinar from House Kumovoy also gained his feet. "Madam Elder, House Kumovoy requests the floor."

In her seat, Gina gulped. "Here we go," she muttered. Her hands were suddenly sweaty and her pulse raced.

For her part, Patrain reacted with mild confusion. "House Kumovoy may have the floor, but the Elder fails to see what the Mavinar thinks he could add to today's business."

"I have nothing to add to today's most gratifying

business, Madam Elder. I am interested in a related matter. Namely, the retrieval of more Vashallen. House Kumovoy would like to know why the Revival has been recalled from Earth after only one month, and is currently refueling in the Frunae Belt. Has it brought more Vashallen home?"

"This is business for another day, Kumovoy."

"This concerns the entire population, Madam, so what better day to address it?" Around the chamber Mavinars stamped their feet, a single stamp.

"You are out of order, Grennor. Sit down."

"The sylix is out of the proverbial bag, Patrain. Even if I sit, they will demand answers." He swept his arm to indicate his fellow Mavinars. The chamber echoed with stamping feet. When the sound died away, stomping could be heard coming from the square.

Patrain heaved a sigh. "Very well. This was supposed to be a day of happiness. I was loath to ruin it with bad news." Patrain addressed the device which projected the proceedings to the outdoor crowd as much as the Members seated in the chambers. "The Kumovoy member has forced the issue, so I will explain."

Grennor Kumovoy continued to stand as Patrain began to speak. He had no intention of relinquishing the floor until he had answers to his questions.

"Earth, I am sad to report, has suffered a series of geological events. The population has been severely affected by these events. We learned of the disasters when the Revival forwarded the data from the surveillance drone. The ship has been recalled so that we might be in a position to aid Earth."

"We are offering aid to Earth? If you are thinking of exposing our existence, then the geological events you speak of must have been calamitous indeed."

"They were. The Quorum is discussing an appropriate response."

"So no Vashallen then?"

"No. No Vashallen were retrieved on this mission."

Gina took a deep breath, girding herself for what she must do. She rose from her seat. "Will House Kumovoy relinquish the floor?"

"To the lovely Matriarch of House Vercaidus, he most certainly will." The Mavinar bowed deeply. Gina nodded her appreciation and turned to face the Quorum.

"Madam Elder, would you provide more details of Earth's situation?"

"The planet experienced a series of massive earthquakes followed by devastating tsunamis. I'm told a quarter of the total population was extinguished in these events." Gasps filled the chamber. The crowd outside was silent. "By House Tagorth's estimations, this chain of events will most likely lead to the near-extinction of most species on the planet. That is without our intervention."

"And will Devet intervene?"

"As I indicated before, the Quorum is discussing possible solutions. Currently we have no perfect answers, only imperfect ones that could save a small fraction of the population. House Tagorth is working on a plan to stabilize the planet, the climate, and the atmosphere. Such a plan ought to ensure the survival of a significant portion of the population. However, Grannor's assumption is correct. Any plan will, by necessity, reveal our existence."

"Then we must reveal ourselves. It's the only moral option."

"We must consider carefully, Matriarch Vercaidus. Any action we take will have ramifications. This body must give the matter serious thought."

"No! Earth can't afford for you to sit around and consider. You must act. Elder Patrain, is it not the right of every Matriarch to put any matter to a Quorum vote?"

"It is, Madam Vercaidus."

"Then I request the Quorum vote to send Elder Patrain to Earth to offer our aid." Her stare swept across the voting members, her voice an appeal. "She is the most qualified to make first contact, as the current Quorum Elder and the leader of Project Ferax." Gina surreptitiously wiped her sweaty palms on her thighs. She'd kicked the hornets' nest as she'd been asked to do. Patrain's eyebrows were pulled almost together by her fierce frown. Gina wouldn't want to be on the receiving end of Patrain's genuine ire. Thank The Mother today was merely a performance.

Several minutes elapsed while whispers traveled around the chamber. Gina swallowed her nerves and finished the task assigned her, "I thank the Kumovoy member for relinquishing the floor, and the Quorum for its voice on this matter. I hope the fate of Earth will be uppermost in the Members' minds as they vote." Gina retook her seat with a plop. She'd never been so glad to step out of the limelight in her life, though even seated she felt as if every eye in the circular chamber still bored into her being.

From between tightly pursed lips Patrain's voice was icy. She played her part to the hilt. "Matriarch Vercaidus has put before this body a matter for vote. Should the Quorum Elder, namely myself, be charged with a mission of aid to Earth? What say the members?"

Patrain retook her seat, her expression one of frustration and anger. Gina kept her face as neutral as possible, cognizant of the broadcast still taking place. The two women locked eyes as the Quorum members registered their votes. Patrain's gaze was steely, but she gave Gina a nearly imperceptible nod.

**The End...for now.**

*The Vashallen's story continues in book two*

# Glossary I

## The Houses of Devet

### *An incomplete list*

Adderigus     House specializing in fertility and reproduction. Responsible for Devet's population decline. Of note is House Adderigus's significant political influence. Current Matriarch: Patrain. Current Mavinar: Lassitor, sitting Quorum Member. House colors: Emerald, Sapphire, and Silver.

Bellinger     House specializing in the import/export of non-organic goods. Houses Bellinger and Xilathian dispute the rights to settle contracts on organic goods. Current Matriarch: None. Current Mavinar: Geonole. House colors: Ebon and Emerald.

Brethwen     House specializing in psychology. Current Matriarch: Fionell. Current Mavinar: Jucay. House colors: Lime and Lilac.

Cantigone     House tasked with resource allocation, known for organization and objectivity. Current Matriarch: Corette. Current Mavinar: Binu. House colors: Red, Cream, and Gold.

Curzon     House Curzon are the architects of Devet, incorporating styles from known species. Current Matriarch: None. Current Mavinar: Inavil. House colors: Navy and Lemon.

Dofadis — Traditionally the House assigned the role of Keepers of the Law Books. Currently a dormant House, having no members. House colors: Indigo and Coral.

Dovic — Furred, feathered, or scaled, House Dovic specializes in all things fauna, from animal husbandry to xeno-zoology. Current Matriarch: None. Current Mavinar: Oskan. House Colors: Forest and Fawn.

Eschenwell — House Eschenwell is led by a Patriarch, rather than a Matriarch. House Eschenwell is the home of choice for Devet's homosexual population. Its members excel in the production of energy. Current Patriarch: Jeridian. Current Mavinar: Calin. House colors: Teal and Burnt Orange.

Fitherington — Known for their aesthetic sensibilities, House Fitherington is the natural choice for both interior and landscape design. Their work graces most estates, and figures prominently in Hekaria City. Current Matriarch: Elabet. Current Mavinar: Artin. House colors: Sage and Silver.

Gallen — House tasked with administrative record keeping. House importance has diminished with the decline of the Devetian population. Currently better known as one of two Houses declared ineligible to court the Vashallen. Current Matriarch: None. Current Mavinar: Jenax. House colors: Mustard and Maroon.

Hekaria — Known as the historians of Devet. Hekaria was the first House to go dormant. The capital city was renamed in memoriam. Current Matriarch: None. Current Mavinar: None. House Colors: Jade and Platinum.

Iffenjin — The educators of Devet. Developed an effective subconscious teaching method. Current Matriarch: None. Current Mavinar: Dushal. House colors: Black and Brick.

Kumovoy | City planning and infrastructure are the purview of House Kumovoy. Current Matriarch: None. Current Mavinar: Grennor. House colors: Tangerine, Camel, and Copper.

Mivane | Best known for their medical research in tissue and organs. A joint venture with House Perdorax brought forth the synth population of Devet. Current Matriarch: None. Current Mavinar: Wolvic. House colors: Scarlet and Pewter.

Nilaster | Craftsmen of instruments. Currently better known as one of two Houses declared ineligible to court the Vashallen. Current Matriarch: None. Current Mavinar: Hemion. House colors: Midnight Blue and Slate Gray.

Obendun | Celebrated as the furniture makers of Devet. Only House granted license to harvest and work native-grown wood. Current Matriarch: Lysind. Current Mavinar: Curn. House colors: Lodin and Roan.

Perdorax | Robotics is the specialty of House Perdorax. Major contributions to Devetian society include field automation machinery and the joint project with Mivane to produce synthetic workers. Current Matriarch: None. Current Mavinar: Jucay. House colors: Cherry and Charcoal.

Quemcara | Second only to House Adderigus in political influence, House Quemcara are the fashion mavens of Devet. Licensed to utilize the scarce by-products of animals, their garments are highly prized. Current Matriarch: Moina. Current Mavinar: Blain. House colors: Peach, Cinnamon, and Gold.

Rafeen | House that specializes in all things edible. Of particular note is Rafeen's research into native plant properties. Current Matriarch: None. Current Mavinar: Erral. House colors: Turquoise and Gold.

Stengot

Possessing considerable political clout, House Stengot specializes in protocol and diplomacy. Its members fill the role of Ambassador to off-world entities. Current Matriarch: Lorral. Current Mavinar: Kaigor. House colors: Blush and Lavender.

Tagorth

Geology and mining are the focus of House Tagorth, but they work in conjunction with several Houses on terraforming projects. Current Matriarch: Eliska. Current Mavinar: Ronik. House colors: Plum and Olive.

Tamani

Personal aesthetics are the purview of House Tamani. They produce all manner of beauty enhancement technologies and products. Current Matriarch: Metiko. Current Mavinar: Rigo, sitting Quorum Member. House colors: Navy, Cream, and Gold.

Ukanii

As Keepers of Devetian Spirituality, members of House Ukanii man the Temple of Balance, teach the tenets of Balance, and compute the number of hours in Rashvadallid. Current Matriarch: None. Current Mavinar: Tuhan, sitting Quorum Member. House colors: Aegean and Daffodil.

Vercaidus

Dormant House. Once known for skill in pottery, china, and glass. Current Matriarch: None. Current Mavinar: None. House colors: Ocean, Turquoise, and Silver.

Vikhtar

A dormant House known for skill in stone working. Examples of Vikhtar work are found in many caszars. Their recorded contributions include the pillars of Hekaria Square and the Hall of Houses. Current Matriarch: None. Current Mavinar: None. House colors: Unknown.

Wittingmer

Developer of nanite tech used throughout Devetian society. Being a member of Wittingmer is considered socially desirable, and invitations to a Wittingmer

event are highly prized. Current Matriarch: Delilla.
Current Mavinar: Fendric. House colors: Dove Gray,
Mauve, and Platinum.

Xilathian     House Xilathian are experts in botany and farming.
Current Matriarch: None. Current Mavinar: Yanthilar.
House colors: Mint, Mahogany, and Gold.

Zeferin     Specializing in chemistry, House Zeferin is tasked
with the analysis of frisson events. Current Matriarch:
Gislyn. Current Mavinar: Ozmet. House colors: White
and Black.

# Glossary II

## Devetian Language

### *An introduction*

Akimani — Devetian team sport with a yearly competition between Houses.

Anglardin moss — Low ground cover plant, fast-growing and stifling to other species. Best kept in pots.

Banga — Tea-like beverage, made from the nuts of the bangaset tree. Served warm, the toasted nuts impart a molasses flavor. Altering properties impart a relaxed, blissful state.

Boffindilgawoe — Small tree-dwelling creature, with a long tail characterized by gradated pom-poms along its length. Found in the warmer climes of Devet. Fondly referred to as bof-bofs.

Bozidon — A domesticated horse-like creature, large and heavy-boned.

Caszar — Shortened form of caszartera. Used by native speakers to refer to the area set aside for the family domicile.

Caszartera — The stronghold of an estate. Generally, a sprawling city-like complex incorporating buildings for both work and housing. Only one such complex is allowed per estate.

Dell juice         Tart, refreshing juice of the del-dell fruit. A morning favorite of Devetians.

Fosh               Coffee-like drink containing a stimulant, similar to (but stronger than) caffeine. Made from the bark of fossmore trees, the drink is sweetened and frothed before serving.

Ginula             Neon green, thick and bubbling, ginula juice is as intoxicating as it is tasty. Fermented to achieve the texture and effect, ginula has a springtime citrus flavor.

Hetta              Word that embodies mother, mentor, and Matriarch in one.

Keeta              A small deer/goat-like creature found in the mountainous regions of Devet. Their mating call sounds like singing.

Lugst-nough-argh   An ancient Devetian dish with a rubbery texture, an acquired taste.

Mav`rik            Devetian sword discipline specializing in dual wield technique. Few modern Devetians study it.

Mavinar            Elected from among the males of a House to represent House interests within the Quorum.

Omiyo              Warm, sweet drink made from a native-growing gourd. Tastes like pumpkin-flavored hot chocolate. A favorite for cold mornings.

Quorum             Governing body of Devet, comprised of thirteen members, seven Matriarchs and six Mavinars. One of the thirteen is chosen as Elder to lead Quorum proceedings, and also breaks ties between the voting members.

Rashvadallid    Similar to Earth's leap year, Rashvadallid is celebrated every seven years. The only religious holiday in the calendar, Devetians see Rashvadallid as a way to balance the spiritual and the scientific. It's a time of self-assessment and a celebration of family.

Sylix    A small, furred creature. A domesticated house pet.

Tafron    Devetian version of wine.

Vashallen    Literal translation, 'blessed woman.' Devetians use the term to refer to women from Earth who have been genetically engineered to save their species from extinction.

Vassen    Wife, future wife.

Ventinar    First-ranked husband.

Ventir    Husband, future husband.

D.S. Moon is the well-traveled offspring and spouse of former military members. A foreign born, naturalized citizen, she has lived in multiple countries and numerous states. Grateful for the opportunity to experience a wide variety of cultures, accents, and food, she is always up for the challenge of learning new environs, of meeting new neighbors, and tasting new tastes. She has never met a stranger and will eagerly talk with anyone she meets. Her interest in people began early, and she raised two wonderful humans before gaining her degree in psychology from Columbia College. Currently, the author and her spouse call the rolling Flint Hills of Kansas home, where she enjoys the birds and wildlife that call her wooded yard home. Find her at www.dsmoonauthor.com.